# SELENE

## BY STEWART GILES

Text copyright ©2018 Stewart Giles

All Rights Reserved

## Contents

CHAPTER ONE
CHAPTER TWO
CHAPTER THREE
CHAPTER FOUR
CHAPTER FIVE
CHAPTER SIX
CHAPTER SEVEN
CHAPTER EIGHT
CHAPTER NINE
CHAPTER TEN
CHAPTER ELEVEN
CHAPTER TWELVE
CHAPTER THIRTEEN
CHAPTER FOURTEEN
CHAPTER FIFTEEN
CHAPTER SIXTEEN
CHAPTER SEVENTEEN
CHAPTER EIGHTEEN
CHAPTER NINETEEN
CHAPTER TWENTY
CHAPTER TWENTY ONE
CHAPTER TWENTY TWO
CHAPTER TWENTY THREE
CHAPTER TWENTY FOUR
CHAPTER TWENTY FIVE
CHAPTER TWENTY SIX
CHAPTER TWENTY SEVEN
CHAPTER TWENTY EIGHT

CHAPTER TWENTY NINE
CHAPTER THIRTY
CHAPTER THIRTY ONE
CHAPTER THIRTY TWO
CHAPTER THIRTY THREE
CHAPTER THIRTY FOUR
CHAPTER THIRTY FIVE
CHAPTER THIRTY SIX
CHAPTER THIRTY SEVEN
CHAPTER THIRTY EIGHT
CHAPTER THIRTY NINE
CHAPTER FORTY
CHAPTER FORTY ONE
CHAPTER FORTY TWO
CHAPTER FORTY THREE
CHAPTER FORTY FOUR
CHAPTER FORTY FIVE
CHAPTER FORTY SIX
CHAPTER FORTY SEVEN
CHAPTER FORTY EIGHT
CHAPTER FORTY NINE
CHAPTER FIFTY
CHAPTER FIFTY ONE
CHAPTER FIFTY TWO
CHAPTER FIFTY THREE
CHAPTER FIFTY FOUR
CHAPTER FIFTY FIVE
CHAPTER FIFTY SIX
CHAPTER FIFTY SEVEN

CHAPTER FIFTY EIGHT
CHAPTER FIFTY NINE
CHAPTER SIXTY
CHAPTER SIXTY ONE
CHAPTER SIXTY TWO
CHAPTER SIXTY THREE
CHAPTER SIXTY FOUR
CHAPTER SIXTY FIVE
CHAPTER SIXTY SIX
CHAPTER SIXTY SEVEN
CHAPTER SIXTY EIGHT
CHAPTER SIXTY NINE
CHAPTER SEVENTY
CHAPTER SEVENTY ONE
CHAPTER SEVENTY TWO
CHAPTER SEVENTY THREE
CHAPTER SEVENTY FOUR

**FOR MAGGIE.**

The most beautiful creature ever to
walk on this earth.

# CHAPTER ONE

**Borsa, Northern Romania**

*Saturday 4 May 1985*

The crowd of people waited. The clouds were preventing them from starting. Eighty or ninety figures huddled together in the cold May mountain air. In brown cloaks with black hoods - all of them naked underneath and barefoot, they waited. All eyes were on the sky. Time seemed to stand still in Borsa. Nestled in the valley below the Carpathian Mountains, a few miles from the Russian border, Borsa appeared to be stuck in another time zone - a time when superstition triumphed over reason. A time when pagan rites thrived. It was the time of the full moon.

From her hiding place tucked inside the rocky outcrop, Selene had a perfect view of the proceedings. The cloaked figures seemed to mingle into one brown mass of movement. They swayed to and fro. Selene was ten years old. She knew she shouldn't be there. If anyone found out what she was doing she knew she would be their next sacrifice, but Selene didn't care. Her curiosity was stronger than her fear of being discovered. Besides, her hiding place had been well chosen. It would take a very keen pair of eyes to make out her slender form hidden between the rocks.

The clouds started to play their part in the performance. Slowly, they dispersed and there it was. The full moon shone down on the squirming mass of bodies. Hoods were removed, and eighty or ninety pairs of eyes were fixed on the lunar display. Selene watched as the figure in the red cloak stepped forward and raised his hands in the air.

Her heart was beating so quickly, she was scared that somebody might hear it. The man in the red cloak lowered his arms and began to speak. Selene couldn't hear the words that came out of his mouth, but it didn't matter - she knew she wouldn't be able to understand the strange language anyway. The noise was more of a drone of sound than words being spoken. The people bowed down before the man in the red cloak as he walked amongst them. His hand came to rest on the shoulders of one of them. The chosen one stood up and walked the few paces to the small incline and stopped. He removed his cloak and stood naked in the moonlight.

Selene closed her eyes and breathed deeply. She opened them again and watched. Her eyes were focused on the naked man on the hill. She knew who he was - he was a farmer from a neighbouring village. The figure in the red cloak started to speak again. His voice was much louder now. Selene could make out every word - his voice rising and falling like the waves on the Black Sea. She watched as he stepped forward and raised the ancient dagger in the air. The cloaked disciples started to chant. It was a sound that Selene would never forget. It was not a sound that ought to come from the mouths of human beings.

The man in the red cloak gazed at the moon and ran the dagger over the naked man's throat. The man didn't move. He stood transfixed. A trickle of blood ran down his neck. The man in the red cloak shouted something at the moon and sliced open the naked man's throat. The crowd started to scream, and the naked man fell to the ground. Blood was gushing from the wound in his neck. Selene let out a high shriek and the crowd fell silent. The man in the red cloak looked up to where she was hiding. She could feel his eyes boring into her soul. He started to walk quickly towards her. The crowd of people followed closely behind him. Selene shot up and ran. She ran as fast as she could. She could hear the footsteps behind her. They were also running, and they seemed to be getting closer. The moon wasn't helping her - she may as well have been running in daylight. She veered off the path and ventured deeper into the forest. At least here she would be able to hide. She tripped over a tree root and fell to the ground. A sharp pain ran through her leg. She put her hand to the source of the pain and felt the warm blood. She'd cut herself quite badly. She crouched down behind a dead tree stump and waited. She could hear the footsteps on the path. She was breathing very heavily. She tried to calm herself down - they would hear her panting. The footsteps were getting further and further away now. Selene stayed where she was.

*Maybe they'll give up the search,* she thought although she knew that wouldn't happen.

She had seen them. She was not supposed to be there, and they wouldn't stop until they found her.

Selene could no longer hear the footsteps. The crowd was far away now. She took a risk and re-joined the path. She ran back towards the place she had been hiding earlier. The pain in her leg was getting worse. She ran down to the valley below and stopped. There was nobody around. She carried on running, making sure not to look at the dead man on the ground as she ran. She came to the part of the valley where it met up with the imposing mountains.

Russia is not far away, she thought, I'll cross the mountains and hide on the other side. They'll never find me there.

She started to climb. The hope of escape seemed to have given her more energy and she climbed quickly. She stopped for a rest on the mountainside. She looked down to the valley. There was nobody there.

She was about to resume her climb when she felt a strange sensation. It was as if somebody was watching her. She walked quickly upwards. The feeling was still there. She looked around her but saw nothing. The moon was about to disappear behind a group of clouds. A pair of hands appeared from nowhere and Selene turned around. She looked into the black eyes of the man in the red cloak. His hands were tightening around her neck.

"Esti al meu acum," he said in a deep voice. "You're mine now."

## CHAPTER TWO

**York, England**

*Saturday 25 December 2010*

The full moon reached its peak of brightness over the city of York at exactly eleven o' clock on Christmas Day. Even the lights on the twenty foot high Christmas tree across the road from the old Minster couldn't compete with the lunar light show in the sky. All around the city, the bars were calling last orders to the unfortunate souls whose Christmas Day celebrations consisted of drowning out the festive loneliness with a bottle or two.

Christopher Riley was one of the wretched ones. His first Christmas alone since the divorce had been strangely painless. Christopher ordered two bottles of Brown Ale at the bar, promising to drink both before the pub closed. The Christmas carols that had been pouring out of the jukebox all night were turned off as a subtle hint to tell the patrons that they were overstaying their welcome. Christopher finished one of the beers and made a start on the second one. As he raised the bottle to his lips he noticed a pair of eyes on the other side of the bar. The eyes were focused on him. Christopher broke eye contact but he could still feel the gaze. He glanced over again and smiled. The woman with the raven hair smiled back. Christopher took a deep breath. What the hell, he thought.
He stood up, picked up his beer and walked over to the other side of the bar.
"Hello,' he said to the woman. "Do you mind if I join you?"

"What took you so long?" The woman said. "I've been checking you out all night."

"I'd buy you a drink, but they've just called last orders."

"I wouldn't accept it anyway."

Christopher's heart sank.

"I don't even know your name," she said. "How can I take a drink from a man I don't even know the name of?"

Christopher detected a hint of an accent when she spoke.

"Christopher," he said. "But most people call me Chris."

"Nice to meet you, Chris," she stuck out a slender hand. "I'm Carol. What happens next is entirely up to you."

Christopher thought that this was a strange thing to say but he was feeling so drunk he pushed the thought aside.

"Do you want to go on to a club? There should still be a few places open even though it's Christmas."

"I hate clubs, they're so crowded. I was thinking of something a bit more private."

Christopher decided to take a chance.

"We could go back to my flat," he suggested. "It's not much but it's all I can afford after the divorce."

"Interesting," Carol smiled. "Sounds perfect."

Christopher unlocked the door to his flat and switched on the lights.

"Go through," he said to Carol. "I'll make us something to drink."

He found an old bottle of Scotch and poured two large measures. He took the glasses through to the small area that served as a living room and bedroom. The moon was shining through the window. The ethereal glow made the woman sitting on Christopher's bed appear different. There was something in her eyes - something Christopher couldn't quite figure out.

"Don't you just love the moonlight?" Carol said. "Come and sit here on the bed."

Christopher walked over and sat next to her. He realised he was feeling very drunk now. He took a long sip from his glass.

"So Chris," Carol said. "Tell me your story. What are your dreams?"

"I don't have much of a story. I'm just a sad old divorced loser knocking on for forty."

"Everybody has a story."

"What's yours?" Christopher finished the whisky in the glass.

He realised that Carol had not touched a drop of hers.

"My story is a long one," she said.

"I've got all night."

## CHAPTER THREE

Borsa

*Sunday 5 May 1985*

Selene woke up and flinched. The sun was burning her face through a small window. It was shining directly into her eyes. She sat up and looked around. She didn't know where she was. She was in a small room made from old stones. There was only one tiny window. On the floor next to the mattress she was sitting on was a glass of water and a plate with two slices of bread on it. Selene stood up and walked over to the window. It was just big enough to let in a tiny sliver of light. There would be no way a person would be able to escape through it - even a person as small as Selene. She went to the old wooden door and tried the handle. It was locked. Selene felt a stabbing pain in her leg and her neck was incredibly sore. She sat back down on the mattress and tried to remember what had happened. She'd watched the sacrifice under the full moon and she had been discovered in her hiding place. She'd been halfway up the mountain when he'd caught up with her. She remembered the hands around her neck. He'd been too strong, and Selene had passed out. That was all she could remember. She stood up and looked out of the window. Fields spread out before her; they seemed to go on forever. They were not the fields around her village - she did not recognise them.

    Selene started to panic. She tried the door again and yanked as hard as she could. It still wouldn't open. The stone walls were too thick, and the window was too small. She was stuck. She went to the window and screamed.

"Help me," she shouted. "Help me."

The door opened, and a big man stood in the doorway. He stepped inside and locked the door behind him.

"Good morning," he said. "You're awake. Nobody can hear you here."

Selene backed up against the wall. She recognised the man as the one in the red cloak from the previous night. He had killed the farmer. His black eyes bored into hers.

"Selene," he said in an unusually soft voice. "I'm not going to hurt you, but you cannot leave. You realise that don't you? You saw too much last night."

"Who are you?"

Her voice was raspy. She put her hands to her neck.

"I'm your family now. I will take care of you, but you cannot leave."

Selene started to cry.

"Eat something," the man said. "And drink some water. You need to keep your strength up."

"Who are you?" Selene asked again in between sobs.

"You will have plenty of time to learn everything. This is fate. Don't you see it?"

He turned around and unlocked the door. He opened it and went outside. Selene could hear his heavy footsteps as he walked off.

Selene lay down on the mattress and wiped the tears from her face. She knew her mother would be wondering where she was. Natasha, her younger sister would have woken up alone.

They'll come looking for me, she thought.

She closed her eyes and thought about what would be happening at home. Her father would be gone already - he would've set off at first light to plough the fields. There would be the smell of coffee and porridge in the house. Natasha would be clinging to her mother's apron.

Selene opened her eyes again and studied her prison carefully. There was nothing in the stone room apart from the mattress she was sitting on. The stones were old - moss had started to grow in the corners and parts of the wall had crumbled away over time. An idea came to her. She thought that if she could manage to scrape away at the edges of the stones, she may be able to loosen one or two, just enough for her to crawl through and escape. She stood up and looked around the room. There was nothing she could see that could be used to loosen the stones. She ran her fingertips between the gap in two particularly worn stones and some of the mortar crumbled away.

After twenty minutes, Selene's fingernails were broken, and blood was running down her hands. It was no use. The pain in her fingers was unbearable. She had only managed to scrape away a handful of crumbled stone. The door opened, and Selene jumped. She turned round. Two stocky women approached her and grabbed her by the arms.

"Come with us," one of them said. "Don't be afraid, you'll grow to like it here."

# CHAPTER FOUR

York

**Sunday 26 December 2010**

Detective Sergeant Jason Smith stood under the shower and felt the powerful warm jets blast down on the top of his head. He ran his fingers over the scar on his stomach - two inches long and shaped like the map of Chile. It'd been over three months since the crazed Harlequin had murdered his entire family. He had stabbed DC Yang Chu, Smith's colleague and then he had stabbed Smith when Smith caught up with him. He'd plunged the knife into Smith's stomach. Three weeks in hospital and another four away from active duty had left Smith drained.

He turned off the shower, dried himself and got dressed. He went downstairs and turned on the kettle to make some coffee. Theakston, Smith's Bull Terrier was banging his head against the back door as a hint that he wanted to go outside. Smith opened the door and a gust of freezing air blew in. It had been one of the coldest Decembers on record. Snow had cut off the remote areas of the moors for days now and more cold weather was forecast. Theakston quickly did what he had to do outside and ran back inside.

"It's not warm out there is it, boy?" Smith closed the door, made the coffee and sat at the kitchen table.

"Laura would've been twenty one today," Smith said to the dog. Laura was Smith's younger sister. She'd disappeared from a beach in Western Australia when Smith was sixteen. He'd found her again, years later in Talinn but she was taken away from him again. The people who had abducted her from the beach then took her away for good. She had been pulled out of the River Ouse with a young boy she had been trying to protect.

Smith finished the coffee and made another one. He wasn't sure what he was going to do - he had a day off. There wasn't much going on at work and half the team were on leave.

"I've had far too many days off recently," he said.

He stood up, picked up his car keys and left the house. The River Ouse was a raging torrent of brownness when Smith crossed the bridge and headed for the city centre. It flowed dark and sinister. The heavy snowfall had melted and raised the level of the river to almost flood point. The people who lived close to the river had been warned to brace themselves for trouble. Smith left the river behind and turned on to the road that led to the station. The Minster stood proudly in the distance.

Smith parked in the car park and ran inside the station. The weather forecast had predicted minus five degrees, but the wild wind had made it much colder. PC Baldwin was sitting behind the front desk as always.

"Don't you ever go home?" Smith asked her.

Baldwin always seemed to be at work.

"I was off yesterday," Baldwin said. "Happy Christmas."

"You too," Smith said.

Smith hadn't found a reason to celebrate Christmas in years.

"I thought you were supposed to be off today," Baldwin said.

"I've been off for weeks. Who's in today?"

"Yang Chu, DI Brownhill and I think I saw Bridge earlier. There's not much going on. I think the weather is keeping the criminals indoors."

DI Bryony Brownhill walked through to the front desk. Smith thought she looked different. She was wearing a long woollen coat that reached her knees and her face was made up. Smith realised what was different about her. The growth of hair that usually sprouted from her top lip was gone. She had obviously had a shave or waxed it off.
"Morning, boss," Smith said. "You look nice."
"Less of the cheek," Brownhill said. "I thought you were off today."
"I was, but I was climbing the walls at home."
"There's nothing happening. Go home. Enjoy the break. You know what it's like. It can all change in a blink of an eye in this place. I'm finished here. I just had to clear up some paperwork."
"Going somewhere nice?"
"I beg your pardon?"
"You're all dressed up," Smith said.
He couldn't stop himself. He smiled and ran his finger over the two days of stubble on his top lip.
Brownhill glared at him.
"I'll see you tomorrow," she turned and walked out of the station.
"You're terrible," Baldwin said when Brownhill was gone.
"I think I preferred her with the moustache," Smith said. "She looks almost female now, if you like that sort of thing."
"Webber seems to like it," Baldwin said.
Grant Webber was the head of forensics. He and DI Brownhill had been in a relationship for a few months.
"Webber deals with blood samples and fingerprints all day. Shrek would seem attractive after that. I'm going to check my emails."
He walked down the corridor towards his office. The place was eerily quiet. Smith didn't like it one little bit. It was as though all the criminals in York had taken a break over the festive season. He went

inside his office and turned on the computer. While he waited for it to boot up, he looked at the photographs on the wall above his desk. He'd put them up when he had returned to work after the stabbing. One was of his sister Laura. It had been taken when she was eight years old. She was standing on the beach in Fremantle with the ocean behind her. She had a perfect smile on her face. The other photograph was also taken in Fremantle. Lucy Maclean was standing by the ocean. She was pulling a face and sticking her tongue out. Smith and Lucy had become close after the death of her husband. She had been killed by a maniac who was out for revenge for something Smith's father did years earlier. At first, Smith didn't know why he had hung the photographs on the wall but afterwards he realised he was starting to come to terms with his own mortality.

I'm twenty eight years old, he thought, and I've stared death in the face far too many times.

Smith opened up his emails. There were just three new messages. One was from Superintendent Jeremy Smyth reminding him of the upcoming crime stats presentation in January. Smyth insisted that everyone should attend this annual bore fest. Smith deleted the email. The second message was to inform him that a sum of two million dollars had been allocated to him by a government official in Nigeria. All Smith had to do was pay the administration fee. Smith smiled. Does anybody ever fall for this crap? He thought.

The third email was from an unknown address. Smith opened it. The main body of the email consisted of just four words.

'Beware the full moon.'

"I thought you were off today," Yang Chu stood in the doorway. He was eating a chocolate bar.

"I am," Smith deleted the remaining two emails. "I was going mad at home. What are you doing here?"

"I'm supposed to be on duty, but there's bugger all happening."

Yang Chu had joined the team halfway through the Harlequin murder investigation. His father was Vietnamese, but Yang Chu had been born in York. Smith thought he was much more of a Yorkshireman that he would ever be. In the few weeks Smith had worked with Yang Chu he had proven to be a very competent detective.

"How's the stomach?" Yang Chu said.

"Still sore. How's the chest?"

"Hundred percent," Yang Chu said.

He'd been stabbed in the chest minutes before Smith was stabbed. An instant bond had been formed and Yang Chu and Smith had been friends ever since. In fact, apart from DC Whitton, Yang Chu was the only other person he considered a friend.

"I need some advice, Sarge," Yang Chu said.

"Fire away," Smith said.

"It's a bit personal."

"Then you're definitely speaking to the wrong person. In case you haven't noticed, my personal life isn't exactly thriving at the moment."

"It's about Whitton."

"Don't do it," Smith knew what was coming.

"You don't know what I'm going to ask yet."

"Yang Chu," Smith said. "Take a piece of advice. We've got a bloody good team at the moment. Best we've ever had. OK, Bridge can be a bit erratic at times and Brownhill is an acquired taste, but we work well together. Don't ruin it by letting your emotions get the better of you."

"I can't stop thinking about her."

"Yes, you can, go home and take a cold shower. If that doesn't work, take another one. That's an order."

"I think she likes me too," Yang Chu wasn't giving up.

"Forget about it," Smith said. "Relationships in this job don't work. That's just the way it is."

"What about Webber and Brownhill?"

"They're both freaks. They're not normal. They deserve each other." Smith stood up.

"I'm going home, I'm going to have a few beers and watch a new ACDC concert on my ridiculously loud home theatre system. The neighbours are going to love it. Forget about Whitton. She'll eat you alive anyway. I'll see you tomorrow. Let's hope the new day throws us something juicy to work on."

## CHAPTER FIVE

### *Monday 27 December 2010*

The woman and the small girl walked up the stairs to the flat above the Chinese takeaway on Mary Gate. The woman walked tentatively as though afraid of stepping on something undesirable. The smell on the stairwell was a mixture of stale sweat and something else - something the woman didn't want to think about.
"How can Daddy live in a place like this?" The young girl said. "It smells funny."
"Your Daddy is still trying to get back on his feet."
They reached the top of the stairs and the woman knocked on a door that was badly in need of a coat of paint.
There was no answer.
She knocked again.
"Come on," she said. "Answer the door."
You'd better have bought the kid a bloody present, she thought.
There was no sound from inside the room. The woman took out her phone and dialled a number. The familiar drone of the answering service was heard.
'The person you are trying to reach is not available. Please leave a message after the tone.'
The woman waited for the beep.
"Christopher," she always used his full name when she was angry with him. "Where are you? We're standing outside your flat."
She rang off and knocked on the door again.
Nothing.
"It's alright, Mummy," the little girl said. "Maybe he forgot."

"It's not alright, baby," the woman dialled the number again.

"Christopher," she said after the beep. "One day. One bloody day and you can't even be bothered to show up. It's Christmas and you can't even spend one day with your daughter. She was looking forward to it if you even care."

She ended the call.

"Come on," she said to the girl. "I'll take you for a milkshake."

"Maybe he had to work," the girl suggested.

"Let's go."

They were about to walk back down the filthy stairs when the woman heard a noise from inside the flat. It was a strange beeping sound - the sound of a voice message being received on a mobile phone. She turned round and banged on the door.

"Christopher," she shouted. "Are you in there?"

She knew her ex-husband never went anywhere without his phone. He was obsessive about it.

"Christopher," she shouted again. "You'll be hearing from my lawyer. The terms were very clear, and you've broken them."

Another beep was heard from inside the flat.

The woman tried the door handle. The door was unlocked. She pushed the door open and was met with the stench of stale whisky and cheap perfume.

He's drunk, she thought, and he definitely doesn't wear perfume. He's got someone in there with him.

"Wait here, baby," she said to the girl. "I just want to have a word with Daddy."

"But I want to see him."

"Wait here."

The tone of her mother's voice told her it was pointless arguing.

Christopher Riley was lying face down on the bed in the middle of the room. His arms were by his side. The woman knew straight away that something was wrong. In the years they had been married, Christopher always slept on his back. She slowly walked towards the bed. A wrapped Christmas present was on the floor next to it. The name 'Maggie' was written on a plain white tag.
"Chris," she said.
The man on the bed didn't move.
"Christopher," she said, louder this time.
She touched one of his hands and flinched. It was cold.
"Can I come inside?" A voice was heard from the doorway.
"Maggie. Stay there."
She looked at the lifeless body lying on the bed. She picked up one of her ex-husband's hands and felt for a pulse. Four years working as a nurse in the operating theatre told her that it was futile, but she had to know anyway. There was nothing.

The woman sat on the edge of the bed and took out her mobile phone. She felt strangely calm considering her ex-husband was lying dead a few feet away from her. They'd been together for eight years and now he was dead.
"Police," she said. "My name is Emily Riley. My ex-husband is dead."
She gave them the address and rang off. She stood up, left the flat and closed the door behind her.
"Daddy's not here," she said to her daughter. "Let's go and get a milkshake."
"He promised. He said he would get me the Barbie with the racing car."
Emily Riley didn't know what to say. She took Maggie's hand and led her down the stairs.

Fifteen minutes later a red Ford Sierra parked outside the Chinese restaurant and two men got out. Emily and Maggie were standing in the doorway of the shop next door sheltering from the wind.
"Mrs Riley?" The taller of the two men asked. "DS Smith and this is DC Yang Chu. Are you the one who called us?"
"Wait here," Emily said to Maggie.
She nodded to Smith and Yang Chu and led them down the street. She stopped outside a deserted night club.
"I don't want Maggie to know anything yet. I'll break the news to her in my own time."
"You said your ex-husband is dead?" Smith said. "Are you sure?"
"I'm a registered nurse," Emily said. "I know when somebody is dead."
"I'm sorry, when did you find him?"
"About thirty seconds before I phoned you. Can I go now please? I have to try and figure out how to tell an eight year old girl that her daddy is dead."
"OK, but we'll need to speak with you again."
"I'm not going anywhere."
She walked back to her daughter and they walked off down the street.

"She seemed very calm," Yang Chu said when Emily Riley was out of sight. "Considering that she's just found her husband dead."
"Ex-husband," Smith said. "She's probably still in shock and she has the unpleasant task of telling her daughter that her Dad is not coming back. Let's have a look upstairs, shall we?"
They walked back to the Chinese restaurant and went up the stairs to the flat.
"It stinks in here," Yang Chu said.
His shoe got stuck on something on the stairwell.
"How can people live like this?" he added.

"Divorce," Smith said. "He probably didn't have much choice."
"I'm never getting married."

Smith put on a pair of rubber gloves. Yang Chu did the same. Smith slowly opened the door to the flat and looked inside. The smell that oozed out was a mixture of stale whisky and perfume.
"Don't touch anything," Smith said and instantly regretted it.
Yang Chu knew the drill.
The curtains were open inside the room. Two glasses stood on a small table opposite the bed. One of them was empty but the other still contained an amber coloured liquid. Christopher Riley lay on the bed.
"What do you think?" Smith said.
Yang Chu took a deep breath. This was the first dead body he had been called out to investigate. His eyes seemed drawn to the figure on the bed. He looked around the tiny flat.
"The curtains are open," he said.
"What does that mean?"
"I'd say he died during the day," Yang Chu said. "The curtains would have surely been closed if he had died when it was dark outside."
"What else?"
"He had company," Yang Chu pointed to the two glasses on the table. "And I'd rule out suicide."
"What makes you say that?"
"The Christmas present, it has the name Maggie on it. That's his daughter. No, he didn't kill himself."
"Slow down," Smith said. "You'll soon learn not to assume anything in this job. We'll know more when Webber gets here. In the meantime, let's have a word with the people in the Chinese restaurant below."
"I hate Chinese food," Yang Chu said.

The Big Wok restaurant had just opened its doors when Smith and Yang Chu walked inside. A short thin man in an apron approached them almost immediately.
"Good day," he said. "Table for two?"
"No thanks," Smith took out his ID. "We'd like to speak to the owner of the restaurant.
"Problems?" The waiter said.
"Could we speak to the owner please?"
"Come through," the waiter said. "He's in his office in the back."
He led them through to a small office. There was barely room for a desk and a chair, let alone the enormous bulk of human being sitting behind the computer screen. He was typing something with the fattest fingers Smith had ever seen.
"Mr Yin," the waiter said. "These men would like to have a word with you. They're from the police."
Yin looked Smith and Yang Chu up and down.
"What seems to be the problem?" he asked in a voice so high that Smith found it hard to suppress a laugh.
"Mr Yin," Smith said. "We need to ask you a few questions about the man who rents the flat above your restaurant."
"Mr Riley?" Yin squeaked. "Very nice man. Never gives me any trouble. Poor man - he's very sad after the divorce."
"When was the last time you saw Mr Riley?" Yang Chu asked.
"I hardly ever see him. He pays rent on time. He always pays it straight into the bank. He's a good tenant."
"So, you haven't seen him recently?" Smith said.
"No, what's this all about? What's he done?"

"He's dead," Smith said. "He's lying dead right above your restaurant. Are you sure you haven't seen or heard from him in the past few days?"

"Christmas day," Yin said as if a sudden memory had come back to him. "I saw him Christmas day. The restaurant was open. He came in to wish me happy Christmas. It was funny. I don't celebrate Christmas."

"What time was this?" Smith said.

"Around three."

"And you haven't seen him since?"

"No," Yin said. "Restaurant closed at ten. I'm sorry he's dead. He was a good tenant. Never made any noise."

"Thank you, Mr Yin," Smith handed him one of his cards. "If you think of anything else, give me a call."

# CHAPTER SIX

Borsa

***Sunday 25 August 1991***

"I bought you these," the big man handed Selene a brown cloak and a silver wristwatch.

Selene took the cloak and put it on. She stared at the watch. It was the most beautiful thing she had ever seen.

"It knows the phases of the moon," the man said. "It's magic. Put it on. See if it fits."

Selene fiddled with the strap, but she couldn't quite figure out how the intricate clasps worked. The man took hold of her slender wrist and undid the clasp. She put the watch on her wrist.

"Do you see that," he pointed to the dial. "That is so you will always know when the moon is at its brightest."

Selene gazed at the watch. According to the dial there would be a full moon in approximately two hours' time.

"You're ready," the man said. "When you were given to me six years ago, I had my doubts but you're ready now. You've come a long way, Selene. Shall we go?"

By the time they reached the valley, the sun had already disappeared behind the mountains in the distance. It was a very hot evening and the goat herders had left their animals on higher ground for the night. Despite the warm temperature, Selene shivered under the thick cloak. It'd been six years since she had hidden in the rocks and watched the sacrifice. Then, she hadn't been invited - she had been an intruder but now she was a part of it. She was one of them.

She stood close to the man in red and watched the figures in brown cloaks as they approached from all directions.

"Don't be afraid, child," the big man said. "They are the ones who need to be fearful."

The sky was cloudless and the air still as the moon gradually rose above the Carpathian Mountains. It was a perfect night for what lay in store.

"Stay here," the man said to Selene. "I have work to do."

Selene watched as the big man walked among the crowd and started to speak. The words that came out of his mouth flowed effortlessly off his tongue. He didn't have to think about what to say - his lips moved on their own. Selene joined the line of cloaked disciples and waited. The man in red stopped in front of a short man a few metres to Selene's left. The chosen one gasped. Everybody knew what was about to happen. Selene had seen enough. She watched the men in the brown cloaks. All eyes were on the man who'd been chosen. She shuffled back a few metres and waited. Nobody seemed to notice her in her new position. The chanting became louder.

*Now,* Selene thought.

She crept further back and stood up. Then she ran. She ran faster than she had ever managed to run before. She ran towards the mountains in the distance. This time she was going to make it to the other side. She didn't stop until she was high above the valley. Nobody was following her. She was safe.

# CHAPTER SEVEN

YORK

*Monday 27 December 2010*

Smith stepped over the tape that Grant Webber, the head of forensics had placed in the doorway of Christopher Riley's flat to prevent unauthorised access to a potential crime scene. Webber was dusting one of the whisky glasses for prints.
"Afternoon, Webber," Smith said. "What can you tell me?"
Webber didn't look up.
"I can tell you that I was in the middle of a very pleasant lunch when I got called out."
"I see the DI has started to shave," Smith said. "She must really like you."
"I've just this minute got here," Webber ignored Smith's comment. "Do we know who the dead man is?"
"Christopher Riley," Smith said. "Divorced. Thirty eight years old. Do we know how he died?"
"You were first on the scene. What do you think?"
"Webber, how many times have you told me that your job is to find out how and then it's up to me to figure out why and try to catch who did it?"
"I'll get to him in good time, but I can tell you now he didn't drop off peacefully in his sleep."
"Murder?"
"Looks like it."

"About bloody time," Smith said. "It's been far too quiet around here recently."

"Do you ever take anything seriously?" Webber poured the amber liquid from one of the whisky glasses into a small glass vial.

"I've lost count of how many times I've nearly died. I'm not even thirty and I've faced death far too many times. Life's too short for seriousness."

"Very philosophical," Webber said. "Let me show you something."

He walked over to the bed and turned Christopher Riley's head to the side. Smith gasped. There was a gaping wound in his neck. It had been sliced open.

"How did I not notice that when I first came in?"

"I don't normally speculate," Webber said. "But I'd say he was killed whilst lying on his stomach. The blood will have gushed out but most of it has been soaked up by the bed sheets and the mattress."

"Interesting," Smith said.

"What are you thinking?"

"Nothing. How soon will you be able to tell us anything?"

"When I'm ready. The path guys will give us the time and cause of death. In the meantime, I have to go through this pigsty with a fine-toothcomb and I would appreciate a bit of peace and quiet. Don't you have something else to do?"

Smith looked out of the window. On the opposite side of the street there was a building that Smith knew had been converted into student accommodation.

"Let me know as soon as you find anything," he stepped over the tape and walked back down the stairs.

DC Whitton and DI Brownhill were standing next to an ambulance when Smith emerged onto the street. The wind had picked up and

Smith wished he'd worn something warmer. Yang Chu was nowhere to be seen.

"Afternoon, boss," Smith said to Brownhill. "Whitton."

"What have we got?" Whitton said.

"Dead divorced guy. His throat was slashed. Webber's going through the flat now. Sorry about interrupting your romantic lunch, boss."

"Do we know anything yet?" Brownhill said.

"Not yet. We spoke to the owner of the Chinese restaurant, but he hasn't seen Riley since Christmas day. Where's Yang Chu?"

"He went home," Whitton said. "He wasn't feeling well."

"This is his first dead one isn't it?"

Whitton nodded.

"He'll soon get used to it."

"What now?" Brownhill said.

"It's a long shot, but I want to see if anyone in the student flats across the road saw anything. I know that most of the students will have gone home for the holidays but there might be some who've stuck around. The curtains in Riley's flat were left open. It's worth a shot."

"I'll come with you," Whitton said.

Smith pressed the buzzer on the door of the student accommodation. A few seconds later a woman's voice was heard.

"Hello," she said.

"Police," Smith said. "Can you let us in please?"

"Give me a minute," she said.

"Probably stashing away all the drugs these students use these days," Smith whispered to Whitton.

"You don't like students do you, Sarge?"

"They're useless wastes of space. Self-important idiots."

"That's a bit harsh," Whitton said. "And I remember it wasn't that long ago that you stopped smoking weed."

The door opened and a woman with green hair stood in the doorway. Smith cast Whitton a knowing smile.

"Afternoon," he said. "DS Smith and this is DC Whitton. Can we come in?"

The woman looked Smith up and down.

"Do you have any identification?" she said with an accent that indicated she didn't come from York.

Smith took out his ID.

"Sorry, you don't exactly look like a detective sergeant. You can't be too careful these days. What's this all about?"

"Can we come inside?" Whitton said. "It's brass monkeys out here."

"You should spend a winter in Bergen," the woman stepped aside and let Smith and Whitton inside.

Smith stared at her. He had a blank look on his face.

"Norway," the woman said. "I'm Norwegian. Kjersti Sorenson."

"How many people stay here?"

"Normally there are eight of us, but right now it's just me and Kim. It's the holidays."

"Do you or Kim live on the second floor?"

"I do," Kjersti said. "Why?"

"Can we see your room? I want to see the view from your room."

Kjersti appeared confused.

"Just humour him," Whitton said.

Kjersti shook her head and led them up a narrow staircase. She stopped outside a red door.

"You'll have to excuse the mess," she opened the door. "I wasn't expecting guests. I've been working nonstop since the term finished."

They went inside. The student flat consisted of a kitchen area cum dining room and a small space for a bed and a wardrobe. A huge map of Norway covered one of the walls. Smith walked over to the window and looked outside. He could see the flat above the Chinese restaurant. Grant Webber was clearly visible. He appeared to be collecting samples from Christopher Riley's clothing.

"You say you've been working nonstop?" Smith said. "Where do you work?"

"At a bistro in the city centre," Kjersti said. "I work weekends and out of term time. The money gives me a bit of independence."

"This may sound odd, but you didn't happen to see anything unusual going on in the flat across the road in the last few days, did you?"

"Unusual? Like what?"

"People coming and going. People you haven't seen before."

He decided to come straight to the point.

"The man who lives in the flat above the Chinese restaurant was killed," he said. "Sometime between Christmas day and this morning."

"Oh my God," Kjersti sat down on the bed. "Murdered?"

"Looks like it, can you remember seeing anything strange?"

"No," Kjersti said. "It's not as if I sit here and spy out of the window all day."

"Did you know the man who lived above the Chinese restaurant?" Whitton asked.

"No," Kjersti said straight away. "I have to get going. I have to get ready for work. Will there be anything else?"

"That's all for now," Smith said. "Come on, Whitton."

Smith was halfway down the stairs when he turned around and walked back up to Kjersti Sorenson's room. He knocked on the door. Kjersti opened it a few seconds later. She no longer had green hair - it had obviously been a wig. Long black hair flowed down her back.

"Sorry," Smith handed her one of his cards. "Just in case you think of anything else. By the way, the black hair suits you much better."

## CHAPTER EIGHT

"She was a bit weird," Whitton said as they drove through the dimly lit streets back to the station.
"Weird?" Smith said.
"There was definitely something not right about her. I didn't like her."
"Whitton, since I've known you there hasn't been a woman you have liked."
"I like Baldwin," Whitton said. "I just think she was odd that's all. And what's she doing in York? Did you know that anybody from anywhere in the world can study in Norway for free? Why come to York and pay the exorbitant tuition fees they charge these days?"
"Maybe she's here for the weather," Smith parked his car outside the station.
The wind had picked up to almost gale force strength and when Smith opened the car door an icy blast almost tore him in two.
"She's obviously here for the weather," he said and ran inside the station.
Whitton followed closely behind.
 Baldwin was sitting behind the front desk when they got inside.
"Hi, Baldwin," Smith said. "What's with this weather? I've never seen anything like it."
"Afternoon, sir," Baldwin said. "Brownhill wants everyone in the small conference room in half an hour."
"Come on, Whitton," Smith said. "We've got time for a cup of God awful coffee before all hell breaks loose. It might warm us up a bit."
Bridge, Yang Chu and DCI Chalmers were sitting in the canteen. Chalmers was staring out of the window at the dark grey clouds coming in from the east. He had a faraway look in his eyes.

"Afternoon, boss," Smith said to him. "Long time no see. I wasn't sure if you still worked here or not."

"Smyth is driving me nuts," Chalmers said. "You know his bloody crime stats lecture is coming up next week, don't you? He's got me going through the whole stats from the last year. All I can see in front of my face are figures and more figures. I see them in my bloody sleep for God's sake. Have you got anything on this Christopher Riley murder?"

"Nothing, Webber seems to think that his neck was sliced open while he was lying on his stomach."

"That's a bit odd isn't it?"

"Yes, it is."

Smith turned to Yang Chu.

"How are you feeling?" he said.

"Fine, it was just a bit of a shock that's all."

"First dead one?" Chalmers said.

Yang Chu nodded.

"I remember my first one," Chalmers mused. "You never forget the first one. It was over twenty years ago now. Down past St Mary's on the river. We got a call out to a suspicious object in the river. It was only when we pulled it out that we realised it was the body of an old man. Bloated as hell he was. I had nightmares for days afterwards. Turns out he slipped and fell, and nobody was around to help him - poor bugger. Anyway, you'll get over it."

Whitton handed Smith a cup of coffee.

"Thanks, Whitton," Smith put both hands around the cup and felt them warming up straight away.

"The weather's going to get worse," Bridge said. "They say we're in for a long cold spell."

"Great," Smith said.

"What's the plan?" Chalmers said.

"Brownhill has called a meeting," Smith said. "She seems to know what she's doing. I'm actually starting to like her."

"Have you noticed she's started shaving?" Bridge said. "Her and Webber must be getting serious."

Chalmers started to laugh.

"They deserve each other," Smith said. "Anyway, it won't last. Relationships on the job never do."

He glanced over at Yang Chu. Yang Chu's face turned a deep crimson colour.

"I'm off for a smoke," Chalmers said. "And then it's back to more bloody crime stats. The DCI job will be the death of me."

"I miss Chalmers," Whitton said when he had left the canteen. "He's a grumpy bugger but he's alright."

"Where's Thompson?" Smith said.

"He's off with a cold," Bridge said.

"I don't think I've ever had a cold," Smith finished his coffee and put the cup on the table. "We'd better get moving. We wouldn't want to keep the fulsome Bryony Brownhill waiting, would we?"

DI Brownhill was sitting alone in the small conference room. Smith, Whitton, Bridge and Yang Chu took seats around the table and waited. Brownhill looked agitated. Something was obviously bothering her.

"Afternoon," she said suddenly, as if she had snapped out of a trance. "Let's get started, shall we? We have a lot to get through. What do we know so far?"

"Not much," Smith decided to open the proceedings. "Christopher

Riley, thirty eight year old divorcee. Throat sliced open on the bed. No murder weapon found yet. Webber seems to think he was killed while he was lying face down on the bed."

"Does he now? Well, if Grant thinks that then it's probably true. What else have we got?"

"His ex-wife found him. She was dropping their daughter off at his flat. She found him this morning."

"Have you spoken to her?"

"Briefly, but she didn't say much. She seemed very calm under the circumstances. She phoned the police straight away."

"OK," Brownhill said. "Do we know if anybody saw anything?"

"We've spoken to Riley's landlord - he owns the Chinese restaurant below Riley's flat. He hasn't seen Riley since Christmas Day."

"We also spoke to a student," Whitton said. "A Norwegian woman who lives across the road from Riley's flat. She claims she didn't see anything either."

"What do you suggest we do?" Brownhill looked at Smith.

"The forensics and path reports should be in later today," Smith said. "We'll know a bit more then but in the meantime, I reckon we should try and retrace Riley's tracks."

"Go on," Brownhill said.

"He was last seen around two on Christmas Day," Smith said. "By the obese Chinese man who happens to be his landlord. We need to find out where he went between then and this morning when his ex-wife found him."

"Good, get onto it then."

"Whitton," Smith said. "You come with me."

"I disagree," Brownhill said. "You and Whitton have the most experience here. Whitton can team up with Yang Chu and Bridge can go with you."

"I'll take Yang Chu," Smith said. "Come on."

He walked out of the room before Brownhill had a chance to argue.

## CHAPTER NINE

"That was a bit obvious, Sarge," Yang Chu said to Smith by the front desk.

"I don't care," Smith said. "I'm keeping you and Whitton apart. I need you to stay sharp and you can't do that if you're thinking with your todger."

He stopped by the front desk.

"Baldwin, have you got the photographs of Christopher Riley?"

Baldwin handed him two black and white photographs.

"Good luck out there," she said. "Stay warm. It's getting colder and colder by the minute. It'll be dark soon."

"Thanks, Baldwin."

They drove back towards Christopher Riley's flat.

"I'm not thinking with my todger," Yang Chu said. "I happen to have a lot of respect for Whitton and since when was the word todger in the Australian vocabulary?"

"I've been here too long, and you might not believe this, but I've been infatuated a few times myself. You and Whitton are not going to happen. Get used to it."

He parked outside the Chinese restaurant. The flat above was in darkness but the restaurant was well lit up. Smith and Yang Chu went inside. Mr Yin was sitting at a table at the back of the restaurant. He was polishing off his third plate of chicken chow mein. He spotted Smith and Yang Chu and sighed.

"Mr Yin," Smith said. "Sorry to interrupt your feast but we need to ask you a few more questions."

"Have a seat," Yin said. "Would you like something to eat? The chicken chow mein here is almost bearable."

He started to laugh.

"No thanks," Smith sat down opposite him. "Do you know where Mr Riley went after you saw him on Christmas Day? Did he tell you what his Christmas Day plans were?"

"It was his first Christmas after the divorce," Yin wiped his mouth with a napkin and belched loudly. "Excuse me. I asked him if he wanted to join me here, but he said no. He said he was going to drown his sorrows in the pub all day."

"Which pub?"

"How should I know? I have work to do. They need help in the kitchen. We have a party of twenty five coming in later. I'm not looking forward to it."

"Are there many pubs around here?" Yang Chu asked.

"I don't drink," Yin said. "Eating is my vice as you can probably tell. Mr Riley set off on foot if that's any help to you."

"Yes, it is," Smith said. "Thank you, Mr Yin."

Ye Olde Yeoman was a hundred metre walk from Riley's flat. By the time Smith and Yang Chu went inside they were both frozen to the bone. There was a log fire burning in the corner of the room. A jukebox was blasting out an old Alice Cooper song. Smith rubbed his hands together and approached the bar. A man in his early twenties was typing frantically on a mobile phone behind the bar.

"Excuse me," Smith said. "Do you work here?"

The man looked up from the phone and stared blankly at Smith and Yang Chu.

"Of course, I work here," he said. "What can I get you?"

Smith shivered.

"Double Jack Daniel's," he said. "No water, no ice."

Yang Chu looked shocked.

"Make that two," Smith said.

He smiled at Yang Chu.

"It'll warm you up."

The barman poured the drinks and placed them on the bar counter. Smith took out one of the photographs of Christopher Riley.

"Do you recognise this man?" He showed the photo to the barman.

"Might do, who's asking?"

Smith drained the double whiskey in one go. It burned his throat as it went down and then hit his stomach. The warming effect was felt immediately.

"Do you know him or not?"

"What is this?" the barman said. "Who are you? Some kind of heavies?"

"Yes," Smith said. "I'm an underworld boss and this is my protection." He patted Yang Chu on the shoulder.

"He knows fourteen different kinds of lethal martial arts. Do you know this man or not?"

He pushed the photograph in front of the barman's face.

"Yes," the barman said. "Chris comes in here quite often."

"Was he in here on Christmas Day?"

"He was."

"Now that wasn't too hard was it? Was he here with somebody?"

"He was on his own," the barman said. "He's just got divorced. He's quite a sad case. What's this all about? What's he done?"

"Nothing," Smith said. "What time did he leave?"

"Just after last orders. He finished his last brown ale and left. It's quite depressing really. I mean, who wants to be on their own on Christmas Day?"

"Did he leave on his own? Are you sure there wasn't anybody with him?"

"I don't think so."

"Think harder," Smith pressed him.

"I didn't see him leave," the barman said. "I was busy clearing up the place. You're police, aren't you? I've seen you somewhere before."

"Let's go," Smith said to Yang Chu.

"That'll be eight quid."

Smith looked at Yang Chu. He hadn't touched his drink.

"I don't have any cash on me," Smith said.

Yang Chu took out a ten pound note and placed it on the counter. Smith picked up the untouched glass of Jack Daniel's and drained it in one go.

"You caught the clown killer," the barman said. "That's where I've seen you before. You were in all the papers."

He handed Yang Chu a two pound coin.

Smith and Yang Chu were about to leave when Smith had the feeling he was being observed. A bald man in his fifties was staring at him. Smith walked over to him.

"I couldn't help overhearing," the man said. "I'm not nosy but it's quiet in here. The name's Bill. You were asking about Chris."

"That's right," Smith said. "Do you know him?"

"Only to say hello to. We're not really friends. He gets in here every now and then. I was in here Christmas Day. I'd had a row with the wife and I came in here for a few quick ones before they closed."

"Did you speak to Mr Riley?"

"No, but I did see him leave. He wasn't on his own if you know what I mean."

He winked at Smith.

"What *do* you mean?"

"From where I was sat, it looked like he'd pulled. Lucky bugger. On Christmas Day of all days."

"Do you know this woman?"

"No," Bill said.

"What did she look like?"

"Bit of a looker. Long black hair. Weird eyes though. She looked right at me when they left. She had eyes that stared right through you."

# CHAPTER TEN

It was dark when Smith and Yang Chu emerged onto the street outside Ye Olde Yeoman. The wind had eased off slightly but the chill in the air was biting. Smith fumbled with the key in the lock on his car. He was feeling extremely light headed. The whiskey had affected him straight away. He realised he hadn't had a drink since before the stabbing a few months earlier.
"Do you think you're alright to drive?" Yang Chu asked. "You had two double whiskies back there."
"I'll be fine," Smith managed to get the door open.
He started the engine, engaged reverse gear and took his foot off the clutch too soon. The red Ford Sierra stalled.
Concentrate, he thought.
He turned the key in the ignition again. The car was still in gear. It stalled again.
"Third time lucky," he smiled at Yang Chu.
He started the car again. It shot backwards and slammed into a parked Mercedes Benz.
"Shit," Smith said. "Do you want to drive?"
Yang Chu got out and walked round to the back of the car. He inspected the damage and got in the driver's side.
"You bust the Merc's headlight. Your car doesn't seem to be too badly damaged."
"She may be old," Smith said. "But she's a tough bugger."
"What do you want to do?"
"Get out of here. There's nobody around - nobody saw anything. The owner of the Merc will have insurance."

Yang Chu shook his head. He started the engine and drove away from the scene of the accident.

"Not a word to anyone about this," Smith said.

He was starting to slur his words.

"You can drop me off at my house," he said. "And pick me up in the morning."

They drove in silence for a while. Smith knew he should've reported the accident, but he also knew that it would only mean trouble. He was probably over the legal limit for driving and he could risk losing his job. Yang Chu stopped the car outside Smith's house.

"Thanks," Smith said. "See you tomorrow. And remember, not a word to anyone about what happened. It's been a while since I had a drink."

He stumbled out of the car and concentrated on walking in a straight line up the path to his front door. Yang Chu drove off without saying a word.

Theakston was waiting in the hallway when Smith managed to get inside.

"Hey, boy," Smith patted him on the head. "I'm slightly pissed. Are you hungry?"

*Stupid question,* he thought.

The dog was always hungry.

He went through to the kitchen and put some food in the dog's bowl. He suddenly felt like smoking a cigarette. He had stopped smoking after the stabbing and the time in hospital, but he decided he wanted to start again. He opened the kitchen cupboard. He remembered there was still a full carton in there. He opened it up, took out a pack of cigarettes and went outside to the back garden. The cold air froze his head immediately. He lit a cigarette and took a long drag. His vision went black. The buzz from the nicotine hit him at once after such a long time without smoking. Smith smiled as his sight came back. He took another long drag and sat back in the chair. The freezing air was helping to clear his head. He thought about the accident. It had been a while since he'd had a car accident and then it hadn't been his fault. Someone had loosened the wheel nuts and his front wheel had come off while he was driving.

Smith stood up and went back inside the house. He was feeling quite awake now. He realised he hadn't eaten all day, but he wasn't hungry. He went through to the living room, opened the side board and took out the bottle of Jack Daniel's. He took a long swig straight out of the bottle. He switched on the television. The news was finished, and the weather report was on. Heavy snowfall was forecast for the entire country.

"Great," Smith said. "That's all we need."

Smith turned off the television and stared at the blank screen. He took a long drink and thought about what had happened earlier that day.

The mystery woman with the raven hair, he thought, we need to find this woman.

He took out his phone and dialled Whitton's number. Whitton answered straight away.

"Sarge," she said. "Where are you?"

"I'm at home," Smith said, "I'm getting reacquainted with a couple of old friends. Have you got anything for me?"

"Nothing, we spoke to Riley's wife again. She's not exactly a friendly woman. She didn't seem to care too much either. Are you alright? You sound a bit down."

"I'm fine," Smith said. "Jack is starting to cheer me up."

"Are you drunk?"

"A little bit. We need to find a mysterious woman with black hair and peculiar eyes."

"Sarge?"

"Christopher Riley was seen with a woman on Christmas Day," Smith said. "She's one of the last people to see him alive. We need to find out who she is."

"It's getting late, get some sleep."

"I will," Smith said. "Oh, and Whitton."

"Yes,"

"Yang Chu is smitten with you."

"Goodnight, Sarge," Whitton rang off.

Smith put the phone down and went upstairs. He lay on the bed and was asleep in seconds.

## CHAPTER ELEVEN

*Tuesday 28 December 2010*

The woman ran through the fields. The rain was falling on her long black hair. Something was chasing her. The full moon lit her way. Her pursuers were gaining on her. A pack of wolves. Their teeth were bared, and saliva dripped from their fangs. The woman increased her speed, but it was futile. The snarling beasts behind her were faster. They snapped at her heels as she ran. She was holding a knife, but she knew it would be useless. There were too many of them. A cloud drifted across the face of the moon and the field was cloaked in darkness. The woman was tiring - she wouldn't be able to keep going for much longer. The cloud revealed the glow of the full moon again and the wolves moved in for the attack. The woman raised the knife in the air and brought it down on the head of one of the wolves. It wasn't enough - two more pounced and pinned her to the ground. She looked up at the moon as the biggest wolf locked his teeth on her neck. Her throat was torn open and the blood gushed out.
"Holy shit," Smith shot up in the bed.
He was drenched in sweat. Theakston was fast asleep at his feet, oblivious to what was going on. It was still dark outside. He looked at the clock on the bedside table, it was seven in the morning.

Smith got out of bed and went to the bathroom. He looked at his face in the mirror, there were heavy dark bags under his eyes. He washed his face with some water and breathed deeply. Suddenly, he experienced a peculiar sensation - it was as if someone was watching him. He looked in the mirror again.
"I need to get more sleep," he said to the face in the mirror.

He was about to go back to the bedroom when he spotted something. There was a woman standing in the doorway behind him. He could make out her features in the bathroom mirror. It was the woman with the long black hair and unnerving eyes. Blood was pouring down her neck.

Smith shot up in his bed again. He woke up with such a jolt that Theakston fell off the bed and started barking at him.
"What the hell is happening to me?" he said.
He looked at the clock. It was still seven in the morning. Sweat had drenched the sheets in the bed. He got out of bed, dressed and went downstairs and turned on the kettle. He tried to brush the dream aside, but it was still fresh in his mind. He hadn't had a nightmare for a very long time. In the past it was Laura, his sister he used to dream about on a regular basis, but those dreams had stopped. There was a knock on the door.
Yang Chu's early, he thought.
He walked through and opened the door. Snow had fallen during the night and a thick blanket of white covered the streets. There was nobody outside. A small package had been placed on the doorstep. Smith went outside and looked around. The streets were deserted. There were footprints in the snow leading up to his house. He picked up the package and went back inside. He made some coffee and opened the back door. Theakston appeared in the kitchen, stretched languidly and strolled outside. Smith picked up the coffee, a pack of cigarettes and followed after him. The back garden was white. He lit a cigarette and smiled. He picked up a handful of snow, packed it together into a tight ball and threw it at the dog. There was a soft thud and the snowball fell from Theakston's rear end. He didn't look

impressed. He shook the remaining snow off and went back inside before Smith had the chance to make another snowball.
"Sorry, boy," Smith laughed loudly. "I couldn't resist it. We never had much snow when I was growing up."

Smith finished his cigarette and lit up another one.
"Morning," Yang Chu stepped outside. "I knocked but you didn't answer. The front door was open. How are you feeling? You don't look too well."
"I'm fine. I had a weird dream though. I've never had a dream like it before. Do you want some coffee? The kettle's just boiled."
Smith made two fresh cups of coffee and sat down at the kitchen table. Yang Chu sat opposite him.
"What's that?" Yang Chu pointed to the small package on the table.
"I have no idea. Someone left it on my doorstep this morning. They knocked but when I went outside there was nobody about."
"That's weird," Yang Chu said. "Don't you want to see what's inside?"
Smith opened up the box. All it contained was a Michelin map of Romania. There was no note to indicate where it had come from.
"Romania?" Yang Chu said. "Are you planning a trip to Romania?"
"I don't even know where Romania is," Smith opened up the map and spread it out on the table.
A small portion of the map had been highlighted with a green marker pen - a section in the north east of the country.
"Why would someone leave a map of Romania on your doorstep?" Yang Chu studied the map carefully. "I've never heard of any of these place names."
"I have no idea. I suppose we should get going."
He stood up and left the map on the table.

Whitton and Bridge were in the canteen when Smith and Yang Chu walked in. Bridge looked like he'd had a rough night - his eyes were red, and he hadn't shaved.

"You look like you had more to drink than me last night," Smith said to him.

"New lady friend," Bridge smiled. "She can drink anyone under the table. She's gorgeous though. I met her at a club on Boxing Day."

"I don't want to know," Smith walked over to the coffee machine and got a cup of strong coffee.

"Coffee break's over," Brownhill marched into the canteen. "We have some news about the murder. My office now."

She marched out again. Smith took a sip of the coffee and winced. It tasted awful.

"What is it about coffee in police canteens?" he said. "Read any detective novel and there's one thing they all have in common - all the police canteens serve shit coffee."

"We'd better go," Whitton said. "Brownhill looks quite scary this morning."

Two minutes later, Smith, Whitton, Bridge and Yang Chu stood against the wall in Brownhill's office.

"Firing squad," Smith whispered to Whitton. "Looks like we're about to face a firing squad."

"Where's Thompson?" Brownhill walked inside.

"I thought he was off with a cold," Smith said.

"He's due back in today. It's not acceptable to be absent from duty because of a common cold. I told him as much. Anyway, we can't wait for him. Take a seat."

Everyone sat in front of Brownhill's desk.

"Grant has finished his report," Brownhill began. "All the fingerprints found in the flat were Riley's. That's the bad news. The good news is this. He found a good few hairs on the bed sheets that definitely didn't belong to Riley."

"Let me guess," Smith said. "They were long and black."

"That's right," Brownhill looked surprised. "How did you know that?"

Smith told her about the woman who had been seen with Riley at Ye Olde Yeoman on Christmas Day.

"We need to find this woman," Brownhill said.

Smith smiled.

"The path report came up with something even more intriguing," Brownhill continued. "Riley had a very impressive blood alcohol count. He died due to loss of blood from the wound in his neck. This is the interesting part. The path guys found traces of Trichloromethane in the membranes of his nose and throat."

"Trichloro what?" Bridge said.

"Chloroform," Brownhill said. "It appears that Mr Riley was anaesthetised before he was killed."

"That ties up with Webber's theory," Smith said. "That he had his throat cut while he was lying on his stomach. But why bother to knock him out if you're going to kill him anyway? If he'd had so much to drink anyway, surely that was a bit unnecessary."

"We don't know yet. I'm just giving you the facts."

"Chloroform," Smith found himself thinking out loud. "I thought that was now illegal."

"It is, you can't just get it over the counter in a pharmacy, but I suppose when you're planning on murdering someone, you don't exactly worry about the law do you?"

"There are ways to get hold of anything if you're willing to pay for it," Whitton said.

"I still don't get why the murderer would use it in the first place," Yang Chu joined the conversation. "Like the Sarge said, if you're going to murder someone, why knock them out first?"

"One thing's for sure," Smith said. "This wasn't some argument that got out of hand - it was a meticulously planned murder."

The door opened, and DS Thompson walked in. He looked like he had been running. His face was wet and sweat was dripping from his nose.

"Nice of you to join us," Brownhill said. "You really don't look well."

"You try to catch a bus in this weather," Thompson sniffed. "All the routes have been cancelled due to the snow. I had to walk the whole bloody way."

"Bus?" Smith said. "What's wrong with the faithful Audi?"

"I traded it in. Mrs Thompson persuaded me to buy another car. She's always wanted a Mercedes Benz. Her brother in law has one. Anyway, to cut a long story short, we were visiting the in laws yesterday - Mrs Thompson wanted to show off the new car and when we were ready to leave I noticed that some moron had smashed one of my headlights in. Smashed it to bloody pieces they did. Now the car's in for repairs. It's only done ten miles."

Smith glanced across at Yang Chu and smiled. Yang Chu also had a huge grin on his face.

"I'm going to find out who did it," Thompson was adamant. "There was red paint on the smashed light. I'll find the bastards and they're going to pay."

"Sorry to hear about the car," Smith said. "It was probably a drunk driver. They probably didn't even realise what they'd done. Anyway, we have a lot to get through."

He gave Thompson a summary of the information they had so far.

"Chloroform?" Thompson said when Smith had finished. "Where did they get chloroform from? I thought it was banned."

"We've gone through that," Brownhill said. "This is what we're going to do. Thompson, seeing as though you're a bit under the weather, you and Yang Chu can enjoy the warmth of the station and find out everything you can about Chloroform. Where you can obtain it - that kind of thing. Smith, you and Whitton need to get hold of the witness who saw Riley with the unknown woman. See if you can get a better description of her. Bring him in if you have to. Bridge, you and I are going to speak with Riley's ex-wife. In my experience it's those closest to the victims who tend to know much more than they think."

## CHAPTER TWELVE

Snow had started to fall again when Smith and Whitton left the station. The thick flakes were settling on the tarmac in the car park. A thin layer had formed on the roof of Smith's car.

"Do you think it's safe to drive in this?" Whitton said.

"I don't know," Smith said. "I suppose we'll soon find out."

He opened the car and they got inside. He turned on the windscreen wipers to remove the snow from the windscreen and drove slowly out of the car park.

The streets were deserted as they drove. Smith could feel that the car was handling strangely on the slippery roads.

"I had the weirdest dream last night," he said. "I woke up after a nightmare, got up and went to the bathroom. It turned out that this was also a dream, but I was aware of what was happening. I could even control what I did in the dream. I woke up again, this time for real."

"Wow," Whitton said. "I've read about that. It's known as a double awakening. A lucid dream. It's very rare."

"Great, it freaked me out anyway. It's never happened before."

"It's supposed to be a form of psychosis," Whitton said. "But we all know you're not quite right in the head."

"Are you saying I'm psychotic?" Smith stopped the car outside Ye Olde Yeoman.

"You're a bit weird, but I wouldn't say you were a full blown psychopath. What was the nightmare about?"

"I'll tell you another time. Let's see if we can find out where our friend Bill is likely to be today."

Ye Olde Yeoman was closed. It was still two hours before opening time. Smith banged on the door. A few moments later it was opened by a young woman with short red hair.

"We're closed," she said.

"I know," Smith took out his ID. "Sorry to disturb you but we're looking for a patron of yours. A man by the name of Bill. We need his help in finding someone."

"You'd better come in," the woman said. "I'll get my dad."

The early morning atmosphere of a pub always made Smith feel melancholy. The smell of stale beer and the silence of the morning after was depressing. It didn't matter where it was, pubs all around the world were exactly the same. A balding man with an impressive beer belly limped towards them.

"Morning," he said. "Shane Littlewood. I'm the landlord here. How can I help you?"

"We're looking for a man by the name of Bill," Smith said. "Mid-fifties - he may be an important witness in a serious crime investigation."

"Bill?" Littlewood scratched his nose. "That's probably Bill Smithies. He's always in here. What's he seen?"

"We're not sure yet. Do you know where we can find him?"

Littlewood looked at his watch.

"It's almost nine," he said. "Bookies will be open soon. You'll probably catch him there. Ladbrokes on Monk Street."

"Thanks for the help," Smith said.

Ladbrokes on Monk Street was surprisingly full when Smith and Whitton went inside. It was still early in the morning but a large number of people, most of them men were crammed inside, gazing hopefully at the numerous television screens scattered around the room. Smith spotted Bill almost immediately.

"Morning, Bill," he said. "Are you winning?"

"Don't know yet," Bill sighed. "The nine-fifteen at Harrogate is about to get under way."

He glanced over at Whitton.

"This is DC Whitton; can we have a word? It's about the woman who was with Christopher Riley on Christmas Day."

"Can it wait ten minutes? I've got fifty quid on a sure thing. Twenty to one. Got a tip from a guy at the pub. Maggie's Millions."

Smith laughed.

"It's got no chance," he said.

Twenty minutes later, Smith, Whitton and Bill Littlewood sat in the small coffee shop down the road from the Ladbrokes. Bill was fifty pounds poorer.

"I was sure I was onto a winner there," he said. "I stood to make a grand less tax."

"You win some you lose some," Whitton said.

"This woman," Smith came straight to the point. "Would you recognise her again?"

"Yes," Bill said without thinking.

Whitton looked across at Smith.

"I have an eye for faces," Bill said. "I'm terrible with names but faces I always remember."

"Great, in that case would you mind working on a photofit down at the station? It shouldn't take long."

Bill had a faraway look in his eyes.

"I was going to watch the ten forty five at Redcar, but I've got a feeling that this isn't my lucky day."

## CHAPTER THIRTEEN

Emily Riley lived in a three bedroom detached house three streets from the river. It was not one of the more exclusive properties where the new millionaires lived but it still belonged in the upper middle class bracket. Riley lived among doctors, accountants and lawyers.
"How on earth did Christopher Riley go from this to renting a grotty flat above a Chinese restaurant?" Bridge said.
"Divorce," Brownhill sighed. "It's never a pleasant thing for anyone."
"I'm never getting married," Bridge said."It's the single life for me."
"We'll see," Brownhill knocked on the front door of number eighteen.
Emily Riley opened the door immediately. It was as if she had been expecting them.
"Hello," she said sheepishly.
She was dressed in a black tracksuit with some designer logo neither Bridge nor Brownhill recognised on it. She obviously visited the gym on a regular basis. Bridge couldn't help but admire her toned physique.
"Good morning, Mrs Riley," Brownhill said. "DI Brownhill and this is DC Bridge. Can we come in?"
"Of course, but you'll have to excuse the mess. The cleaner won't be in until tomorrow. I gave him time off for Christmas."
Cleaner? Bridge thought, Him? Who the hell has a male cleaner?
Emily led them into a medium sized sitting room. A small girl was busy working on a jigsaw puzzle in the corner of the room.
"Maggie," Emily said. "Go to your room, baby. I need to speak with these people for a while."
"But the tiger's face is almost done," Maggie protested. "It'll take me less than five minutes to finish the whiskers."

"Maggie."

The look on Emily's face seemed to say more than any words could. Maggie put down the jigsaw piece she had in her hand and left the room.

"She's still confused about this whole business," Emily said. "We all are. Can I get you anything to drink? Coffee? Tea?"

"No thanks," Brownhill spoke for Bridge and herself. "Mrs Riley..."

"Please call me Emily," Emily said. "Mrs Riley doesn't sound right. Especially after everything that's happened."

"OK, Emily, I know this is a difficult time but perhaps you've had a bit of time to think now. Can you think of anyone who would want to do this to Christopher?"

"No, who would do such a thing?"

"Did he have any enemies?" Bridge asked.

"Christopher was a quiet man," Emily said. "He kept himself to himself. He wouldn't hurt a fly."

"If you don't mind me asking," Brownhill said. "Why did you and Mr Riley get divorced?"

"What's that got to do with all this?" Emily was suddenly on the defensive.

"We're just trying to gather as much information as we can," Brownhill decided to change tack. "I know what it's like - my husband and I have recently divorced. I know how painful it is."

Brownhill's openness appeared to work. Emily seemed to relax a bit.

"I didn't realise how hard it would be," she said. "Chris and I met at University. We were inseparable from day one. I thought we were soul mates. I thought we would grow old together, but things changed when Maggie came along. You always assume a child will bring you closer, together don't you? In our case it had the opposite effect. Chris loved Maggie, I'm not denying that, but I don't think he could handle sharing me with someone else. Do you have children?"

"No," Brownhill and Bridge said in unison.

"You'll understand when you do. Are you sure you won't have something to drink?"

"Coffee would be great," Brownhill said.

Emily stood up and left the room. Bridge looked at the jigsaw in the corner of the room. He was surprised - there had to be at least a thousand pieces and Maggie had started the puzzle from the centre.

Emily returned with a tray of coffee and biscuits. She put the tray on the table next to Brownhill and Bridge.

"Thanks," Bridge made a beeline for a custard cream.

"What did Christopher do for a living?" Brownhill asked.

"He was some kind of computer programmer - don't ask me what he programmed. All I know is he provided us with all of this."

She glanced around the room.

"He used to divide his time between London and York," Emily continued. "And it suited us all. His head office was in London and he was often away for a few days but as technology improved so his working life was supposed to improve - he was able to work from home more and more. That was when the problems started. We weren't used to having him around and he wasn't used to having us around. He started drinking more and more. He was close to losing his job a few times."

"And you're a nurse?" Bridge wiped a crumb from the corner of his mouth.

"Yes, when Maggie started school, I went back to nursing. We don't need the money, but I wanted to do something meaningful with my time."

Bridge finished his coffee and put the cup on the table.

"Mrs Riley," he said. "Sorry, Emily, there's something I don't understand. You're obviously not short of a few bob. How on earth did Christopher end up living in a pigsty above a Chinese restaurant?"

Brownhill glared at him.

"I'm sorry, Emily," she said. "My DC is not renowned for his tact."

Emily smiled.

"It's alright, he's a Yorkshireman. I like it - it's actually quite refreshing these days. Chris wasn't broke, nor did the divorce cripple him financially. I think he was punishing himself. He was trying to ease his guilt by suffering."

"Guilt?" Bridge said.

"He felt guilty for failing us. For failing himself. For a computer geek, he was a sensitive soul."

She smiled at Bridge and Bridge could feel his cheeks burn.

"Thank you, Emily," Brownhill stood up. "Thank you for your time. You can be sure that we will do everything in our power to find out who did this. You have my word."

Emily led them out of the room. They met Maggie in the hallway. She stared at Bridge with a blank expression on her face.

"Maggie," Bridge said. "I'm curious. Why do you start the jigsaw puzzle from the middle? Surely it would be much easier to construct the frame first."

"Exactly," Maggie said and went back inside the sitting room.

## CHAPTER FOURTEEN

"Let's get started," Brownhill clapped her hands together.
Everybody had met back at the station and they were now seated in the small conference room. Grant Webber had been asked to join them.
"Grant," Brownhill smiled at him. "Do we have anything new?"
"Not much," Webber said. "Time of death has been confirmed as somewhere between midnight and one on Boxing Day. Cause of death is loss of blood due to the deep laceration in his neck. He'll have bled out in a couple of minutes. Most of the blood seeped into the bed sheets and mattress."
"So, you were right?" Smith said. "He was killed while he was lying on his stomach."
"The evidence would suggest that, there was no sign of the murder weapon at the scene, but we have a good idea about what was used, and this is where it gets interesting. It wasn't your everyday carving knife."
"What do you mean?" Brownhill said.
"From the wound in Riley's neck, it would appear that the knife had a rounded blade."
"Rounded?" Bridge said.
"A straight blade," Webber said. "Like the one on a kitchen knife for example, would slice open the neck evenly. The depth of the wound would be the same all across the laceration. In this instance, the wound was deeper in the centre of the neck which suggests a knife with a rounded blade. A razor sharp one at that."
"So, we're looking for an unusual knife?" Smith said. "That's something at least."

"Right, I've checked the databases and we've never come across such a knife before."

"OK," Brownhill said. "What about the chloroform?"

"He was definitely out of it before he was killed. He wouldn't have felt a thing."

"At least that's something," Yang Chu said.

"He's still dead," Smith said. "What about the hairs you found? The long black hairs."

"Nada," Webber said. "They were definitely from a female - we managed to ascertain that but the DNA we pulled from them is not on our system."

"That brings us to the mystery raven haired woman," Brownhill said. "What did your witness give us?"

Smith started to laugh.

Everybody looked at him as if he were insane.

"Sorry," he said. "But our friend Bill and his so called extraordinary memory for faces have let us down."

"What's so funny?" Brownhill said.

Smith took out a file and opened it up.

"This is what the police artist managed to draw from Bill's description of the woman," Smith passed the drawing around.

"But this is Baldwin," Whitton said.

"Yup, our main suspect in the murder of Christopher Riley is working at the front desk right now. Who wants to go down and arrest her?"

"This is uncanny," Brownhill said. "The likeness is uncanny."

"Aren't we at least going to ask Baldwin where she was on Christmas Day?" Yang Chu asked.

Everybody stared at him.

"Yang Chu," Smith said. "Our star witness is a gambling addict with a drinking problem or is that the other way around? Anyway, I don't think Baldwin is some secret psychopathic killer."

The room erupted. Even Thompson had a grin on his face.

"OK," Brownhill said after a while. "That's enough. Thompson, Yang Chu, what did you find out about the chloroform?"

"You can't get it across the counter," Thompson said. "Nobody uses it anymore. They used to use it as an anaesthetic, but the side effects were unpredictable."

"I did a bit of digging too," Yang Chu said. "It's amazing what you can find on the internet. You can get your hands on just about anything these days from bombs to slaves. Chloroform is available to purchase by mail order. Mainly from China and India. The scariest thing I found out is you can actually make it yourself."

"Make it?" Whitton said.

"I couldn't believe it myself, there are over fifty videos on YouTube that guide you through the process. All you need is a simple still, a litre of acetone and a couple of litres of household bleach."

"Bloody hell," Bridge said. "Surely that kind of thing should be banned from the internet?"

"The internet is a useful but often dangerous tool," Smith said.

"A litre of acetone and a couple of litres of bleach will give you about fifty milligrams of chloroform," Yang Chu continued. "That would be enough to knock out everybody in this room."

"I found out something interesting too," Thompson said. "It takes quite a while for the chloroform to work. It's not like you see in the films where a few drops on a hankie renders someone unconscious straight away - it takes much longer than that."

"Riley was very drunk," Smith said. "He probably didn't know what was happening to him."

"Right," Brownhill said. "I hate to admit it but this meeting has left us no further ahead than we were before. Does anybody have any suggestions?"

"What about the ex-wife?" Smith said. "We're assuming the killer is a woman, aren't we? Nobody has dared to say it yet."

"We are," Brownhill said. "Right now, the evidence leads to that fact."

"Say it."

"Christopher Riley was murdered by a woman," Brownhill said. "Me and Bridge spoke to his ex-wife and in my mind she had no reason to kill him."

"What about money?" Smith said. "The motive is always love, hate or money isn't it?"

"Emily Riley doesn't need money," Bridge said. "She's loaded. Fit body too. I wouldn't mind having a crack at her myself."

"That's enough, Bridge," Brownhill said. "But it's true - her ex-husband looked after her very well. She had no reason to want him dead."

"Hate then," Smith said. "Maybe he'd done something to make her angry."

"Emily Riley is not a suspect," Brownhill said.

"We've got nothing, everybody is a suspect."

"Apart from Baldwin," Yang Chu said.

Smith was about to say something but changed his mind. He smiled at Yang Chu.

"It's been a long day, let's leave it for now. Our brains are fried at the moment. Something is bound to turn up tomorrow."

He said the last part with as much conviction as he could muster but he had a sinking feeling that this investigation was going to drag on for a very long time.

# CHAPTER FIFTEEN

LUZHANY, UKRAINE

**_Monday 26 August 1991_**

Selene was woken by slowly dripping water on her face. She opened her eyes and it took her a while for her to remember what had happened the night before. Rain was starting to fall. It wasn't quite light, but dawn was on the way. Selene sat up and surveyed the landscape around her. She didn't know where she was - she didn't even know if she was still in Romania or if she had crossed the border into Russia. She thought about her trek the previous night. Nobody had come after her this time. The rain was falling harder now, and she was getting drenched, but she didn't care. She was free. After six years, she had managed to escape.

The dawn came, and the sun illuminated the most beautiful valley Selene had ever seen. The fields below her were similar to the ones that surrounded her village, but they seemed less sinister somehow. They welcomed her. Selene stood up and started her descent. She felt elated for the first time in years. She ran down through the rain to the green fields below.

"I'm in Russia," she sang as she ran.

She walked for a few miles and stopped to rest under an ancient oak tree. Her stomach was growling. She hadn't eaten anything in a very long time. The rain clouds slowly moved over the mountains and the sun beat down on the meadows. Selene spotted a cluster of buildings in the distance. Two church domes rose far above the village. She set off again in search of something to eat.

The small village of Luzhany was deserted when Selene reached the road that ran through it. There were no people on the streets and the houses appeared abandoned. Their windows were closed up and the doors were closed. Yellow and blue flags hung from every single house. More flags hung from poles in the gardens. Selene jumped - the flags were similar to her own flag. All that was missing was the red section.

This flag is much prettier, she thought.

She carried on walking and stopped outside the church. She couldn't help staring at the strange building. It was constructed almost entirely out of wood and it looked very old. Two domes rose far above it. She opened the door and went inside. The musty smell hit her in the face immediately. She couldn't help but think that all churches smelled the same. She sat down on a wooden bench and closed her eyes.

I made it, she thought, I'm finally free.

    She'd been with the big man for six years. Six years with no contact with her family or friends. Her life had been what he told her it must be. She'd thought about contacting her family again, but she was certain he would come and look for her there. He wouldn't think to search for her in Russia. For six years she had been his student - his prodigy even. She had tended the fields by day and studied at night. She had learned all about the rituals and their origins and once a month the full moon would appear.

Six years, she thought, seventy two months. Seventy two sacrifices. It was almost too much for her to comprehend.

    Selene was woken from her thoughts by a sound behind her. She jumped and turned around. An old man had entered the church and was now staring at her. He was dressed in black and he was wearing a strange black hat. A grey beard hung down to his huge chest. He continued to stare at her. Selene was sure she could smell alcohol on his breath.

"Dobroye Utro Rebenok," he said in the most soothing voice Selene had ever heard.

She didn't understand what he was saying. She'd studied a bit of English from the television programs she had been allowed to watch but she couldn't speak a word of Russian. The priest looked her up and down and smiled.

"Good morning, Child," he said to her in Romanian. "Are you lost?"

Selene looked around the old church.

"No," she said. "I'm not lost. I've never wanted to be somewhere so much in my life."

Her reply seemed to surprise him. He raised his left eyebrow.

"OK, are you hungry?"

Selene nodded. The priest opened the door of the church and gestured with his arm for her to follow him outside.

    The local priest lived in a modest brick building next to the church. An elderly woman also dressed entirely in black was preparing breakfast on a small gas stove when Selene walked in. The smell was something Selene hadn't smelled since she was last at home. It was the smell of coffee, porridge and boiled eggs.

"Zlata," the priest said. "We have a guest. She's come a long way to eat with us."

The old woman looked at Selene and smiled. It was a smile Selene would never forget. Her blue eyes lit up her whole face. Selene had never seen such bright blue eyes before.

"Syad'te," the old woman said. "Kak tvoye imya?"

Selene stared blankly at her.

"Zlata is asking you to please sit down," the priest said. "What's your name?"

"Selene," Selene said. "Selene Lupei."

"Then please sit down, Selene Lupei. Zlata is the best cook in the whole of Luzhany."

Zlata placed a bowl of porridge in front of Selene and said something else she couldn't understand.

The priest started to laugh. He had a hearty laugh.

"What did she say?" Selene tucked into the porridge.

"She said you need to eat more," the priest said. "In fact, she said you're as skinny as a Russian gymnast."

"Am I in Russia?" Selene's heart started to beat faster.

"Not anymore," the priest smiled. "If you had come two days ago you would have been but now we're free. You're in the Ukraine. The opinion was overwhelming. Now we are free."

Selene had no idea what he was talking about. She finished her porridge and made a start on some boiled eggs and a piece of toast. Zlata looked on approvingly.

"Well, Selene Lupei," the priest said when Selene had finished eating. "What's your story? You claim not to be lost. Why are you here? Where are you heading?"

Selene didn't know what to say. How could she explain to this kind man that she had escaped from the grasps of a man who was responsible for the deaths of hundreds of people? She'd seen more than seventy of them first hand.

"I'm all alone," She said. "I have no family or friends. Romania held nothing more for me."

The priest merely nodded his head.

"OK," he said. "Can you sew?"

"A bit," Selene said.

"Good. Zlata has a lot to get through. Some of the celebrations got a bit out of hand and many of the flags were damaged in the excitement. Zlata will show you what to do."

## CHAPTER SIXTEEN

YORK

*Monday 17 January 2011*

Superintendent Jeremy Smyth's annual crime statistics presentation had been postponed. Smyth had been taken ill with a mystery virus and at one stage it appeared as though the whole thing would have to be cancelled altogether. For the entire workforce at York police station this had been a Godsend, but Smyth had made a rapid recovery and a collective groan had been heard around the station when the news hit the grapevine. Smyth's annual four hours of torture was about to get under way.

Smith sat between Whitton and Yang Chu. Thompson and Bridge were seated in the row in front of them. Brownhill and Chalmers had the misfortune of having to sit at the front of the main conference room with Smyth. Smith watched as Thompson took out a silver hip flask, opened it and took a long swig. He tapped Thompson on the shoulder.
"Great idea," Smith said. "If that's what I think it is would you mind passing it around? It might make things a bit more bearable."
"It's cough medicine," Thompson said. "No matter how much of the stuff I get down my neck I can't seem to shift this bloody cold."
"I feel like a drink," Bridge said. "And old Smyth hasn't even started yet."
"Next year," Smith said. "Remind me to bring a flask like Thompson's. Maybe two."

"Could we have a bit of hush please," Brownhill was glaring in their direction. "The Superintendent is about to begin."
Loud sighs were audible all around the room.

"Good morning everybody," Smyth spoke into the microphone. "Is everybody here? The turnout seems to be down from last year."
"It's the flu season, sir," Chalmers said. "Quite a few of them are off sick."
"Very well," Smyth didn't seem perturbed. "Let's get this show on the road, shall we? I'm afraid to say that 2010 was, as Her Majesty most eloquently put it a few years ago, an annus horribilis for me and the York Police Department."
He switched on the huge screen at the back of the room.
"As you can see," he continued. "From January to March last year it was pretty quiet on the crime front. Things were looking good as far as my stats were concerned. We had the usual number of burglaries, a bit above average assault cases but on the whole, it seemed promising. We were looking at a record year but then…"
He paused for effect. He clicked a button and a graph appeared on the screen. It was a pie chart showing the crime statistics for the rest of the year.
"What happened?" he said. "Can anybody here please explain to me what happened from March through to December?"
The officers in the conference room were silent.
"Twenty six murders," he mouthed the words slowly. "Twenty six murders in nine months. That's almost three a month. In York of all places."
Smith could feel his heart beating faster at the thought of what was coming next.

"This is disgraceful. Based on my points system, the stats for this year are a whopping nine thousand percent worse than last year. Several stern letters have already found their way onto my desk, I can tell you that. Nine thousand percent. Is there anybody here that can even attempt to justify it?"

Chalmers stood up. He'd never seen the Superintendent so angry before.

"Sir," he said. "To be fair, all but one of these murder cases was cleared up in a month or two. We're still busy with the other one but I promise you that one won't take long to crack. If you ask me, that's what we should be looking at - the clear up rate. I'd say its bloody good detective work."

"You were in charge of most of the investigations weren't you, Bob?" Smyth said.

"I was, and my team did us proud."

"That's not good enough," Smyth looked like he was going to cry. "We need to find a way to prevent these crimes happening in the first place. It's all very well being adept at cleaning the crimes up, but it still affects my statistics when murders occur."

"With respect, sir," Chalmers said. "That's not our job. We are, as you said, the cleaners and I for one believe everybody here did a very good job last year."

"Do you realise," Smyth wasn't about to stop any time soon. "That in the last calendar year, York had more murders than Manchester? That's virtually unheard of."

"Maybe the killers are just choosing more picturesque locations to commit their murders," Smith whispered to Whitton.

Whitton started to giggle.

"What was that?" Smyth looked directly at Smith. "What did you say? Are you not taking any of this seriously?"

Smith counted to ten, but it wasn't enough.

It didn't help.

"Seriously?" He remained seated.

Everyone in the room tensed up in anticipation.

"Seriously?" Smith said again. "I take two of your precious statistics very seriously. One of them was my girlfriend and the other one was my sister. I also take it seriously when my house gets blown up and everything I own is destroyed. Talk about a fucking annus horribilis."

Superintendent Smyth didn't know what to say. He stood there with his mouth wide open.

He resembled a dead fish.

"A few years ago," Smith hadn't finished yet. "I would have stood up and walked out but now I'm going to respect the authority you've had thrust upon you and sit here and endure the rest of your bullshit. Please carry on."

A few sniggers were heard in the room, but it didn't last long. The room remained silent for what seemed like forever.

"Right," Smyth filed through a pile of papers to regain his poise. "Let's continue, shall we?"

## CHAPTER SEVENTEEN

Smith finished the coffee in his cup and went to the machine to get another one. It tasted like liquid soil, but he needed the caffeine. He felt like going home and rolling the biggest joint he could - he was sure he still had some marijuana left in the tin in the sideboard, but he decided against it. Whitton and Yang Chu came in the canteen. They seemed to be sharing a joke. Both of them had huge grins on their faces.

"Well, Sarge," Yang Chu sat opposite Smith. "I'd heard about it, but I'd never seen it for myself."

"Heard about what?" Smith said.

"The famous DS Smith 'couldn't give a shit about anything' attitude." Yang Chu said, "Old Smyth didn't know what to do in there."

"Did you notice that he kept the rest of the presentation short too?" Whitton said. "You did us all a favour."

"The man's an idiot," Smith said. "And he's very dangerous."

"Dangerous?" Yang Chu said.

"Any idiot with that much authority is dangerous."

"There's more snow on the way," Whitton said to change the subject. "Lots of it if the weather forecast is correct."

DI Brownhill marched in the canteen. She had a very grave look on her face.

"Smith," she said. "Can I have a word?"

"Speak," Smith said.

"In private."

Smith stood up and followed her to the other side of the canteen. They sat down at a table by the window.

"What's up, boss?" Smith said.

"Detective Sergeant," Brownhill said. "When I arrived here a few months ago I had preconceived ideas about you. I'd heard all about your antics - a loose cannon with an utter disregard for the rules when it came to solving cases. I didn't like you. I'd made my mind up about that before I even met you."

"Thanks, boss, is this heading somewhere or am I just in for more abuse?"

"Just shut up and listen. I've gone through your file and it appears that you were instrumental in resolving every single one of the twenty five murder investigations that Smyth was crying about in there."

"I had a bit of luck," Smith said.

"Nobody has that much luck. The jury's still out as to whether I like you or not but that's irrelevant - you're one of the best detectives I've ever come across, if not the best and if you repeat that to anybody I'll deny it."

"Smyth's going to suspend me again, isn't he?"

"Why do you say that?" Brownhill said.

"I'm not stupid, all this pre-bollocking praise. You're letting me down gently."

"Smyth does want to see you," Brownhill said, "but…"

"I thought so," Smith stood up.

"Sit down. He does want to see you, but I want you to know that you have my full backing. Chalmers will stick up for you too - I've spoken to him. We need you on the Christopher Riley murder. It's been almost a month and we're still no closer to finding out anything."

Smith stood up again.

"Let's get this over with then."

The door to Superintendent Smyth's office was open. Smith knocked. Some kind of South American pipe music was playing softly inside.

"Come in," Smyth said. "Take a seat."

Smith sat down. Smyth did not bother to turn off the music.

"It helps me to relax," Smyth said. "It's an Andean troupe from Bolivia. Their El Condor Pasa is pure genius. You've got to hear it to believe it."

Smith's reply was somewhere between a nod and a grimace.

"You probably already know why you're here. I will not tolerate insubordination at this station."

Smith sat in silence.

"But, on this occasion, not only am I prepared to turn a blind eye - I believe I owe you an apology."

"An apology?" Smith couldn't believe what he was hearing.

"Yes," Smyth said. "An apology. It was extremely insensitive of me to harp on about statistics considering what you've been through in the past twelve months. Your girlfriend, your house being destroyed, and you mentioned something about a sister?"

"She was pulled out of the river. After the football players were shot."

"Ah yes, I remember it now. Well I'm terribly sorry about all that. This ought to cheer you up though. In many countries they have such a thing as officer of the year - an award for outstanding commitment to the job."

"Sir, all I want is to be left to get on with my job."

"We don't have such a thing as officer of the year here," Smyth carried on. "But my position as Superintendent allows me certain powers. One such power is the ability to create such an honour. I've spoken at length to the Chief Constable and he thinks it's a splendid idea. Also, I've been able to back date the award."

Smith didn't like where Smyth was going with this.

"And as such," Smyth smiled a grotesque grin. "I'm proud to inform you that you've been awarded the police officer of the year award for 2010. I'm hopeful that more stations will follow suit when the publicity of your achievements comes to light."

"There's no need," Smith said.

"Detective, I learned a long time ago that modesty is not a virtue. Modesty slows down progress. Anyway, this isn't up for debate - I've already set the ball in motion. There will be a small informal ceremony of course. You should be very proud."

Smith had never wanted to get out of somewhere so quickly. The pipes of the Andes were starting to give him a headache.

"Thank you," he said to indicate that the conversation was over.

"You'll be informed of the details in due course," Smyth said but Smith was already halfway down the corridor.

He needed a drink. He needed a lot of drinks.

"What did Smyth say?" Whitton said to Smith as he was about to leave the station. "Are you suspended again?"

"Let's go for a drink," Smith said. "I'm buying."

Fifteen minutes later they sat at the bar at the Hog's Head. Smith had finished a pint of Theakstons and was a good way through the second.

"Well?" Whitton said. "Are you suspended or not?"

"They want to pin a bloody medal on me. Top cop for 2010."

"You're kidding me?"

"I wish I was. Smyth arranged the whole thing off his own bat. What an imbecile. I humiliate him in front of the whole station and he wants to give me an award."

"But that's great news," Whitton raised her glass. "Top cop."

"It's not great news," Smith drained his glass and tried to catch the eye of the man behind the bar. "I'll be the laughing stock of the station. Bang goes my street-cred. People like me don't win awards for outstanding commitment to the job."

"You're always selling yourself short. I don't know anybody who's more committed to the job than you."

"Two more pints," Smith managed to catch the attention of the barman. "Where's Marge today?"

"She's not feeling well," the barman said. "She's having a lie down upstairs."

"Nothing serious I hope?"

"Just a touch of the flu," the barman put the drinks on the counter. Smith had known Marge, the owner of the Hog's Head for years. She had become a kind of Grandmother figure to him.

"Will there be a ceremony and all that?" Whitton said. "An award ceremony?"

"Let's talk about something else," Smith said. "That's an order. What's going on between you and Yang Chu?"

"Nothing, he's more like a little brother than anything else. He's a good detective too."

"Make sure it stays that way," Smith said.

"Are you jealous?"

"Of course not," Smith took a long sip of his beer and smiled.

"Anyway, Yang Chu's not my type. I prefer green eyes."

Whitton laughed. She looked into Smith's eyes. They were very bloodshot. He looked like he hadn't slept properly for a while. They stared at each other for quite a long time. Smith had forgotten what an unusual shade of green Whitton's eyes were. He broke eye contact.

Smith finished his beer and ordered two more. He was starting to feel quite drunk, but he liked it.

"I'm still having the dreams," he said. "The ones where I think I've woken up and then realise I'm still dreaming. They're becoming more and more frequent. The last one scared the hell out of me. It started out like the ones I used to have all the time - the one where I'm in the water and my sister is sinking below me. I reach out and I can't save her in time. Then I wake up, or at least I think I've woken up. I open the curtains and Laura floats past the window like she's in the sea. She reaches out to me, but I can't get hold of her. Then she isn't Laura anymore - she's this evil animal with cruel eyes and sharp fangs dripping with blood. Then I woke up for real. It's starting to freak me out."

"Maybe you should see someone about it," Whitton suggested.

"A shrink?" Smith said. "You've got to be kidding?"

"Don't come with all this macho crap. Something is causing these dreams. Maybe if you find out what it is they'll stop."

"Whitton, there's no way in hell that I'm going to see a head doctor."

"You've had a rough year. Anybody else would probably have had a nervous breakdown by now - lost the plot completely. Everything is building up inside that stubborn head of yours and it needs to be released somehow. The dreams are a part of this essential release."

"Where did you come up with this bollocks?"

"Psychology 101," Whitton said. "Three semesters a few years ago."

Smith started to laugh.

"Two pints please," he said to the barman.

He turned to Whitton.

"Are you tired?"

"I feel wide awake."

"Me too, a bit drunk maybe but I'm still awake. I'm starving though."
"Why don't we order a couple of steak and ale pies?" Whitton said.
"Marge is ill," Smith said. "The other chef doesn't know how to cook them like she does. I'll tell you what, I'll treat you to a frozen pizza, a few beers and a new Metallica DVD. You should hear it through my surround sound system."
"You old romantic you," Whitton said.
"Is that a yes then?"

## CHAPTER EIGHTEEN

LUZHANY, UKRAINE

***Friday 30 August 1991***

The small village of Luzhany was preparing for another weekend of celebrations. Boris Yeltsin had finally recognised Ukrainian independence. The festivities were set to carry on for weeks throughout Ukraine. Selene had woken early, and she was busy in the kitchen. She was helping Zlata prepare a modest feast for the revellers. An ox had been slaughtered and was slowly roasting on an open fire in the village square. Zlata and Selene were busy with sacks of potatoes, cabbages and beetroot. Selene had come to like working with Zlata - they worked well together despite the fact that neither of them spoke the other's language. They communicated with gestures. Zlata indicated what needed doing and Selene got it done. They made an excellent team.

Ivor, the priest entered the kitchen and removed his hat. His brow was soaked with perspiration. It was promising to be an extremely hot day. He kissed Zlata on the cheek and rested his hand on Selene's shoulder.
"You are a gift from God indeed," he smiled.
Selene smiled back. She'd been with Ivor and Zlata for only four days, but they'd been the happiest four days of her life. These strangers had treated her well - she felt like part of a family once more. Not once had either of them questioned her reasons for being there and Selene was happy not to have to divulge them.

"We have enough potatoes here to feed the Ukrainian army," Ivor said. "I think we're going to need more cabbage."
"What are the celebrations for?" Selene asked him.
"Freedom. Russia is dissolving before our eyes and not before time. Yeltsin is a wise man. He has spared much bloodshed. It was futile to ever expect such a diverse group of people to live under one flag. It has finally happened, and we must embrace the change the only way we Ukrainians know how. With drinking…"
He took Zlata by the shoulders and turned her round.
"And dancing," he added.
They danced a slow waltz. Selene was amazed at how nimble Ivor's feet were considering the weight they were carrying.
"Ivor," Zlata laughed.
She said something Selene couldn't understand.
"Zlata seems to think that there is always work to do," Ivor said. "But life's not always about work. Selene, you've done enough for today, take a break. The river here is especially beautiful at this time of the year."

Selene followed Ivor's orders and went outside. The sun was high in the sky and there wasn't a cloud in sight. She walked past the old church and headed for the river. She spotted a group of boys in the distance. They were kicking a ball around between some trees. They stopped playing as Selene approached.
"Salut," Selene said.
The three boys looked her up and down. One of them, a tall gangly boy with thin blond hair said something in Russian and the other boys started to laugh. The gangly boy's chest seemed to swell up with pride.
"What's your name?" one of the other boys said in English.

He was tall and athletic with dark hair. Selene looked into his eyes. They were the darkest eyes she had ever seen. They were almost black like her hair. Long black eyelashes hung on either side of them.
"Selene," she said. "My name is Selene. I'm heading for the river."
She set off again. After a few paces she turned around. Two of the boys had returned to their game but the boy with the dark eyes was watching her. Selene turned around, smiled and continued on her way.

She heard the river before she could see it - a soft trickle of water over rocks. She jumped down a small embankment and sat on an old tree stump. Ivor had been right. This was a most beautiful place. The river wound down through the valley. It flowed at its own pace. It didn't seem to be in any hurry.
I could stay here forever, she thought.
She'd never felt such peace before.
"You're the Romanian girl," a soft voice was heard behind her.
Selene turned around. It was the boy with the dark eyes. He was staring at her. His long eyelashes didn't seem real.
"Yes," she said and turned back to face the river.
Without asking, the boy took a seat next to her on the tree stump.
"I'm Luka," he said. "I'm almost eighteen."
"Congratulations."
Selene didn't know why she said it, but it was the first word that came into her head.
"You speak English?"
"From the television. I don't speak it well though."
"You speak it well enough," Luka said. "I'm going to work in London next year. When I'm eighteen. I'm going to work in a big hotel. I've been learning English from a tape. Are you going to be at the dance tonight?"

"I think so," Selene didn't know what was happening to her.
She felt strange. It felt like something was burning inside her stomach.
"Then perhaps we'll dance," Luka said.
Selene focused on the river as it flowed slowly between its banks. She stared for some time.
"Perhaps," she said.
When she turned around Luka was gone.

As the sun disappeared behind the mountains in the distance, music could be heard in the valleys below. The smell of beef and potatoes and roasted onions had drawn people from miles around. Blue and yellow flags were flying from anywhere they could be fixed. The ox had been carved and plates and plates of delicious beef had been placed on a huge table in the village square. Enormous vats of vodka and wine were standing next to the table. The music stopped.
"People," a loud voice resonated through the square.
It was Ivor the priest.
"People," he said again. "We have waited a long time for this and we must embrace it for as long as possible. We must stand together proudly as Ukrainians and do what Ukrainians do best. Now let's drink."
A loud cheer was heard, and the music started up again.

Selene watched the whole spectacle in awe. The people of Luzhany and the surrounding villages were singing, dancing, eating and drinking together. The atmosphere was euphoric. The sound of the music mesmerised her. She felt a hand on her shoulder and jumped.
"Would you like to dance?"
It was Luka.
"Perhaps," Selene looked into his dark eyes. "But I don't know this music."

"Follow me," Luka put one hand on her shoulder and the other on the small of her back.

His touch made her shiver.

"It's easy," he said.

He led her through the first part of the dance - a traditional waltz with a quick three-four time. Selene quickly got the hang of it and they moved closer to the rest of the dancers. Suddenly, Luka spun her round and she was grabbed by somebody. She was about to scream then realised this was part of the dance. She was in the arms of a hefty man with a beard who smelled faintly of cabbages. Soon she was reacquainted with Luka and she smiled. He deftly danced her away from the crowd and any further competition.

    The music stopped, and another song began; a quicker, more upbeat song.

"I don't like this dance," Luka said. "It has far too many complicated changes. I prefer to keep things simple. Let's get something to eat."

He led her to the huge table laden with food. He piled a plate full of beef and potatoes for Selene and took a plate for himself. They sat down on the grass a short distance from the dancers.

"Do you like it here?" Luka asked.

"It's like heaven," Selene said. "I want to stay here forever."

"I don't, I want more than this."

"What can be more than this? I thought you liked to keep things simple."

They ate in silence for a while. Selene had never felt so happy. She watched Luka as he ate. He seemed to take it very seriously. He had a very solemn expression on his face.

"Selene," a familiar voice was heard.

It was Ivor.

"You have to go," Ivor sounded different.

He sounded almost frightened.

"Go where?" Selene said.

"You need to get away from here. They know you're here. He's found you. Go now."

## CHAPTER NINETEEN

YORK

***Tuesday 18 January 2011***

Smith woke up from a dream he instantly forgot. His head felt like somebody was hitting it with rocks. He rubbed his eyes and looked around the room. Theakston was nowhere to be seen.
He must have slept downstairs, Smith thought.
He turned his head and gasped. Whitton was lying in the bed next to him. She was breathing softly. Smith gently peeled the covers off and crept out of bed. He realised that he was completely naked. He tried to remember pieces of the night before. He recalled the conversation at the Hog's Head. Then he remembered coming home with Whitton. They had eaten a pizza, drank a few beers and watched a DVD. Then the Jack Daniel's had come out.
"Fuck," Smith whispered.
Whitton stirred in her sleep and rolled over. Smith slowly lifted the sheets off her. She was also naked. He quickly replaced the sheets.
What have I done?
He got dressed quietly and tiptoed down the stairs.

Theakston was waiting by the back door to be let out. The map of Romania that had been lying on the kitchen table was now in hundreds of tiny pieces on the floor.
"I know, boy," Smith said. "I didn't mean for it to happen. We were drunk."
He opened the back door and the dog marched out in disgust. Smith turned on the kettle. While he waited for it to boil he took a packet of

aspirin out of the cupboard and popped three in his mouth. He washed them down with water straight out of the tap.

"Are you making coffee?" Whitton was standing in the doorway. "My head hurts."

Smith couldn't look her in the eyes.

"I thought you didn't get hangovers," he said.

"Urgh," Whitton rubbed her temples. "I must be getting old. What happened here?"

She pointed to the pieces of the map.

"Jealous dog. He gets destructive when he's not allowed to sleep in the bed."

"About that," Whitton said.

"Do you take sugar?" Smith said in a futile attempt to change the subject. "It's been a while since I made you coffee."

"Two," Whitton said. "About last night."

"We don't need to mention it again," Smith started to make the coffee and dropped the tea spoon on the floor.

"I think we should at least talk about it," Whitton sat down at the kitchen table.

"Talk about what?" Smith couldn't think of anything better to say.

"Sorry, my brain isn't working properly yet."

"We had quite a bit to drink, and somehow we ended up in bed together. It happens."

"Does it?"

"Is that coffee going to take long?" Whitton said. "My head is pounding."

An awkward silence ensued. They sipped their coffee. Smith stood up and started to clear away the pieces of the map.

"What's the map?" Whitton said. "Or at least what was the map?"

"It's a map of Romania, someone left it outside my house."
"Why?"
"I have no idea. Maybe they got the wrong house. I think we should keep what happened last night to ourselves. I think its best. Can you imagine the tongues wagging at the station when they find out?"
"I'm going to have a shower," Whitton stood up.
She looked very upset.
"Maybe it'll clear my head a bit," she added.

Smith put the pieces of the map in the box it had been delivered in.
"Bloody dog," he said.
Theakston walked in and stared at his empty bowl.
"You're far too sensitive," Smith filled the bowl with dog food. "Far too sensitive."
Smith could hear the sound of the shower running upstairs. He tried to piece together the blanks from the previous night, but nothing came to him.
Whitton, he thought, things are never going to be the same.
He suddenly realised what an idiot he'd been. Whitton had seemed quite upset. He was about to switch on the kettle to make some more coffee when he changed his mind. He went upstairs to the bathroom. The steam from the shower had filled the room and condensation had covered the mirror above the sink.

Smith took off his clothes.
"Whitton," he said.
She couldn't hear him over the sound of the jets blasting over her ears.
"Whitton," Smith said again, louder this time.
"What?" Whitton had heard him.

Smith pulled the shower door open. Whitton stared at his naked body in disbelief.

"What are you doing?" She said.

"Last night, there are a few bits I don't remember."

"Me too, but why the hell couldn't this conversation wait until I got back downstairs?"

What am I doing? Smith thought.

He could hear his heart pounding in his head.

"Because I've got a feeling," Smith said. "I've got a feeling that the parts I can't remember were the best parts."

Whitton looked at him. Smith felt like he could look at her green eyes forever. She smiled.

"You need to work on your chat up lines," she said.

"It's been a long time," Smith stepped inside and closed the shower door behind him.

## CHAPTER TWENTY

Smith parked outside the station and he and Whitton got out of the car. The sky was clear, but an icy wind cut straight through to the bone. Smith didn't even notice the cold - he had a smile on his face he couldn't seem to shift. They'd driven the whole way to the station without saying a word but each of them could tell that the other was thinking hard. A million thoughts had rushed through Smith's head. Was he making a mistake? He felt like a hypocrite after warning Yang Chu about relationships in the force. Did he have an ulterior motive without even realising it?

"Sarge," Whitton said when they had reached the door to the station. "What just happened at your house?"

"Was I that bad?" Smith said. "That you've forgotten already."

"No, I'm being serious here."

"To be honest, I don't know what happened. It was odd. I stood in the kitchen when you went up for a shower and I thought about last night. I didn't want you to think that I make a habit of instantly forgettable one-night stands."

"So you thought you'd make it two?"

"Yes, I mean no. Whitton, I'm crap with this sort of thing. Talking about feelings and stuff. Let's go inside – it's freezing out here."

Baldwin was not at her usual post behind the front desk. A man Smith had never seen before was talking loudly on the phone when they approached.

"Calm down," the officer said. "I'm pretty sure he'll be back soon. I mean, it's only been a few hours for Pete's sake."

He held the phone away from his ear and Smith could hear screaming on the other end.

"OK," the officer said. "I'll send someone round. What's the address?"
He wrote the address on a piece of paper.
"I said I'll send someone round," he said and put the phone down.
"Trouble?" Smith said.
He saw from the man's name tag that he was PC Jarvis.
"So called missing person," Jarvis said. "God, he's only been gone for twelve hours. If I had a wife like that I'd be gone for a hell of a lot longer than that, I can promise you that."
"Twelve hours can feel a lot longer when someone doesn't come home. You're new, aren't you? Where's Baldwin?"
"Off sick. Perfect bloody timing if you ask me. It was supposed to be my first day on the beat. I mean, who the hell wants to walk the streets in this shit weather?"
"PC Jarvis," Smith said. "Can I give you a bit of advice? Watch your language in here. I personally couldn't give a rat's arse, but this is a public area and a lot of people don't appreciate it."
He walked down the corridor towards his office.
"Is he for real?" Jarvis said to Whitton.
"Yes," Whitton said. "And he's right. Curb your swearing - it doesn't impress anyone."

Smith turned on his computer and waited for it to boot up. It seemed to take much longer than usual. The cold seemed to slow everything down. Smith thought again about what had happened between him and Whitton. He'd worked with Whitton for four or five years and nothing had ever happened before.
*Why now?* he thought.
He typed in his password and opened up his emails. There were five new messages. Two were from Superintendent Smyth. One was a copy of the crime stats for the previous year and the other was to inform

Smith of the upcoming award ceremony. Smith deleted both emails. The third email detailed the new pension scheme structure for the new year and the fourth was to tell him how much leave he had remaining. He needed to use up twelve days of holiday before the end of March or he would forfeit them. The fifth email was from an unknown address and consisted of just seven words: 'The full moon is upon us again'. There was no indication of who sent the email. Smith closed down the computer and stood up. He'd forgotten about the fifth email by the time he had walked up the stairs to the canteen.

There was nobody in the canteen apart from DI Brownhill. She was sitting by the window staring vacantly at the clouds which appeared to be moving faster than they should.
"Morning, boss," Smith sat opposite her.
Brownhill jumped.
"Oh," she said. "I didn't hear you come in. I was miles away there. It looks like it's going to snow. Those sinister looking things are definitely snow clouds."
"Is something wrong?"
"No, of course not. Do we have any new developments on the Christopher Riley investigation?"
"Afraid not, boss," Smith said. "It's an enigma. We've interviewed the ex-wife again and she's got nothing more to add. I'm afraid if we talk to her anymore she's going to have us on a harassment charge."
"What about the mystery woman?"
"Still a mystery. Nobody seems to have seen them together apart from the drunk guy and his word is hardly reliable. I don't know where else to start looking."

"I know," Brownhill said. "Grant and I had a huge fight about it last night. I asked him if there wasn't maybe something he had overlooked at the crime scene."

"Oh dear."

"I should have known better, I know his work is exemplary. Frustration is getting the better of me."

"I know," Smith said. "This sounds terrible but sometimes I think it would be easier if this murderer struck again - at least then we'd have a bit more to go on."

"I know what you mean. I've called a meeting in my office for what it's worth. Maybe we can bounce a few ideas off each other."

Smith, Whitton and Yang Chu sat opposite Brownhill in her office. Thompson was off sick again and Bridge had not shown up for work.

"This is the team is it?" Smith looked around the room. "The fantastic four. Where's Bridge?"

"He hasn't turned up yet," Brownhill said. "He'd better have a damn good reason."

"What's happening to this place? Even Baldwin's off sick. She's never sick. I don't like the look of the guy who's taken over at the front desk either."

"He's new," Brownhill said.

"He won't last long with his attitude."

"Let's make a start," Brownhill said. "Does anybody have anything new to add?"

Silence.

"Nothing at all?"

"We've been over everything a million times," Whitton said. "We've spoken to everyone who knew Riley and none of them could give us anything to go on."

"Let's start at the beginning once more," Smith said.

Everyone sighed.

"I know it's tedious," Smith said. "But that's what our job consists of. Ninety percent tedium, nine percent disappointment and one percent elation when we finally nail the bastards."

"I'm going to have that printed out and stuck on the walls all around the station," Brownhill said.

The mood seemed to lift slightly.

"Christopher Riley was seen at the Chinese restaurant underneath his flat at around two in the afternoon on Christmas Day," Smith began. "The last confirmed sighting was at Ye Olde Yeoman just before closing time. A witness claimed he saw Riley with a woman with black hair."

"A woman who looked just like Baldwin," Yang Chu added. "Maybe that's why Baldwin is off today - maybe she's out stalking her next victim."

"Yang Chu," Brownhill said. "This isn't helping."

"Nobody seems to know who this woman is," Smith said. "The few friends that Riley had didn't recall him being in a relationship, so we have to assume it was someone he met that night. Nobody has reported seeing her since that night. Riley was found on the morning of the twenty seventh. The path report has confirmed that he died between one and three in the morning of the twenty sixth. We need to find this woman."

"How many times have we heard that?" Yang Chu said. "She's disappeared into thin air."

"Nobody simply disappears."

"What do you suggest we do?"

"We keep digging. We do what we always do - we dig until we find what we've been digging for."

"Whitton," Brownhill said. "You're very quiet. Do you have anything to add?"

"No, Ma'am," Whitton said. "I mean, Smith's right. We can't give up."

"I still say we keep a close eye on Baldwin," Yang Chu said. "She claims to have been on her own the whole of Christmas Day. There's nobody to back that up - nobody to vouch for her."

"Yang Chu," Brownhill said. "I said that's enough. Baldwin is not our murderer."

"I just think it's strange that's all," Yang Chu wasn't giving up. "That our only witness described Baldwin to a T. Why's she not at work today?"

"Enough," Brownhill said. "Smith, you and Yang Chu can have another word with Riley's ex-wife. I get the feeling she doesn't like women very much. Maybe you two will be able to get more out of her."

"What about me?" Whitton appeared annoyed.

"Webber has come up with a beautiful reconstruction of the knife that was used," Brownhill said. "He's based it on the shape of the wound. You and I are going to do some research on knives. Suppliers, manufacturers, that sort of thing. This is a very unusual knife; maybe if we find out where it came from we'll be a step closer."

Brownhill's phone started to ring on her desk. She picked it up. "Brownhill," she said.

Smith, Whitton and Yang Chu watched as Brownhill listened to whoever was on the other end of the line. She didn't appear to be too impressed.

"I have a meeting with the Super," she said when she had finished on the phone. "Something to do with an officer of the year award."

"That'll be me," Smith said with a wry smile on his face.

"You're joking, right?" Brownhill said.

"Nope."

"This place is turning into a madhouse," Brownhill said. "Get out, the lot of you."

## CHAPTER TWENTY ONE

The woman with the long black hair crossed the street again and walked past the bakery. Again. The door to the house with the green door across the road from the bakery opened. She checked her watch, five minutes to two.
Like clockwork, she thought.
She smiled. She watched the slightly overweight man struggle with the lock on the door and turn left. She knew exactly where he was heading.
Look up at the sky.
As if he had heard her, the man lifted his head and gazed up at the snow clouds that were circling wildly above him. He shook his head.

Arnold Mather was a creature of habit. He disliked anything out of order. For twenty two years, he'd spent eight hours every day, Monday to Friday, as a dispatch clerk at AB Jennings Logistics. From five in the morning until one in the afternoon, Arnold was in charge of making sure the deliveries and collections were taken care of. Arnold had suggested these hours himself claiming that if he arrived an hour before the six until two shift clocked in, he could have things organised and things would run much more smoothly. In fact, Arnold had suggested these hours for his own benefit. He didn't care about waking early and when one o clock came around he would hop in his car and beat the mad rush leaving the industrial estate where AB Jennings had their warehouse. He would arrive home no later than fifteen minutes past one. A quick bite to eat and a shower and he'd still have plenty of time to make it to the Fox Inn for two.

Arnold turned left at the Post Office and walked the remaining fifty metres to the Fox Inn. He looked up at the sky again. The snow clouds looked ominous. He'd have been better off looking behind him for then he'd have spotted the woman with the long black hair who was following a short distance behind. If Arnold had been the observant type, he'd have noticed that the woman had followed him every day for over a week. Five beers in the pub, no more, no less and Arnold would be home at six. In time to watch the news. After that, he'd read for precisely an hour and a half and settle into bed at eight. It'd been like this for ten years and Arnold liked it that way. There were too many changes in the world as it was, some kind of normality was important. He'd been married for ten years but the daily drudge had taken its toll on her and she had finally succumbed to the charms of an older, more interesting man. That was over ten years ago.

    Arnold entered the Fox Inn and approached the bar. A complete stranger was washing glasses behind the counter. Arnold didn't know who he was nor did he particularly like strangers interfering with his routine - they upset the equilibrium somehow.
"Where's Ted?" Arnold asked the imposter.
"He's sick," the man said. "There's a lot of flu going around."
"Oh," Arnold said. "Pint of Best please."
The barman poured the beer and placed it on the counter. Arnold paid and took the drink to his usual table in the corner. He sat down and opened one of the newspapers the pub provided for paying customers. An Iraqi suicide bomber had killed sixty three people in Tikrit - Barclays Bank was ordered to pay out millions to customers it had conned, a nasty weather front was set to grip the whole country for days. Arnold leafed through to the crossword. He cursed when he realised that somebody had beaten him to it. The grid was half filled in. Arnold hated completing someone else's crossword. He didn't notice

the woman walk past the window, peer in, and continue in the direction of the river.

The woman with the black hair opened the door to her house and went inside. She realised that her hands were shaking. She opened the sideboard, took out a bottle of brandy and poured herself a large measure. She took a long swig and felt the brandy burn her throat as it went down. She sat in the leather arm chair and stared out of the window. Snow was starting to fall. Thin flakes were hitting the window and melting on the warm glass. Heavy snow had been forecast for the next few days. The woman finished the brandy in the glass and started to panic.

The clouds, she thought - the snow clouds are going to obscure the moon.

There was a knock on the door and she dropped the glass on the floor.

## CHAPTER TWENTY TWO

"Nice place," Yang Chu said. "Her husband obviously did alright for himself."

"Ex-husband," Smith knocked on the door again. "She's at home. I saw something move inside."

The front door opened, and Emily Riley stood in the doorway. She was wearing a thick black sweater and a pair of jeans. Smith could smell the alcohol on her breath straight away.

"Mrs Riley," he said. "Sorry to bother you again. Can we come in?"

"This is getting ridiculous," Emily said. "How many times must we go over the same things?"

"I know. The snow is really coming down again, can we come inside?"

Emily sighed, looked up at the sinister grey clouds and stepped to the side. Smith and Yang Chu walked in.

"Would you like something to drink?" Emily said. "Coffee? You lot solve all your cases with gallons of coffee, don't you?"

"That's only in detective novels."

Emily led them through to the sitting room. A huge jigsaw puzzle lay completed on the floor. It was a photograph of the Eifel Tower. One of the pieces was missing.

"I hate it when that happens," Yang Chu said. "All that effort and you're left with an incomplete picture."

"Rather like police work I imagine," Emily said. "And that's why you're here aren't you?"

"Mrs Riley," Smith sat down on a leather arm chair.

"Emily, and I've reverted back to my maiden name. It seems right don't you think? Under the circumstances. But please just call me Emily."

"What's your maiden name?" Yang Chu said.

Smith glared at him.

"Eastman," Emily said.

Yang Chu took out a notebook and wrote the name down.

"Emily," Smith said. "We're sorry to have to keep harassing you like this, but it's been almost a month now and I'm afraid we're still no closer to figuring out who would want to do this to your ex-husband. Is there anything else you've thought about that might be important?"

"No," Emily said. "Like what?"

"Why did you and Christopher get divorced?" Yang Chu said.

"Boredom," Emily said matter of factly. "Do you mind if I make myself a drink?"

Smith shook his head. Emily poured herself a glass of whisky.

"Chris was a good, old fashioned, salt of the earth type," she said. "Solid as a rock but God was he boring. I used to look forward to him being away from home. I used to count the hours. When he started working more and more from home I couldn't take it anymore."

"So, it was you who filed for divorce?" Smith said.

"Yes. I'd had enough. That wasn't living - I merely existed. I was Mrs Riley, Chris's wife. I'd had enough."

"Did you have much contact with Christopher after the divorce?"

"Not much," she sipped her whisky. "He had Emily every second weekend and some holidays, so I had to see him then but apart from that I didn't have much contact. I moved on."

"But he didn't?" Yang Chu mused.

"What's this got to do with his murder?" Emily said.

"We don't know," Smith said.

"Where's Maggie now?" Yang Chu asked.

"At school of course. Life goes on, even for a nine year old. How much longer do I have to endure these interrogations?"

"Like I said," Smith said. "We're sorry but we don't have much to go on at the moment. Do you know if Christopher was involved with anyone before he was killed?"

"A woman?" Emily started to laugh.

She almost spilled what was left in her glass.

"I doubt it. Chris was hardly what you would call a Casanova. That was another problem in our marriage. He wasn't interested if you know what I mean. Will there be anything else? Maggie will be home from school soon. I'd rather you weren't here when she gets home. It unsettles her, having all these strange people around although she does quite like the other police officer."

"Other police officer?" Smith said.

"The one who was here first," Emily said. "The one with the boyish charm."

"Bridge?"

"That's him," Emily smiled. "DC Bridge. He's a real charmer if you like that sort of thing. He was here yesterday."

"Are you sure?"

"Of course, I'm sure. I might like a drop to drink but I'm not a lush. He came asking more questions. More about me than Chris but it was nice seeing someone taking an interest in me for a change. He sat with Maggie for ages helping her with her jigsaw."

"Thank you, Emily," Smith stood up. "Once again, sorry for bothering you."

"Looks like the snow's set in for the next few days," Emily said.

Her eyes seemed to glaze over.

"I hope you find whoever did this," she added.

"What the hell was Bridge doing here yesterday?" Smith said to Yang Chu as they drove through the blizzard back to the station. "He didn't mention paying Emily Riley a visit."

"And he wasn't at work today. Maybe he was hiding upstairs while we were talking to her."

"You've got a hell of an imagination," Smith took out his phone and dialled Bridge's number.

"Do you think you ought to be talking on the phone while you're driving?" Yang Chu said.

Smith glared at him.

"I'm doing twenty miles an hour," he said. "There's a blizzard out there. I'd say that talking on the phone is the least of my worries."

Bridge's phone went straight to voicemail.

"Bridge," Smith said. "Phone me as soon as you get this. I want to have a few words about a jigsaw of the bloody Eifel Tower."

He rang off.

"Let's hope Whitton's found out something about the knife," Yang Chu said. "I had a dream about her the other night. A very nice dream if you know what I mean."

Smith slammed on the brakes so hard that the car skidded for fifteen metres before it came to a dead halt.

"Yang Chu," he said. "Forget about it. It's never going to happen. Get that into your thick skull."

Yang Chu had never seen Smith so angry before.

"Alright," he said. "Chill. What's your problem?"

"My problem?" My problem is we have a man who's been dead for four weeks and we don't have a clue about any of it. You and this schoolboy fixation on Whitton and Bridge's little escapade yesterday are not exactly helping. Do I make myself clear?"

A car hooted behind them.

"Alright, can we get moving before we cause a pile up?"

## CHAPTER TWENTY THREE

LUZHANY

**_Friday 30 August 1991_**

"How did he know I was here?" Selene said.

"I don't know," Ivor said. "There were a couple of women here a few days ago. They were asking about a Romanian girl with black hair. Somebody must have told them. You have to leave right now. I'm an old man. I can't protect you. Go well, my child."

"I can protect you," Luka stood up. "I won't let anybody hurt you."

"Go to the church," Ivor said. "You can't hide there forever but at least it will give you some time. There's a hidden compartment to the left of the pulpit. Wait there until I come to get you. Go now."

Luka took hold of Selene's hand and they ran towards the church. The music had stopped, and a sinister voice could be heard. Selene knew the voice very well.

Luka opened the door to the church and they went inside. He slammed the door behind them. Candles were burning throughout the church. Selene was about to blow one out, but Luka took her by the arm.

"No," he said. "Leave them. If the candles are not burning, he'll know we're here. He'll be able to smell it."

They walked to the back of the church and searched for the secret compartment. Luka slid the wooden panel to the side and looked inside. The space inside would barely be enough to hide one person, let alone two.

"You hide here," Luka said. "I'll stand guard. I won't let anything happen to you."

"No," Selene said. "You don't know him. We can both squeeze inside."

They crept inside, and Luka slid the panel back again. Selene was breathing heavily.

"Shh," Luka said. "He'll hear you. Try to calm down. I won't let anything happen to you."

Luka's words seemed to work. Selene's heartbeat slowed down, and her breathing became calmer.

Moments later they heard the sound of the church door being opened and heavy footsteps could be heard. Selene gasped but Luka managed to put his hand over her mouth just in time. The footsteps were getting closer. Selene realised there were many of them. She could pick out the big man's footsteps over the others. They seemed to be much heavier and more full of purpose. He stopped next to the pulpit and knocking sounds could be heard.

He's looking for a secret compartment, Selene thought, he's going to find us.

The knocking continued for a few more seconds and then it stopped.

"Burn down the church," the man said.

Selene felt like she was going to be sick. Luka held her more tightly. The knocking started again. Selene realised that if he knocked on the panel hiding them he would know that there was a hollow space beyond. She stretched out her hands and pressed them against the panel. Luka did the same.

The big man rapped on the wooden panel. Selene flinched. His knuckles were mere millimetres from her outstretched palms. He knocked again. Everything went quiet and Selene held her breath.

He's going to find us, she thought, he'll kill Luka and take me back with him.

The knocking ceased, and the footsteps could be heard again. They appeared to be getting further away. The church door slammed so violently that the vibrations reverberated throughout the church. Selene started to slide the panel back.

"Wait," Luka whispered. "It could be a trick. Wait a while longer." They listened carefully. Their pursuers could be waiting silently for them to emerge from their hiding place.

Selene didn't know how long they had waited inside the hidden compartment but by the time Luka slid the panel back slivers of light streamed inside the church. She crept out and looked around. The church was deserted. Her legs were extremely stiff from being cramped inside the small compartment all night. Luka emerged and smiled at her. He looked extremely tired.

"We're safe," he said. "They've gone. They're probably halfway to Kiev by now."

"I need to find Ivor," Selene said. "He said he would come and find us when everything was alright. Something's wrong."

They opened the door and went outside. The sun was still low in the sky and Selene reckoned it to be still early. They reached the village square. The fires from the previous night were still smouldering. Stray dogs were fighting over the remnants of the slaughtered ox. A small crowd of people were gathered in a circle around something on the ground. Selene could hear sobbing as they approached. A young woman was crying, and a man was trying to pull her away from whatever it was on the ground. As they got closer, Selene realised what it was on the ground. It was a man and a woman. It was Ivor and Zlata. Selene knew at once that they were dead. Luka pulled her away, but she fought back.

"What happened?" She said.

Luka spoke to the woman whose sobbing had become louder. She managed to get a few words out between the wails.

"The people last night," Luka translated. "They killed the priest and Zlata. Ivor wouldn't tell them where you were hiding so they killed them both."

# CHAPTER TWENTY FOUR

YORK

### Tuesday 18 January 2011

The snow had fallen so heavily on the city that by the time Smith and Yang Chu parked in the car park at the station a blanket five centimetres thick had covered the entire area. Superintendent Smyth's green Jaguar had a perfect layer of snow on the roof and bonnet.
"We're going to be snowed in before long," Yang Chu said. "I remember the winter of ninety two. I was still small, but we had snowball fights that seemed to last forever. Schools had to be closed. The whole of the North came to a standstill."
Smith ignored him and ran inside the station. He shook the snow off his jacket and went to the front desk. Baldwin was back.
"I thought you were sick," Smith said.
"I don't get sick," Baldwin said. "Who told you I was sick?"
"The new guy, arrogant idiot if you ask me."
"Jarvis? He is a bit of a moron. Three complaints against him in four hours. They sent him out on the beat. Anyway, I had a dentist appointment. Nothing serious."
"Glad to hear it. Where is everybody?"
"Whitton and Brownhill are in Brownhill's office. They're going through something together on the internet. Thompson's off sick again and I've no idea where Bridge is."
"You and me both," Smith said. "It's good to have you back."
Yang Chu eyed Baldwin with suspicion.

"Yang Chu," Smith said. "Don't worry, Baldwin's been at the dentist, she hasn't been stalking her next victim."
Baldwin looked at Smith as if she had no idea what he was talking about.

Whitton and Brownhill were glued to a computer screen when Smith knocked on the door.
"Come in," Brownhill said.
"Found anything?" Smith said.
"Maybe," Whitton said. "The closest match to Webber's reconstruction of the knife is this one."
Smith looked closely at the photograph on the screen.
"Szankovits?" he said. "If that's how you pronounce it. It does appear to be similar."
The photograph on the screen was of a hunting knife with an extravagant wooden handle and a slightly curved blade.
"Hungarian," Brownhill added. "Apparently the Szankovits brothers are legends in the world of knife making."
"Never heard of them. Where can someone get their hands on one of these?"
"That's the interesting part," Whitton said. "They're not available anywhere in the UK. You can see them in museums but they're not for sale here."
"You'd have to go to Hungary to get one," Brownhill said. "People sometimes bring them back as souvenirs. The workshop is in Ostnor, outside Mora in Hungary."
"So, we're looking for someone who's been to Hungary? That narrows it down a bit. We just need to speak to a few hundred thousand people who've been to Hungary in the last few years."
"Don't be so pedantic," Brownhill said.

"Sorry, I hate it when we've got bugger all to go on. I've got a feeling that this is going to be one we don't get to the bottom of."

"Stop right there," Brownhill said. "What did you find out from the ex-wife? Anything interesting?"

"Oh, I found out something very interesting, but nothing that will help us in this investigation."

"Where's Yang Chu?" Brownhill asked.

"In the canteen, we had a bit of a fight."

He looked at Whitton and smiled.

"Well get over it," Brownhill said. "Let's leave it for today. It'll be dark soon and the snow is going to cause chaos. I'm sure I'll be dreaming about knives tonight."

"What have you got planned for this evening?" Smith asked Whitton in the corridor.

"I don't have any," Whitton said.

"Me neither, do you feel like not having any plans together?"

"Are you asking me out? During work hours? That could be construed as harassment seeing as you're the superior officer and I'm bound by duty to follow your orders."

"Report me, I'm top cop of 2010 remember, you'll never make it stick."

Whitton started to laugh.

"I don't feel like frozen pizza though," she said.

"I've got frozen lasagne too, and I'm sure there's some frozen chips in there too."

"How can I say no to an offer like that?"

Yang Chu was talking to Baldwin at the front desk when Smith and Whitton walked through.

"Is this man bothering you?" Smith asked Baldwin.

"Not really," Baldwin said. "He's just asking me a few questions."

"You do realise, that Yang Chu thinks you're our main suspect in the Riley murder?"

"Not anymore," Baldwin said. "I think I've put his mind at rest once and for all."

"Good, Brownhill has given us time off for good behaviour. It doesn't happen very often, so I suggest we make the most of it."

Yang Chu moved a step closer to Whitton. He appeared to be about to say something.

"Come on, Whitton," Smith said. "I'll give you a lift home. I'm going that way anyway. I want to have a look at the music shop before they close - I'm in the market for a new guitar."

Yang Chu watched as Smith and Whitton left the station together.

The snow was falling at an alarming rate as Smith parked outside his house. The streets were white and layer after layer of snow was collecting in drifts.

"Let's get inside," Smith turned the key in the lock. "Do you want a drink?"

"I could drink a beer," Whitton said.

"Me too."

They sat at the kitchen table. Theakston banged his head against the back door. Smith let him out and watched as the dog began to explore his new white environment. Theakston had never seen so much snow before. He did what he had to do quickly and came back inside. He shook the snow off his fur right next to Whitton.

"Thanks," Whitton said. "You've got the manners of a pig."

"I don't know where he gets it from," Smith took out two beers and handed one to Whitton.

"Cheers," he took a long sip. "Here's to going backwards in the investigation and to whatever it is that's happening between us at the moment."

"What is happening?"

"I have no idea, all I know is it shouldn't really be happening."

"Thanks," Whitton slapped him on the shoulder.

"I haven't finished, it shouldn't be happening but I'm glad it is. I like it. Besides, life's too short. Ask Christopher Riley about that."

"I'm starving," Whitton said. "You mentioned something about a frozen gourmet feast."

"Coming right up," Smith kissed Whitton on the top of the head.

After eating, Smith and Whitton sat on the sofa drinking beer.

"Are you sure about this?"

"No," Smith said. "If you really want to know, I feel like a hypocrite."

"A hypocrite?"

"One minute I'm warning Yang Chu about relationships in the job and next thing I'm doing this."

"You warned him off? I didn't even know he liked me."

"He's smitten," Smith said. "I told him to forget about it. I'm starting to think that I put him off for other reasons."

"You had an ulterior motive," Whitton moved closer and put her hand up Smith's shirt.

"I suppose I did, do you want to smoke a joint?"

"No," Whitton said. "Are you mad?"

"Come on, you'll be surprised what it does to the mind. I figured out most of that Harlequin business under the influence of old Joanna."

He stood up and took the tin out of the cupboard. He opened it up. There appeared to be enough marijuana left for a decent sized joint.

He rolled it awkwardly – it'd been a long time but when he had finished he had managed to produce a passable effort.

"Let's go outside," he said.

"It's freezing out there."

"It's not that cold," Smith took her hand and led her outside.

It had stopped snowing when they walked out to the back garden. The snow was packed tightly on the lawn.

"There's more on the way," Whitton pointed to the clouds.

The moon was barely visible through the grey clouds. It would be a full moon soon. Smith lit the joint and passed it to Whitton.

"I don't think I should," she said.

"Life's too short, live dangerously for once."

Whitton looked at the joint. She put it in her mouth and inhaled. The smoke burned her throat, but she managed not to cough. She took another drag and passed the joint back to Smith. The effect hit her almost immediately. A snowflake landed on Smith's nose and Whitton started to laugh.

"You're getting flaked," she said.

More snow started to fall. Smith handed Whitton the joint again and she took a few long drags. They stood together looking up at the sky. They let the snow fall on them. Smith put his arms around Whitton and kissed her on the lips. She tasted like beer and smoke. They stayed locked in each other's arms for quite some time. Whitton broke off the embrace first.

"I can't feel my feet," she said. "We're getting drenched out here."

"Let's have a hot shower."

"If it carries on like this, we'll be snowed in. Just imagine it. Snowed in - we could be stuck here for days."

## CHAPTER TWENTY FIVE

*Monday 24 January 2011*

Whitton had underestimated the extent of the chaos the snowfall would cause. It had continued to pelt down for four days. Schools were forced to close; the city centre had become inaccessible and businesses were left counting the cost from lost revenue. People had been advised to stay indoors and only essential travel had been advised. The snow stopped suddenly on Saturday night and by Monday morning all that was left were a few snow rings where snowmen once stood. It was as if nothing had happened. The schools were reopened, and it was business as usual for everybody who worked in the city. Business as usual, for everybody apart from Arnold Mather, that is. When Arnold had failed to turn up for work on Thursday and Friday, everybody had assumed it was due to the weather but when he didn't arrive at AB Jennings logistics on Monday morning, eyebrows were raised. Arnold Mather had never been late for work nor had he taken a day off sick without phoning in first.

Alan Jennings hung up the telephone and dialled another number - Arnold's mobile number. It rang for a while and then stopped. Arnold didn't appear to have an answering service.
"Where is he?" Alan said to his brother Brian. "What does he think he's playing at? We've got a load of work to catch up on after the balls up last week."
"Maybe he's sick," Brian suggested.
"Arnold doesn't get sick, he's a robot. Besides, he'd phone in if he was sick."

"What are we going to do then?"

"We can't just wait for him to turn up, we've got fifteen trucks to get out this morning. We'll have to handle it ourselves like we used to in the old days."

"Damn it," Brian said. "Do you realise how much work that involves?"

"It can't be helped," Alan said.

"He'd better have a good excuse, or he's in for a right bollocking when he gets back."

By half past two that afternoon, the Jennings brothers were not the only ones who were concerned about Arnold's whereabouts. Ted Turner, the barman from the Fox Inn had known Arnold for five years. At two on the dot, every day from Monday to Friday, Arnold had walked through the door of the pub. He always ordered a pint of best bitter and made his way to the table in the corner. Ted could set his watch by him.

"Where's Arnold?" Vernon Simmons asked Ted.

Vernon was the landlord at the Fox Inn.

"He hasn't been in for a while," Ted said. "The snow probably kept him at home but it's all melted now. I was sure he'd show his face today. I wonder where he is."

"This is very strange," Vernon said. "I've never met such a creature of habit before."

"Maybe he's found himself another local," Ted suggested.

"Never. People like Arnold never change. They hate change. Go and check on him. You know where he lives don't you?"

"Of course, I do, across the road from the bakery. What about the bar?"

"I'm sure I can manage for twenty minutes or so. Go and see if he's alright. He might have had a fall or something."

"He's only forty, it's old people who fall over and can't get up."
"Just check on him. It'll take you half an hour at the most."

Ted reached the bakery and crossed the road to Arnold's house. The curtains were open upstairs and downstairs and nothing appeared to be amiss.

Maybe he had to work overtime, Ted thought, that's what it is. He had to work overtime to catch up on the lost business caused by the snow. He knocked on the door and waited.

This is ridiculous, he thought, any minute now Arnold will park his car outside and wonder why I'm bothering him just because he didn't show up at the pub.

Ted knocked again. He could hear no noise from inside the house. He was about to walk away when he realised that Vernon would probably only send him back to check if Arnold had not hurt himself inside the house.

"This isn't part of my job," he said to himself.

He tried the door handle. The door was unlocked.

Maybe he's sick, he thought, if he's asleep in bed. He won't thank me for waking him up.

There was a strange smell inside the house - a sharp, acrid smell. It seemed to be coming from the kitchen. It smelled like burnt coffee. Ted went inside and closed the door behind him. He went through to the kitchen and discovered the source of the strange odour. The coffee percolator next to the microwave had been left on, the water had boiled dry and the coffee beans had burned to a crisp. Ted switched the machine off.

"Arnold," he shouted.

He realised that his voice was trembling. An uneasy feeling swept through him. Arnold Mather wasn't the kind of person who would let a coffee percolator burn dry.

"Arnold," Ted shouted again.

He checked the living room. It was spotlessly clean. Arnold was nowhere to be seen.

Ted climbed the stairs.

"Arnold," he shouted.

He felt like an intruder. He was invading another man's territory. He checked the bathroom and the spare room. There was no sign of Arnold. The door to the bedroom at the front of the house was closed. Ted turned the handle and went inside. The curtains were open, and the room was incredibly warm. A foul smell had filled the room. It smelled like an animal had died in there. Arnold Mather was lying on the bed under the covers. He was lying on his side facing an old sideboard.

"Arnold," Ted said. "It's Ted, from The Fox Inn. I just came to see if you're alright."

The figure in the bed didn't stir.

"Arnold," Ted moved closer.

He noticed a crumpled up handkerchief on the sideboard. He turned Arnold's head towards him and screamed. He'd never screamed before. Arnold Mather's face was a bluish black colour and there was a gaping hole in his throat.

## CHAPTER TWENTY SIX

Baldwin took the call ten minutes later. Ted Turner had raced down the stairs and made it to the Fox Inn in less than two minutes. It had taken a while for Vernon Simmons to figure out what Ted was babbling about. It was Vernon who made the call.

"Could you say that again please," Baldwin said.

"There's a dead body," Vernon said. "Arnold Mather. He's dead."

"Where are you calling from?"

"The Fox Inn."

"There's a dead body at the pub?"

"No," Vernon said. "Around the corner on Gibb Street. Opposite the bakery. Number eighteen. One of my barmen found the body."

Twenty minutes later, two police cars, Smith's Ford Sierra and Thompson's new Mercedes were parked outside Arnold Mather's house. Webber and Brownhill arrived minutes later in Brownhill's old Citroen. Webber got out of the car and walked over to Smith.

"What's going on?" he said.

"Dead body," Smith said. "Apparently."

"Apparently?"

"The barman from the Fox Inn found him," Smith said. "Arnold Mather."

"The barman?'

"The dead guy. It seems he had his throat cut open. We haven't had a look inside yet."

"Good," Webber said. "For once I may actually have the luxury of a virgin crime scene."

"Apart from what the barman left in there," Smith said.

Webber ignored him and walked towards the house.

"You're not allowed in there," an officer in uniform said. "Possible crime scene. You could contaminate any evidence we might find."
It was PC Jarvis.
"Get out of my way," Webber was in no mood for an argument.
"I'm afraid I can't do that," Jarvis stood right in front of Webber. "Nobody's allowed inside. Now move along please and let us do our work."
"Jarvis," a loud voice was heard behind them.
It was Brownhill.
"Let Webber through," she said.
"Who's he?"
"Grant Webber," Brownhill said. "Head of forensics and definitely not somebody you want to be on the wrong side of and in case you haven't forgotten, I am a detective inspector. Address me appropriately."
"Sorry, Ma'am," Jarvis stood aside and let Webber enter the house. "But you can't be too careful, can you? He could have been some wacko who just wanted to look at the stiff. How was I to know who he was?'
Brownhill was about to say something, but she knew it would be a waste of time with PC Jarvis.
"Jarvis," she said. "You can go now. We'll take it from here."
"Who's going to guard the door?"
"Get back to what you were doing before."
　　DS Thompson got out of the car and walked up to Smith.
"Do you still work for the police?" Smith said. "That must be some cold you've got."
"I feel terrible, I've never felt so sick in my life before."
"Have you seen a doctor?"

"I don't trust doctors," Thompson said. "They're just glorified drug dispensers. They fob you off with a bunch of pills and hope for the best. What happened here?"

"The barman from the pub around the corner found a dead body in there," Smith pointed to the house. "Arnold Mather. Webber is up there now. He doesn't like to be disturbed."

"Where's Whitton?"

"How should I know?" Smith said rather too quickly. "I'm not her keeper."

"So, it's finally happened."

"What?"

"The inevitable," Thompson said. "I might be getting on a bit but I'm not senile yet. I've seen the signs before. It'll only end badly you know."

"I'm going to have a look inside."

Webber was placing a white handkerchief inside a plastic evidence bag when Smith entered the room. He didn't say a word. After all the years he had worked with Smith, Smith's presence was to be expected by now.

"Not a pretty sight," Webber pointed to the body in the bed.

"Why's it so hot in here?"

"That's going to cause a few problems. The central heating was turned right up. That, together with the fact that he was wrapped in a winter duvet is going to cause havoc with the time of death."

"Shit," Smith looked closely at the dead man in the bed. His face was bloated and greyish blue. The wound in his throat already had maggots wriggling around inside it.

"Amazing isn't it?" Webber said. "A fly can find a dead body from a mile away. Nature's clean up service at its finest."

"Thanks, Webber, I know you're not one to speculate..."
"This time I think I can be pretty certain, the answers to your questions are yes and yes."
"Yes, and yes?"
"Yes, I do believe the wound in the man's neck was caused by the same knife that was used on Christopher Riley," Webber said. "And yes, I have a strong suspicion that chloroform was also used. You've got your wish at last."
"My wish?"
"Bryony and I do talk occasionally," Webber said. "It's not all physical."
Smith cringed at the thought.
"She said you almost wished for another body," Webber elaborated.
"To give you more to go on. Well, your wish has been granted."

## CHAPTER TWENTY SEVEN

LUZHANY, UKRAINE

*Sunday 1 September 1991*

Ivor and Zlata were buried two days later in a small plot next to the river. The whole village turned up for the funeral. After a short but very emotional service, the villagers headed towards the village square to share in a farewell toast. Selene stayed behind and stared at the fresh graves.
"This is all my fault," she said to Luka. "They died because they were protecting me. It's all my fault. I should never have come here. I have to go. More people will die if I stay here."
"Ivor and Zlata did what any one of us would have done. I would have done the same. I'll protect you now."
"No," Selene turned and ran off in the direction of the river.
Luka chased after her. He had to run as fast as he could just to keep up.

Luka caught up to Selene by a copse of trees further downstream. She was sitting with her head in her hands. She was shaking uncontrollably.
"Selene," Luka put his hand on her shoulder. "It's alright."
Selene looked up at him. Her eyes seemed different - there was a fire there that Luka had never seen before. It scared him; he would never forget that look in her eyes.
"It's going to be alright," he looked away.
"I have to go. Nobody is safe while I'm here."

"Then I'll come with you. I'll be eighteen soon. I was going to leave soon anyway. We can go to England together. Meet me at this spot just before nightfall and we'll go together."

He turned and walked away before Selene had a chance to argue.

Selene stayed by the river for quite some time. She watched it as it flowed slowly over the rocks down through the valley.

This river has been here for hundreds of years, she thought, and it will be here long after I'm gone. Nobody will miss me if I leave, least of all the river.

She stood up and looked around her. The small village of Luzhany was roughly half a mile to the south.

I'll head north then, she thought, I'll go as far north as I can. Luka will have to understand - he cannot be found with me.

She considered going back to the village to collect what little belongings she had collected over the short space of time she had been there but quickly changed her mind.

I'm not welcome there anymore.

Besides, she might bump into Luka and he would no doubt try and persuade her to wait for him.

Selene looked up at the sky. The sun was high now. She knew it would peak and then descend behind the mountains far away to the west. She set off north-west and hoped that if she kept the Carpathian Mountains to her left she could somehow make it to central Europe. She didn't know exactly where she was going but she was determined to keep going at all costs.

Darkness fell, and Selene felt exhausted and extremely hungry. She had managed to find water along the way from becks and streams, but her stomach was growling. She needed to find food soon.

She hadn't eaten anything since the previous night and then she had been interrupted by Ivor before she could finish.
Ivor, she thought, the friendly priest, and kind old Zlata.
They'd shown her nothing but kindness and what had they received in return?
Selene didn't know how far she had walked or where she was, but she knew she would have to sleep soon - she couldn't carry on much longer. She selected a spot beneath a cluster of elm trees. The stars were showing their faces one by one and Selene knew it wouldn't rain. She sat down against one of the trees and closed her eyes. Everything was quiet. There was no wind and the trees were still. She drifted off to sleep within minutes.

    Selene woke suddenly. A strange noise had jolted her out of a dreamless sleep. The sound was something that shouldn't be heard out there in the fields. She sat up and looked around. It was starting to get light and the birds were already making their plans for the day. Selene held her breath and listened.
Where had the strange noise come from? She thought.
She heard footsteps - they were getting closer and closer. She looked around, but she couldn't see anything. Then she heard voices. She couldn't make out the words that were being spoken - the language the people were speaking wasn't Russian and it was definitely not Romanian. The voices were getting louder and then a man and a woman emerged from the trees. They stopped dead when they spotted Selene.

# CHAPTER TWENTY EIGHT

YORK

*Monday 24 January 2011*

Arnold Mather's body was taken away in an ambulance just as the sun was setting over the city of York. His body was in such an advanced state of decomposition that Webber had decided it was better to leave it wrapped inside the duvet from the bed. He still had the image of Arnold in his mind. Wrapped inside a warm duvet with his throat slashed open. Webber had photographed the body, but he knew he'd probably not need the photos.
"What are you mulling over in that depraved mind of yours?" Smith said.
"This is all very strange," Webber said.
"When is a murder anything else? To us rational folk that is."
"It looks like the poor bastard was doped up with chloroform first, then he had his throat sliced open."
"What's so strange about that? It makes perfect sense to me. Knock the guy out and then slit his throat. No struggle."
"But why wrap him warmly in a duvet afterwards? It's freaking me out. It's almost as if he was tucked in afterwards."
"Murderers are funny creatures. Logic seems to elude them. Have you found anything useful?"
"Not much," Webber admitted. "No sign of a struggle. Plenty of blood but like the Christopher Riley murder, most of it had been soaked up by the sheets. I'd say he was also killed on the bed."
"Same killer then?"

"I'm ninety nine percent certain," Webber said.

"Seventy five percent would have been good enough for me."

"I'll know more when the path guys have managed to peel the duvet off him. I wouldn't like to be them - I've got a nasty feeling they're going to find half of Arnold Mather stuck to the duvet when they do."

"Thanks, Webber, I've just lost my appetite for the rest of the week. Did you find any prints?"

"A few. As I said, we'll know more later. You know the score - we spend half our time waiting around for other people to do their jobs. These two murders have left a nasty taste in my mouth. Two sad, lonely men killed in their beds. It doesn't make sense."

"You're getting soft in your old age," Smith said. "We live in a sick world. I'm going for a smoke. I need to get the stench of death out of my nostrils."

He walked towards the door, stopped and turned around.

"The central heating," he said. "It's bloody hot in here."

"What are you talking about?"

"The central heating - it's expensive to run these days. Nobody leaves it running on full blast the whole time; they use a timer so it's only on when they're home."

"What's your point?"

"I don't believe Arnold Mather left his heating on full," Smith said. "And I suggest you find out where the thermostat and timer are located and dust them for prints."

"Damn it, why didn't I think of that?"

"That's why they pay me the big bucks. It's time for that smoke."

Whitton was talking to Yang Chu outside the house. Smith took out a packet of cigarettes and lit one. He inhaled deeply and let the smoke out through his nose.

"Yang Chu," Smith said. "Do you have anything useful for me?"

"No, Sarge, we've spoken to all the people in the neighbouring houses - all six of them and nobody recalls seeing anything unusual. It turns out that the dead guy is bordering on the obsessive compulsive."

"What do you mean?"

"One particularly observant old lady two doors down was rather helpful," Yang Chu said. "She spends most of her time looking out of her window. She said that Arnold Mather arrives home from work every day at around one fifteen. At five to two he leaves the house and returns at around six."

"He goes to the Fox Inn," Whitton said. "We spoke to the landlord there. From two until just before six, he sits in the pub, drinks five beers and reads the papers. He's been doing it for years."

"When did the landlord last see Arnold?"

"Five to six last Wednesday. When the blizzards arrived, he didn't think anything of the fact that Arnold didn't show up but when he didn't turn up at two today he thought there must be something wrong and sent the barman to check."

"What a sad existence," Smith mused. "Plodding on and on and waiting for death. What else do we know about lonely old Arnold Mather? Relatives? Friends?"

"He had none. Divorced, no kids, parents are dead. He has a sister, but nobody knows where she is."

"He didn't seem to have any friends either," Yang Chu said.

"No relatives or friends," Smith said. "Sounds a lot like me. Has anybody heard from Bridge today?"

"No," Whitton said.

"Brownhill is going to have his balls on a plate if he doesn't turn up sometime."

"What now, Sarge?" Yang Chu said.

"We'll know more when Webber and the path guys are finished going through everything. I don't mind admitting these murders have confused the hell out of me."

"Do you think they're connected?" Whitton said.

"Almost certainly, I just haven't figured out how Christopher Riley and Arnold Mather fit together yet."

## CHAPTER TWENTY NINE

An hour later, the whole team gathered in the small conference room at the station. Even DCI Chalmers was present. Bridge had still not bothered to show his face and speculations were being tossed around regarding his whereabouts. It was uncharacteristic of Bridge to disappear like this.

"Maybe he's ill," Whitton suggested. "And he can't make it to a phone."

"Hungover more like it," Thompson said. "I'm sick and I still manage to get to work. At least I make the effort."

"You're not ill, Thompson," Smith said. "You've had the same phony cold since I can remember. I'm sure Bridge will turn up sooner or later with a perfectly good excuse."

"Can we get started?" Chalmers said. "I've managed to get away from that public school idiot for a while. I've forgotten what proper police work is like. Smith, do you want to fill me in on what's been going on?"

"Of course, boss, it's good to have you back. Arnold Mather was found by the barman from the Fox Inn this afternoon around three. He didn't show up at the pub, so the barman went to see if everything was alright. Mather had had his neck sliced open. Webber seems to think he was knocked out with chloroform first. He was killed and then wrapped in a duvet on his bed."

"When was Mather last seen?" Brownhill said.

"Last Wednesday, just before six. He left the pub and presumably went home."

"So, nobody has missed him for five days?" Chalmers said.

"The blizzards didn't help, it was chaos remember. He didn't show up for work this morning. He works as a clerk at a warehouse and he didn't turn up to the pub like he normally does."

"So, he died sometime between Wednesday evening and today?" Chalmers said. "This isn't good."

"The central heating in the house was turned right up - permanently. The timer had been switched off. I think whoever killed him turned the heating up."

"What the hell for?"

"I don't know, the way he was wrapped up it was like he'd been tucked in like a child."

"I imagine the heat didn't do much to slow down the decomposition process?"

"No, Webber said the path guys would have to be careful when removing the duvet. The skin from the body would…"

"We get the picture, Smith," Brownhill said. "We're not going to be too exact about the time of death then?"

"What about the central heating people?" Yang Chu said.

"How are they going to help?" Thompson said.

"Pre-paid meters," Yang Chu said. "Most people have got one these days. I've got one. When you can see how much it's costing you to heat the house, you're not too keen to have it on all the time."

"Is it me," Thompson said. "But is Yang Chu being completely irrelevant here?"

He took out a handkerchief and blew his nose.

"Nice thinking, Yang Chu," Brownhill said. "If I'm not mistaken, a pre-paid meter can be analysed. We can check back over the last week and see exactly when the heating peaked. Thompson get onto it right away."

"Onto what?" Thompson sniffed.

"Get hold of British Gas and get them to check Mather's meter. Find out exactly when the heating was turned up. Once we know that I'm pretty sure we'll be closer to finding out the time of death."

"Something's really bugging me," Smith said.

"Spit it out," Brownhill sighed.

"Two men are dead. Both of them middle aged lonely souls. Both were knocked out before they were killed, and both were put onto their beds afterwards. It's almost as if our murderer wanted to make them as comfortable as possible afterwards."

"What do you think it means?" Whitton said.

"I don't know, that's why it's bugging me. I've never seen anything like it before."

"Let's take a short break," Brownhill suggested. "We'll meet back here in half an hour."

Smith, Whitton and Yang Chu walked into the canteen. Bridge was standing next to the coffee machine. He gave it a kick and walked away.

"Where the hell have you been?" Smith said.

"Rough night," Bridge said. "Or should I say rough early morning. I only climbed into bed at nine this morning. I lost my bloody phone somewhere, too."

"The DI is spewing," Smith said. "You'd better make up a good excuse. Where were you anyway?"

"Trade secret, if I tell you I'll have to kill you. It was well worth it anyway if you know what I mean. Baldwin said there's been another murder. Do you think it's the same guy?"

"Woman," Smith said. "We're looking for a woman, I'm pretty sure of that. Have you tried phoning your phone?"

"How am I supposed to do that? I've lost my phone."

"For someone who has moments of intellectual brilliance every now and again you're pretty dumb sometimes. Get someone else to phone it you moron."

Smith took out his phone and dialled Bridge's phone. It went straight to voicemail.

"Voicemail," Smith said. "That's a good sign - if it had been stolen they would have switched it off."

Webber burst into the canteen. He looked exhausted.

"What's wrong with you?" Smith said. "You look like you've seen a ghost."

"I've just spent an hour at the path lab," Webber said. "And then another hour at forensics trying to peel pieces of Arnold Mather off a fetid duvet. It was the most disgusting two hours of my life."

"But you've found something haven't you? I know that look."

"That I did, I found hair. Black hair from a female to be exact. It matched the hair from the Christopher Riley murder."

"So it's the same woman. But we already knew that deep down, didn't we?"

"Your hunch was right for a change," Webber said. "I dusted the thermostat on the central heating system and I pulled a couple of beautiful prints. They didn't come from Arnold Mather."

"Whose are they?"

"I have no idea. My guys are looking as we speak. They're running them through the national database."

"Oh well," Smith sighed. "At least we've got something, even if it isn't much."

"We'd better get back," Whitton said.

"Nice of you to join us," Brownhill said as Bridge took a seat next to Yang Chu.

"Sorry," Bridge said. "I thought I was coming down with the flu."

"But it's mysteriously disappeared has it?"

"No, I still don't feel well but I thought I might be needed."

"Very conscientious of you."

"Anyway," Smith said. "Webber has a bit of good news. He found some hair on the duvet Mather was wrapped up in. It matches the hair he found at the first murder scene. Black hair from a woman."

"It's confirmed then," Brownhill said. "But we already knew that didn't we?"

"There's more, there were fingerprints on the thermostat for the central heating. Webber's guys are checking them out now."

"Where *is* Webber?" Chalmers asked.

"He's gone home to have a quick shower," Smith said. "He's had a pretty disturbing day."

"Thompson is busy checking with British Gas to see if they can see when the heating was turned up," Brownhill said. "Does anybody have any suggestions as to how we move forward on this one?"

"The two victims," Chalmers said. "Always start with the dead ones. What's the connection between them? There has to be something."

"No connection as far as we know," Brownhill said. "Christopher Riley was a computer programmer and Arnold Mather was a warehouse clerk. As far as we know, they didn't know each other."

"There has to be a connection, murderers don't generally select their prey at random. Find out more about them. Find out how they knew each other."

"Boss," Smith said. "With respect, I think in this instance, they were selected at random."

"What brings you to this conclusion?"

"Just a feeling."

"That feeling of yours again? Dig deeper anyway, these men were selected for a reason. Find out what that reason is. Find out who these men really were."

"I don't think it's who they were that's important," Smith said. "I think they were killed because of what they were."

"Once again in English please," Thompson said.

"Both of them were middle aged men - sad cases. Lonely men with nobody in their lives."

"Bollocks," Chalmers said. "You've just described just about every man who works in this station, yourself included. There's a link between these men somewhere. Find it and you'll get a lot closer to finding out who did this."

Thompson entered the room. He looked even more grumpy than usual. He was holding a piece of paper in his hand. He handed it to Brownhill and sat down.

"Those people at British Gas spoke to me like I was an idiot," he said. "There's no respect left in the world. I'm not too good with graphs and all that stuff but they emailed that over."

He pointed to the piece of paper Brownhill was holding.

"It appears we've beaten the path guys to it for once," Brownhill said. "Yang Chu, give yourself a pat on the back."

Yang Chu was beaming from ear to ear.

"According to this," Brownhill continued. "Arnold Mather did have his central heating on a timer. The radiators were set to come on at three in the morning until half past four and then again from twelve noon until nine. That is until last Wednesday. The timer appears to have been switched off and the heating was turned up permanently. It's been on for the past five days."

"So, he was probably killed last Wednesday around eight?" Smith said.

"It appears so. This is one of those rare occasions where creative thinking has triumphed over science. We've beaten the path guys at their own game."

"Arnold Mather was last seen at the Fox Inn just before six," Smith said. "He was killed between six and eight. We know that now but who killed him?"

"And why?" Whitton said.

"The eternal quadrangle," Chalmers said.

Everybody stared at him.

"The four quarters of the investigative quadrant," Chalmers explained. "That's what old DCI Walker used to call it. Before your time I'm afraid. Where, when, why and who? We've got the easy part out of the way - the when and where. Now the shit part begins. We try to find out why."

"What about who?" Bridge said.

"Find out why," Chalmers said. "And the final part usually jumps out and bites us on the arse. I say usually but sometimes it's not that obvious."

"So, what do you suggest we do now, sir?" Brownhill said.

"Find the connection between the two dead men of course. Have I been talking to myself for the last half an hour?"

## CHAPTER THIRTY

UKRAINE

*Monday 2nd September 1991*

The man and the woman stood and stared at Selene for a very long time. Selene didn't know what to do. Her mouth felt incredibly dry and she desperately needed something to eat. She didn't recognise either of them - they looked like they were in their early twenties and they didn't look like anybody Selene had met in the six years she had been away from her family. The woman said something to the man in a language Selene had never heard before.
"Are you alright?" The man said in English.
Selene didn't reply. She didn't feel that she had the energy to make a run for it. She looked them up and down. They didn't appear to be dangerous, but Selene had learned that looks can be deceiving.
"Are you lost?" The man said.
"No," Selene said.
"Are you hungry?" The woman asked her. "Would you like something to drink?"
Selene started to weigh up her options. This young couple didn't seem like they were going to harm her, she was hungry and thirsty, but it could be a trap. The woman said something to the man, he nodded, and they turned around and walked away.
"Wait," Selene said.
They turned back around. Selene walked towards them.
"I am hungry," she said.

"We have food and plenty to drink in the van," the woman said. "Come with us - it's not too far."

Selene followed them for a few hundred metres. They emerged onto a narrow road. A green VW camper van was parked on the grass next to the road. Selene had never seen a vehicle like it before. Two surfboards were strapped to the roof. Selene didn't even know what they were used for.

"There she is," the woman pointed to the camper van. "We call her Mathilde. She's not much to look at but she's reliable. Let's get you something to eat."

Selene thought the woman had a kind voice. She followed them to the camper van and watched the woman go inside and emerge shortly afterwards with a brown paper bag and a plastic container. They sat on the grass next to the van. The woman made a breakfast of meat, cheese and bread while the man prepared some coffee inside the van.

Selene ate greedily. She couldn't remember the last time that food had tasted so delicious.

"Where are you going?" The man asked.

He handed her a glass of orange juice.

"England," Selene said without thinking.

"On foot?" the woman said. "That's quite a trip."

Selene realised she didn't know where she was nor, did she know the way to England.

"Are you alone?" The man asked.

"Yes."

"You're certainly hungry," The woman smiled. "What's your name? I'm Florence and this is Bo."

"Selene," Selene stuffed a large piece of cheese into her mouth.

"Selene," Florence said. "That's a very pretty name. Where have you come from? How old are you?"

Bo said something to Florence.

"Bo thinks I ask far too many questions," Florence said. "I can't help it - I have a curious nature. It's a very long way to England."

Selene finished another bread roll and belched loudly.

"Scuzati Ma," she said.

"You're Romanian," Bo said.

Selene froze.

How does he know that? she thought.

"We spent a while in Costinesti," Florence said. "Bo came up with this bright idea to do something different. We decided to see what the surf was like on the Black Sea. Have you ever heard of anything so absurd?'

"The Black Sea is beautiful," Selene said.

She'd been there once when she was very small. She remembered swimming in the sea with her father.

"But the surfing is terrible," Bo said. "Next year we'll stick to the west coast of France."

"Do you need a lift somewhere?" Florence started packing away the remains of the food. "Our next stop is Poland. Krakow, Prague, Frankfurt and then the final push back to Paris. We've got a week to do it in."

Selene had never heard of any of the places Florence had mentioned.

"Yes please," she said.

"Yes please what?"

"Please take me with you," Selene said.

## CHAPTER THIRTY ONE

YORK

***Monday 24 January 2011***

Yang Chu and Bridge were talking by the front desk. Smith and Chalmers walked through together.
"Dig around a bit," Chalmers said. "You should know the drill by now. Something's bound to turn up. I'm off home. It's my birthday in case you didn't know. Mrs Chalmers is cooking me some liver and onions as a special birthday treat."
"Urgh," Whitton said. "You call that a treat?"
"It is in our house," Chalmers said and walked outside.
"Yang Chu," Smith said. "You and I are going pub crawling."
"Sarge?"
"Just following orders, the last places Riley and Mather were seen happened to be pubs. Let's do a bit of digging. There's something I need to talk to you about too."
The colour seemed to drain from Whitton's face.

Ye Olde Yeoman was surprisingly busy for a Monday evening when Smith and Yang Chu walked inside. The clientele consisted mainly of middle aged men. Smith walked up the bar and tried to catch the attention of a barman wearing glasses with the thickest lenses Smith had ever seen.
"Two pints of Theakstons," he made eye contact with the myopic barman.
"I don't usually drink," Yang Chu said.
"You do tonight, you'll like this stuff."

The barman placed the drinks on the counter.

"Four fifty,' he said.

Smith placed a five pound note on the bar.

"It's busy tonight," he said.

"I know," the barman handed Smith his change. "Sad buggers all of them. Don't they have homes to go to?"

"Were you on duty here over Christmas?"

"Unfortunately, yes, I'm Graham. You're police, aren't you?"

"Is it that obvious?"

"Not really, you don't actually look anything like a policeman - more like a student if you ask me. I saw your photo in the papers. Something to do with those clown murders."

*A student?* Smith thought.

It was the worst insult he had heard in years.

"Christmas Day?" Smith said. "Was the pub busy then too?"

"Packed, it's quite depressing when you think about it isn't it? Who goes to a pub on Christmas Day? It's a day to be with your family isn't it?"

"Do you know Christopher Riley?"

"Chris? The one that got killed? He used to come in here every now and again. Nice bloke. Kept himself to himself. Such a horrible thing to happen."

"Did you see him here on Christmas Day?"

"He came in around three if I remember and left around closing time. He must have had around nine or ten brown ales."

"Was he with anybody?"

"No," Graham said. "Chris is always on his own."

"Are you sure?"

"Positive, I'd better get back to work."
Smith finished the beer in his glass. Yang Chu had barely touched his.
"Two more pints please," Smith said.
He turned to Yang Chu.
"You'd better up the pace a bit," he said. "You're lagging behind."
Yang Chu took a long slug of the beer and winced.
"There was something," Graham put two fresh pints of beer on the counter. "Just before closing, Chris was talking to this woman. They seemed to be very cosy. I think he might have pulled actually. They chatted for a while and left together."
"Did you know this woman?"
"No, never seen her in here before."
"Could you describe her?"
"It was quite dark, but she was quite striking looking. Black hair, unusual eyes. Pretty face though. She looked a bit like her over there if you lose the green hair."
He pointed to a woman sitting on her own at the other end of the bar.
"Can I get back to work now?" Graham said but Smith had already walked over to the woman with the green hair.
"Kjersti isn't it?" Smith said. "You live across the road to the Chinese restaurant. You're a Norwegian student, aren't you?"
"I can see why you're a police detective," Kjersti smiled a sarcastic smile. "Who's your friend?"
She nodded towards Yang Chu.
"Another police detective I'm afraid, can we have a chat?"
"I'm always happy to help the police, can we sit at a table though?"
She led them to the only free table in the pub.
"Would you like a drink?" Yang Chu said.
"A pint of Stella would be great," she said.

"And another two pints of Theakstons," Smith added. "I see you're getting a taste for it."

Yang Chu was halfway through his second pint.

Yang Chu returned with the drinks and sat down.

"You still haven't caught her, have you?" Kjersti took a long swig of the lager. "The woman who killed my neighbour I mean."

"Not yet," Smith said. "But we will. Some new evidence has come to light. Can you remember anything else about Christmas Day? Something you didn't think of before?"

"No, like I told you, I don't sit staring out of the window all day."

"Thank you, Miss Pelge," Smith stood up. "I assume you still have my card. In case you do think of something."

"It's in my flat somewhere. Thanks for the drink."

"Kjersti," Smith said. "There's something I don't understand. You said we still haven't caught her. The woman who killed your neighbour."

"Did I?" Kjersti didn't seem worried at all.

"Yes, you did. Why did you say that?"

"I don't know, I suppose I must have seen it in the papers."

"The newspapers didn't print anything about the murder suspect being a woman, that part isn't common knowledge."

"I must have heard it somewhere else," Kjersti said. "I hope you catch them anyway."

Smith stood up to leave. He was about to walk out the door when he spotted somebody familiar. It was Bill, the man who had helped produce a perfect photofit of PC Baldwin.

"Bill," Smith said to him. "Nice to see you again, "the artist's impression you came up with caused quite a stir at the station."

"Only glad to help," Bill said. "Have you caught em yet?"

"Not yet, I need you to do me a favour. Don't turn around yet but there's a woman sitting over there with green hair. When I say so, turn round and have a look at her. Tell me if she could be the woman you saw with Christopher Riley in here on Christmas Day."

Bill turned his head and looked over at Kjersti Pelge. She spotted him straight away and waved. Bill couldn't stop himself. He waved back.

"Very subtle," Smith said. "Could that be her?"

"I don't know, the green hair is a bit off-putting but she's certainly pretty. It could be her. I don't know."

"Thanks, Bill," Smith said. "You've been a great help."

"Wait," Bill said as Smith was about to leave. "Isn't there some kind of reward? Some sort of payment for me doing my civic duty. If you catch em because of me I mean?"

"We'll let you know," Smith headed straight for the door.

## CHAPTER THIRTY TWO

"Do you think she's the one?" Yang Chu asked as they walked to The Fox Inn. "The Norwegian student, do you think she's our throat slasher?"
He was starting to slur his words.
"I don't know," Smith said. "She didn't seem too bothered about talking to us. She wasn't the least bit nervous. Are you alright?"
"I feel great."
He teetered to the side and had to steady himself on a lamppost.
"What did you want to talk to me about?" He said.
"Not now, we'll talk later. This is the Fox Inn here."

When they went inside the pub, Smith noticed straight away that the Fox Inn was the complete opposite of Ye Olde Yeoman. A grand total of three people were inside the pub and one of those was Ted, the barman who was sitting behind the counter watching a football game on a screen above the bar. He looked extremely bored.
"Two pinths of Sheaksons," Yang Chu said to him and almost fell over.
"I think you've had enough, mate," Ted said.
"It's alright, Ted," Smith said. "He's with me. I'll take full responsibility for him."
"It's your funeral."
He poured the drinks and placed them on the counter.
Yang Chu stared at his beer. He shook his head, pointed to an imaginary beer next to it and started to laugh.
"Which one's mine?" He said.
"All three," Smith replied.
Yang Chu picked up the beer and took a long drink.

"He doesn't usually drink," Smith said to Ted. "It's quiet in here tonight."

"Monday - the quietest night of the week. We used to have a quiz on a Monday. That used to pull the people in, but we had to stop because of all the cheating."

"Cheating?" Smith said.

"Bloody smart phones. People were looking up the answers on their phones. Any news on Arnold? We're all still in shock. I don't think I'll ever get that picture out of my head."

"We're working on it. Do you know if Arnold was in a relationship?"

Ted started to laugh.

"Sorry, I know you shouldn't talk ill of the dead but the thought of Arnold with a woman is absurd. Arnold wasn't the relationship type."

"No female friends then?"

"No friends of any sex as far as I'm aware, he always sat by himself and left here by himself."

"We're trying to find a woman with black hair," Smith said. "Quite pretty with strange eyes."

"We get a lot of people in here."

"In the past few days," Smith said. "She may have been in here in the last few days."

"Like I said, we see a lot of people in here."

Yang Chu started to fumble in his pockets. He retrieved his mobile phone and dropped it on the floor. Smith and Ted stared at him.

"The Norwegian student," Yang Chu said. "I took a thoto when I was at the bar."

Smith picked up the phone and opened up Yang Chu's photo gallery. He noticed there were five photographs of Whitton on the phone. He found the photograph of Kjersti Pelge and showed it to Ted.

"No," Ted said. "I'd definitely remember seeing her. Especially the green hair."

"Try to picture her with black hair, have you seen her before?"

"I don't think so. Do you think she has something to do with Arnold's murder?"

"We don't know yet. Was Arnold acting strange at all when he was last here? Did he appear agitated in any way?"

"No," Ted said. "He was the same as always. He drank his usual five pints, read every newspaper in the place and left just before six like every day."

"And you didn't notice a woman in here at the same time? She may have followed him home."

"Not that I remember. I think you ought to get him home. He doesn't look well at all."

Yang Chu was standing with his head bowed. He was swaying from side to side.

"You're probably right," Smith drained his glass. "Give me a call if you do think of anything."

He handed Ted a card.

"I will," Ted took the card and placed it next to the till.

"I'd better walk you home," Smith said to Yang Chu outside the Fox Inn.

Yang Chu was taking one step forwards and two steps back. Smith took him by the arm and marched him slowly up the street. An elderly woman walking her dog crossed to the other side of the road when they approached. Yang Chu stopped suddenly. He started to make strange gurgling noises and Smith knew what was about to happen. He let go, Yang Chu lurched forwards and sprayed three pints of

Theakstons into some dead rose bushes. Smith waited for him to finish and helped him up again.

"Feel better?" He said.

"No, I feel terrible. I'm never drinking again."

"I've lost count of how many times I've said that."

They continued on their way and stopped outside Yang Chu's house.

"Goodnight," Smith helped him up the driveway. "Drink plenty of water - you won't feel so bad in the morning then."

Yang Chu fumbled with the key in the lock and finally managed to open it. He was about to go inside but turned around instead. It was as if he had suddenly come up with a brainwave.

"I just remembered something," he said. "You said you had something you needed to talk to me about."

"It can wait," Smith did not feel like bringing it up now. "Go to bed."

"No."

He appeared to have sobered up slightly after being sick.

"What is it you wanted to talk to me about?" he said. "Is it about Whitton because I've decided what I'm going to do? You can't tell me what to do in my private time."

"Yang Chu, leave it. Go to bed."

"No," Yang Chu was quite animated now. "You might be my boss at work, but you have no right to tell me who I can or cannot see when I'm not at work. I'm going to ask Whitton out whether you like it or not. I'm in love with her. I don't care what you say. It's none of your damn business what I get up to out of work hours."

It was quite a speech. Smith didn't know what to say.

"So there," Yang Chu banged his hand on the door. "Now you know. What have you got to say about that?"

Smith thought hard. He realised this was neither the time nor the place for the truth, but he decided that'd never stopped him before.
"Me and Whitton are in a relationship," he said.
Yang Chu stared at Smith with his mouth wide open. Drops of spit had formed at the side of his mouth. It was as if he hadn't understood what Smith had said.
"Me and Whitton are seeing each other," Smith said. "It just sort of happened."
Yang Chu appeared to understand now. His whole body tensed up and his fists clenched.
"You fucking bastard," he moved closer and swung a punch.
Smith stepped out of the way and Yang Chu lost his balance. He stumbled to the ground and hit his head on the concrete of the driveway. Smith tried to help him up.
"Get your stinking hands off me," Yang Chu screamed."You bastard. You shit. You devious bastard."
"Go to bed."
"Bastard," Yang Chu managed to get to his feet.
Smith watched as he stumbled inside the house and slammed the door behind him.

# CHAPTER THIRTY THREE

### Tuesday 25 January 2011

The atmosphere in the small conference room was like nobody had ever experienced before. It appeared that an insomnia epidemic had affected the whole team. Everybody sat bleary eyed waiting for DI Brownhill to arrive. Smith sat in between Bridge and Whitton. Yang Chu sat as far away as possible from Smith. Thompson sat next to him. Yang Chu had a bump the size of a small egg on the side of his head. Nobody in the room spoke.

Brownhill walked in with Grant Webber and sat at the head of the table. She eyed the lump on Yang Chu's head with disapproval. "Morning," she said. "I do hope the atmosphere in this room by no means reflects your attitude towards this investigation. Let's get started, shall we? The path report came in late last night and it appears that Yang Chu's idea reaped results. Arnold Mather died at around eight last Wednesday night. Apparently, they used some new technique of analysing the fly larvae to determine this but we don't need to delve any further into that just now. Maggots are the last thing anyone needs to hear about. So, we have a two hour window. Arnold Mather left The Fox Inn just before six and died around two hours later."

"We know all this already," Thompson said.

He looked very pale and his eyes were bloodshot.

"We weren't a hundred percent sure, but now we are. Two hours. What happened in those two hours that resulted in Mather's death."

Silence.

"Anybody?"

"I have a theory," Smith said.

Yang Chu snorted.

"Is there a problem?" Brownhill glared at Yang Chu.

"No, Ma'am," Yang Chu said.

"What on earth happened to your head? That looks very nasty."

"I fell," Yang Chu said.

"OK, Smith, what's this theory of yours?"

"I couldn't sleep last night, and I thought about something Chalmers said. About the connection between Christopher Riley and Arnold Mather."

"Go on," Brownhill said.

"Chalmers reckons there's a connection," Smith said.

"There generally is."

"I agree, but my theory regarding this connection is not about who they were but what."

"I don't understand."

"Riley and Mather didn't know each other," Smith said. "I'm pretty sure of that but they were both similar in one way - they were both sad, miserable middle aged men with no friends or family to speak of."

"Are you suggesting that this woman is preying on insignificant wretches?"

"Look at the facts. Nobody missed Arnold Mather for five days. Christopher Riley was only found because it happened to be his turn to look after the daughter. I reckon they were chosen carefully because of exactly that."

"Interesting theory," Yang Chu said. "But aren't you forgetting something. This woman still had to gain access to them somehow."

"Yang Chu, she watches them. She knows their routines. She preys on the very thing that makes them the sad cases they are. Vulnerability.

From all accounts, this woman is very beautiful. It wouldn't be too difficult for her to charm men like Riley and Mather into letting her into their houses. She could make them do exactly what she wanted, especially considering the amount of alcohol both men had consumed."

"Alcohol?" Brownhill said.

"I spoke to the people working at Ye Olde Yeoman and the Fox Inn," Smith said. "Riley had knocked back almost a crate of brown ale and Mather drank five pints of best bitter. That would have made them even more vulnerable."

"Hmm, but that still doesn't explain the motive. Why is this woman doing this?"

"I haven't quite figured that one out yet, but I am convinced that both Riley and Mather were watched carefully before they were killed."

"Grant," Brownhill said. "Could you please give us a rundown of what you've found so far?"

Webber cleared his throat.

"Not much," he said. "We've confirmed that the same knife was used on both occasions. The same curved blade was used, and chloroform was administered before their throats were cut. Both men were found in their beds. The woman appears to have black hair - traces of hair were found at both murder scenes and we found some fingerprints on the thermostat of Mather's heater."

"Any luck there yet?" Smith said.

"Nothing, they're not on our system anywhere."

"Do we at least have any suspects yet?" Brownhill said.

"Maybe one," Smith said. "A Norwegian student who lives across the road from Christopher Riley's flat. She has black hair and a couple of witnesses claim she could be the woman Riley was seen with on Christmas Day."

"Why hasn't she been hauled in yet? Why isn't she in one of the interview rooms right now?"

"Because I don't think she's our killer, it's just a feeling I get about her."

"I'm not going to ignore a murder suspect on a feeling you get, bring her in."

Forty five minutes later, Kjersti Pelge sat in interview room two with Brownhill and Whitton. She had declined the offer of a solicitor. Brownhill had decided that it would be better for her to be interviewed by two female officers.

"Kjersti," Brownhill said. "Do you know why you're here?"

"I assume it's because I live across the road from where the dead guy was found," Kjersti said matter-of-factly.

"That's right, did you know Christopher Riley?"

"No," Kjersti said.

"You never met him? You lived across the road from him and you've never bumped into him before?"

"No, I saw him a couple of times, but I didn't know who he was. He was just some bloke who lived across the road."

"That's an interesting hair colour," Brownhill said. "Is that the fashion these days?"

"I don't go in for fashion, it's not my natural hair colour - I'm actually blond."

"Blond?" Brownhill said.

"But I dye it black. I mean, come on, all Norwegian's have blond hair, don't they? They have blue eyes and shag like rabbits. I wanted to get away from the stereotypical bullshit."

"You're a student, aren't you?"

"That's right."

"What are you studying?" Whitton asked.

"Psychology and Sociology. What has that got to do with anything?"

"We're just trying to gather all the facts," Brownhill said. "Why are you studying here in York? I believe the Universities in Norway are first class."

"Norwegian isn't exactly widely spoken, I wanted to do my degree in English. Besides, can you believe I actually came here for the weather? I was tired of the snow."

"How old are you?" Whitton said.

"Thirty four."

"Isn't that a bit old to be a student?"

"You're never too old to learn," Kjersti smiled.

Whitton didn't like the smile one little bit.

Kjersti looked at her watch. It was a very unusual watch.

"Is this going to take much longer?" she said. "I have to be at work in an hour. Are we going to drag on with the pleasantries or are we going to get down to the nitty gritty sometime today?"

"Nitty gritty?" Brownhill said.

"The dead guy, I live across the road from where a man was found dead in his bed. I've never spoken to him before, I didn't see him on Christmas Day and I didn't see anything untoward around midnight the night he died. I also don't know anything about how he happened to expire. Can I go now?"

"Not yet, how did you know he died around midnight?"

"The other detective told me," Kjersti said. "The unusual looking one. I think he likes me. He came back to give me his card. He said my hair looked better in black."

"Where were you between six and eight last Wednesday evening?" Whitton said.

"At home, I finished my shift around five then I went home."

"Was there anybody with you?"

"No," Kjersti said. "Kim was out at some swimming gala thing. I was on my own."

"Kim's your flat mate?" Brownhill said.

"She stays in the flat opposite mine."

"So, there was nobody who can confirm that you were actually at home?" Whitton said.

"No, the other girls only came back this weekend."

"Nobody can vouch for you?" Whitton said.

"Vouch for me? Why would I need somebody to vouch for me?"

She shifted her green wig to the side slightly.

"Do you know a man by the name of Arnold Mather?" Brownhill said.

"Never heard of him. Am I a suspect here?"

"Not at the moment, right now we're just looking at things from all angles. We're trying to narrow things down a bit."

"Let me help you then, I didn't kill the guy who lived opposite me nor did I kill this Arnold Mather bloke. I read about it in the papers. Can I please go now? I'm going to be late for work."

"Would you object to providing us with a hair sample?" Whitton said.

"And your fingerprints of course?"

"I thought you said I wasn't a suspect."

"We'd just like to make sure," Brownhill said. "Then we can eliminate you from our enquiries and concentrate our efforts elsewhere."

"If I'm not a suspect in the first place, why would you need to eliminate me from your enquiries?"

"Because it's our job," Whitton realised her voice was getting louder. "Will you agree to have your fingerprints taken and give us a hair sample or not?"

"OK," Brownhill said. "Let's calm things down a bit shall we. I apologise if we've come across as being a bit harsh, but murders tend to stir up the emotions a bit."

"Am I obliged to provide you with my fingerprints and hair samples?"

"If we suspect any involvement in a crime we have the power to enforce it," Brownhill said.

"And do you? Do you suspect my involvement?"

"At the moment," Brownhill said. "No, we don't but it would be in your best interests to cooperate fully at this stage."

"I'm late for work. I assume I'm free to go?"

Whitton looked across the table at Brownhill.

"Yes," Brownhill said. "For the moment, you're free to go. Thank you for your time. We may need to speak with you again."

## CHAPTER THIRTY FOUR

"I can't believe Brownhill let that Norwegian wise arse go," Whitton said to Smith in the canteen. "I don't like her at all. There's something odd about her."

"She's not our killer," Smith said. "Get over it."

"What happened with you and Yang Chu last night? He seems a bit upset."

"He's hungover," Smith said. "He can't handle his drink. I told him about us and he got a bit out of hand. I didn't realise he liked you so much."

"What happened? Why did you tell him about us? I thought we were going to keep it quiet for a while. Your words, not mine."

"I had to tell him, he went off about how I didn't have the right to tell him what he could or couldn't do when he was off duty. He told me he was in love with you and was going to ask you out. I didn't want to watch him make a fool out of himself, so I told him about us."

"How did he take it?"

"He was drunk," Smith said. "He completely lost it. He tried to hit me."

"Oh my God, that's how he got the lump on his head. You socked him one, didn't you?"

"I didn't hit him. He swung a punch at me and missed. I stepped to the side. He fell over and hit his head."

"Poor guy, maybe I should have a word with him."

"You'll do no such thing. Let him calm down a bit first. He'll get over it."

"I couldn't sleep last night," Whitton said.

"Me neither," Smith said. "From the red eyes at this morning's meeting, I don't think anybody slept much last night."

"There must be something in the air - a full moon or something."
"You don't believe in all that crap, do you? About how the phases of the moon affect our moods?"
"It's been proven. Some people are affected more than others. Look at how dogs go crazy when there's a full moon. Where do you think the word lunatic comes from?"
"My dog doesn't go mad when there's a full moon," Smith said.
"Your dog's not quite right in the head, he takes after his owner."
"Anyway, I'm pretty sure there wasn't a full moon last night. Did you find anything useful from the Norwegian?"
"She's stubborn," Whitton said. "Refused to give samples of hair and fingerprints."
"We can't force her. Anyway, she's not the one. I told you that."
"She's weird - she dyes her hair black and then wears a green wig."
"She dyes her hair black?"
"That's right," Whitton said. "She's actually blond."
"Then forget about her, Webber would have mentioned if the hair sample was dyed. He would have spotted it straight away."
"Damn it," Whitton said. "I was really hoping she was the one. This is getting so frustrating. I don't know if we're going to be able to crack this one."
"Something will turn up," Smith said. "It always does."

Bridge burst into the canteen. He was very red in the face.
"Thompson's collapsed," he said. "He's collapsed by the front desk."
"What?" Smith stood up.
"He just collapsed. One minute he was standing talking to me and the next thing he's on the floor. Baldwin's called for an ambulance. It looks like a heart attack."

Smith couldn't believe what he was hearing. He ran out of the canteen and raced down the stairs two steps at a time.

Thompson was lying on his side on the floor by the front desk. Brownhill, Chalmers and Yang Chu were crouched over him. Chalmers was loosening Thompson's shirt and trying to make him more comfortable. Smith stepped closer.

"Thompson," he said.

Thompson's face was a strange grey colour.

"The ambulance will be here in five minutes," Brownhill said.

"What happened?" Smith said.

"He just fell into a heap," Baldwin said. "One minute he was talking to Bridge and the next thing he's on the floor. Do you think it's a heart attack?"

"I don't think so," Chalmers said. "Thompson always kept himself in good shape. He doesn't smoke, and he rarely drinks these days."

"He's had a cold for a while," Smith said. "He couldn't seem to be able to shift it."

"He doesn't look right," Baldwin said.

"He'll be fine," Chalmers said. "Where the hell is that ambulance?"

The ambulance arrived three minutes later. Two paramedics rushed in and moved everybody to the side.

"Is it a heart attack?" Bridge asked one of them.

"I don't think so," the man said. "His heart rate is quite normal. Has he been ill at all recently?"

"He's had a cold for as long as I can remember," Brownhill said. "It's been getting worse over the past few weeks."

"OK," the other paramedic said. "Let's get him out of here, shall we?" I'm sure he'll be fine."

With Smith's help they managed to haul Thompson's considerable bulk onto a stretcher and they wheeled him out of the station to the ambulance.

"I'll go with him," Smith said. "Yang Chu, take my car and meet us at the hospital."

He handed Yang Chu his car keys and ran outside.

Smith sat next to Thompson in the ambulance. He was still unconscious.

"Talk to him," one of the paramedics said.

"Can he even hear me?" Smith said.

"We don't know. Talk to him anyway."

"Thompson," Smith said. "Stop being an arsehole and wake up. We need your help back at the station. There's a dangerous woman out there remember."

Thompson didn't stir.

"Thompson just cut the crap now. You'll probably get a few days off now if that's why you're putting on this performance. Why the hell didn't you just get a doctor's note like anybody else?"

Smith looked up. The paramedic was smiling.

"Nearly there," he said. "We'll have him back at work in no time."

They arrived at the hospital ten minutes later. They were met at the door by two orderlies, three nurses and a man Smith assumed to be a doctor. Thompson was wheeled out of the ambulance and whisked inside the hospital. Smith watched as Thompson disappeared round a corner. A sudden emptiness engulfed him. He'd known Thompson for years – they'd never really seen eye to eye, but Smith still felt a strange affection for the old detective sergeant.

"You can wait in the waiting room," a nurse said to Smith. "Someone will let you know when you can go in and see him."

Yang Chu arrived and patted Smith on the shoulder.

"I'm sure he'll be alright," he said. "I'll wait here with you."

They followed the signs to the waiting room.

"Has anybody phoned Thompson's wife?" Smith said.

"Chalmers called her," Yang Chu said.

"I don't even know her name. In all the years I've known Thompson I don't even know his wife's name. She's always just been Mrs Thompson. Even Thompson calls her that."

"Let's sit down," Yang Chu said. "Do you want some coffee?"

"No thanks."

They waited for a while in the waiting room. Smith watched as a man who was obviously drunk approached the reception desk, was told to sit down and returned to his seat. He repeated this exercise six or seven times before he was escorted out by a burly orderly.

Thompson's wife entered the room and made her way over to Smith. She didn't appear distressed about her husband's condition.

"Mrs Thompson," Smith stood up. "I'm sure he'll be alright."

Mrs Thompson nodded gravely.

"Is there somewhere we can talk?" she said.

"I saw a sign for a canteen back there," Yang Chu said. "I'll wait here in case there's any news."

"What's going on?" Smith said.

He sat next to Mrs Thompson by the window in the hospital canteen.

"It was bound to happen," she said.

"What? What are you talking about, Mrs Thompson? What was bound to happen?"

"Call me Eve, my name's Eve. He didn't want anybody to know."

"Know what? I don't understand."

"Alan is a proud man. Always has been. This is how he wanted it. Those persistent colds - I knew they weren't just colds. I made him get himself checked out. He didn't want to of course but he did it for me. Alan was diagnosed with throat cancer four months ago."

"Cancer?" Smith couldn't believe it. "No?"

"Alan Thompson is the most stubborn man I've ever met, and he distrusted the medical profession more than anything. He refused treatment and I had to go along with his wishes. Some days were fine but on others he couldn't even get out of bed. The pain must have been unbearable, but Alan never let on."

Smith was finding it hard to take it all in.

"The cancer spread," Eve continued. "I suppose that's what cancer does. It's spread to the blood and there's nothing we can do."

"Surely there's something we can do?"

"We can," Eve put her hand on Smith's shoulder. "We can allow him as much dignity a man of Alan's character deserves. He watched as his mother faded away to nothing. It was the treatment that killed her. Alan didn't want to go out like that."

Smith didn't know what to say. The sat in silence for a while.

"He bought a new car you know," Eve said after a few minutes. "He bought it for me even though I can't even drive. A Mercedes Benz."

"I know," Smith thought back to the night he had reversed into the car. "Will you be alright?"

"I'll be fine, dear," Eve said. "Will you be alright? I've had plenty of time to prepare for this. This must be quite a shock for you."

Yang Chu walked in the canteen.

"He's awake," he said. "Thompson has woken up."

## CHAPTER THIRTY FIVE

Thompson was sitting up in the bed when Smith and Eve came in. A drip was feeding a colourless liquid into a vein in his arm. He smiled at his wife and looked at Smith.
"Come to gloat, have you?" he said. "Even in this state I reckon I could still beat you in an arm wrestle."
"How are you feeling?" Smith said.
"I've had better days."
"And I'm sure you'll have plenty more," Smith could feel a lump forming in his throat.
This is what death looks like, he thought, Thompson is dying right in front of my eyes.
"I need to use the ladies," Eve said. "I'll leave you boys alone for a while."
She patted Smith on the shoulder as she left the room.
"How's the investigation going?" Thompson asked. "Bit of a bastard this one isn't it?"
"You're not wrong there," Smith said. "Mrs Thompson has told me everything."
Thompson didn't seem surprised.
"She's a good woman," he added. "But she never could keep a secret. So here we are. Aren't you going to ask me if I have any last requests?"
"Thompson, this is serious. Why didn't you tell anybody? You old fool."
"You can't change an old fool," Thompson mused. "My dad used to say that. I have my reasons and I'd appreciate it if you could respect them."
"Fair enough, how long have you got?"

Thompson started to laugh.

"We'll make a Yorkshireman out of you yet," he said. "Straight to the point. My system is busy shutting down as we speak. That little episode back at the station was its way of letting me know that it can't go on much longer. They've made me comfortable. I'm not scared."

"There's something I need to tell you."

"Here we go," Thompson sighed. "Why do people feel the need to offload their crap onto dying men?"

"Your new car, it was me who reversed into your car."

"I know," Thompson said.

"You knew?"

"Of course I knew. I saw you. I was watching out the window at the sister in law's place. Watching the car was far more interesting than anything they were babbling on about."

"Why didn't you say anything?"

"What for?" Thompson said. "You were probably a bit drunk. What good would it have done? It's only a bloody car."

"Thanks. You're alright, Thompson."

"Bugger off, but while we seem to be getting on for a change, can I give you a piece of advice? Do with it what you will."

"Fire away."

"Whitton's a good woman," Thompson said. "Don't mess her around. It'll destroy her. I've seen the way she is around you - I'm not blind. You only see that maybe once in a lifetime. Don't bugger it up."

"I'll bear that in mind," Smith said.

"I mean it, you hurt that woman and I'll rise from my grave and haunt you for the rest of your life."

Eve returned with a bottle of mineral water. Smith stood up.

"You don't have to leave on my account," she said to Smith.

"No," Smith said. "I'll leave you two in peace. I have something important I need to do."
He winked at Thompson.
"I'll come and see you in the morning. I'll bring Whitton with me."
By the time Smith reached reception, tears were streaming down his face and running down his neck. He took a deep breath and wiped them away. Yang Chu was still waiting.
"Mrs Thompson told me what's going on," he said. "She told me what we can expect. I'm so sorry. You've known Thompson for a long time, haven't you?"
"A few years," Smith said.
"Sarge, about last night. I'm sorry, I was a bit of an arsehole."
"Forget about it, I already have done."

Thompson died peacefully in his sleep four hours later. Smith was watching television with Whitton at his house when Chalmers phoned to tell him the news. Smith put down the phone, stood up and walked over to the sideboard. He took out a bottle of Jack Daniel's, unscrewed the lid and took a long drink from the bottle.
"Thompson died ten minutes ago," he said. "His body just gave up."
Whitton stood up and held Smith in her arms. She was shaking. They stayed locked together in the middle of the room. Theakston walked over and lay by their feet.
"It's strange," Whitton said. "We deal with death almost on a daily basis - it's part of the job but when someone you see every day dies it knocks you for six."
"I know but the death we see in the job is the death of faceless strangers. We put it to one side. We just try and find out what happened to them but what happened to Thompson…"
He took another long swig from the bottle and handed it to Whitton.

"He didn't tell anybody," Whitton drank from the bottle. "How could he keep something like that to himself? He must have been in hell."

"Mrs Thompson told me everything. Thompson didn't want to fade away in a hospital bed with tubes sticking out of him, holding on to some hope that a miraculous cure might pop up at any moment. No, I have to agree with him on this one - I think I would have done the same."

"What? Not telling anyone? It's not right."

She seemed to be getting angry.

"How long have we worked together?" she said. "He owed us something. He could at least have told us what was going on."

"Why?" Smith said. "And have people tiptoeing around him for the last days of his life, offering sympathetic smiles? I have to agree with the old fool. He kept his dignity intact right to the end."

Whitton stared at Smith.

"Since when did you have a head transplant? Where did that wise old head appear from? I think I almost prefer this new mature version."

"Death does funny things to you. It's Chalmers we'd better keep an eye on - he's known Thompson for thirty odd years. He won't admit it but he's going to be the one who takes it hardest."

"I'm going to miss him," Whitton said. "I never really understood what it was he did at work but it's going to be strange not having him around."

"Yang Chu apologised to me," Smith changed the subject. "He told me he was sorry for acting like an arsehole."

"I've been thinking," Whitton said.

"I don't like the sound of this."

"Yang Chu knows about us, and you know what it's like at the station. Pretty soon everybody is going to know. Why don't we just come clean."

"You make it sound like we've committed a crime."

"Haven't we?" Whitton said. "Smith's eleventh commandment. Thou shall not partake in relationships with work colleagues."

"OK, you've got me there. Thompson warned me though."

"About what?"

"He told me you're a good woman, and he said if I mess you around he'll come back from the grave and haunt me for the rest of my life." Whitton smiled. Then a tear appeared in the corner of her eye and her mouth started to tremble. She couldn't stop it - she started to sob uncontrollably.

## CHAPTER THIRTY SIX

**Saturday 29 January 2011**

Thompson's funeral took place four days later. There were no complications as far as the autopsy was concerned - the cancer had spread to the blood and his vital organs had shut down one by one. He was fifty six years old when he died. Thirty two of those had been spent in the service of York city police department.

"Thirty two years," Smith said to Chalmers after the short humanist ceremony.

"That's right," Chalmers said. "He spent more than half of his life catching scumbags."

"It was quite a turnout," Smith said. "I didn't realise Thompson knew so many people."

Ninety six people had turned up to say their goodbyes. At least half of them were work colleagues, past and present.

"Thompson could be a pain in the arse at times, but he was a genuine pain in the arse. What you saw was what you got with him."

"How's Mrs Thompson coping?"

"Better than most. She's a tough bugger that one and besides, she's known for some time remember. She's had time to prepare. The daughter flew in from Canada and she's going to stay for a couple of weeks."

"I didn't even know Thompson had any kids," Smith said.

"Just the one daughter. There's a lot you didn't know about Thompson. He kept himself to himself."

Bridge, Whitton and yang Chu walked up. Smith kissed Whitton on the cheek.

"It's like that is it?" Chalmers said. "Don't tell me you two have finally woken up."

"What do you mean?" Smith said.

"It's been pretty bloody obvious for anyone with eyes in their head to see. Just don't let it bugger up your work."

"Mrs Thompson has booked the Hog's Head," Smith quickly changed the subject. "We're all going back there for a few drinks. Are you coming, boss?"

"Try and stop me," Chalmers said. "Besides, I promised to say a few words."

"Where was old Smyth? Why wasn't he at the funeral?"

"He was supposed to be there. He threatened to be there. He probably went to the wrong church and sat through some other poor bugger's funeral without realising it. Besides, it's probably better he wasn't here. He's not the most tactful person sometimes."

"Can we get going?" Bridge said. "I'm gasping for a pint."

The Hog's Head was already packed when Smith and Whitton walked in. Half of the York police department was there.

"I hope nobody wants to report a crime in the next few hours," Smith pointed to York's finest huddled around the bar. "Even Baldwin has dragged herself away from the front desk."

"I think it's quite touching," Whitton said. "I hope there's as many people at my funeral."

"You're not dropping off any time soon," Smith said. "Can I get you a drink?"

"Pint," Whitton said. "Better make it two. Have you seen the queue at the bar?"

Smith pushed his way through the gaggle of already half-drunk police officers at the bar and caught the eye of Marge, the owner of the pub.

"Jason," she said. "Nice to see you again. Sorry about your friend. Pint of Theakstons?"

"Four please, Marge," Smith said. "I see there's some thirsty policemen here today."

Marge poured the drinks and placed them on the bar counter.

"Thanks, Marge," Smith took out his wallet.

"Put that away, it's been taken care of."

Smith took the drinks back to Whitton who had managed to grab a table by the fire. Chalmers was sitting next to her. He was drinking a large measure of whisky.

"Marge wouldn't take any money," Smith sat down.

"It's been sorted," Chalmers said. "Thompson's daughter stuck three grand behind the bar. Apparently, she's loaded. She wanted a good send off for her dad."

"This should be interesting," Smith said. "A bunch of coppers with a free bar. They'll have to call the police in to keep the peace later."

"Here's to Thompson," Chalmers raised his glass and drained its contents. "It's time for my speech."

He walked up to the bar and said something to Marge. The brass bell behind the counter sounded and a semi hush ensued.

"Everybody," Marge said. "DCI Chalmers would like to say a few words. Could we have a bit of hush please? Food will be served afterwards."

"Thanks, Marge," Chalmers said.

She placed a full glass of whisky in front of him.

"I'll try and keep this short," Chalmers began. "I'm sure you lot want to take full advantage of the free bar. Firstly, my condolences go out to Mrs Thompson and her daughter who has come all the way from

Canada to be here. If there's anything you need, anything at all, we're all here for you. Now, what can I say about DS Alan Thompson?"
He took a sip of whisky. He had prepared two speeches beforehand and, looking around the room, made up his mind to go with the second one.
"Thompson," he said. "Must have held the record for being the longest standing detective sergeant in the history of the York police department. Twenty eight years ago he achieved this distinction and in typical Thompson style he just couldn't be arsed to progress any further."
Everybody started to laugh. Even Mrs Thompson had a grin on her face.
"Thompson had plenty of interesting moments in his career," Chalmers continued. "One such incident involved a nun in a state of undress and, as there are women and children here I won't elaborate on that one. But I will tell you about something that happened when Thompson and me were young DS's together. A young bloke had been brought in after a bit of a drunken brawl at a pub. Thompson escorted him to the cells and suggested he sleep it off. The solicitor was going to sort him out in the morning. This bloke seemed terrified of what his wife would say - he was supposed to be at a night class at the time so, out of the goodness of his heart, Thompson phoned the duty solicitor and asked her to come out to get things speeded up a bit, so the poor drunk could get home without his wife knowing anything."
Chalmers looked around the room. He had a captive audience.
"Anyway," Chalmers said. "The duty solicitor was called, and she arrived about half an hour later in a foul mood. She'd been asleep in bed when Thompson phoned. When she was introduced to her client, we ended up having to pull her off the poor bugger. It turns out, she

was the wife he was so terrified of. Not only did she have to get up in the middle of the night, it was all her husband's fault."

The whole room erupted into laughter.

"No harm was done," Chalmers said. "And I believe they're still happily married although the bloke rarely goes to the pub any more. But that was how Thompson was. He had a kind heart. I hope your glasses are full because I want you all to raise them to the finest man I've ever had the pleasure of working with: Alan Thompson."

"Alan Thompson," the people in the room shouted in unison.

Chalmers returned to his seat. Smith noticed that his eyes were very red. He looked like he had been crying.

"Nice speech, boss," Smith said.

"I'm going to leave you to it," Chalmers said. "I'm knackered. It's been a rough few days."

"Don't you want something to eat?" Whitton said.

"I'm not hungry. I'll see you on Monday morning. That's if Smyth lets me out of his sight."

He stood up and discreetly left the pub.

"He's taking it badly," Smith said. "I knew he would."

"He's older than Thompson, isn't he?" Whitton said.

"I think so. Let's get to the food while there's still some left. These police officers can be a bunch of pigs."

## CHAPTER THIRTY SEVEN

***Monday 31 January 2011***

The snow started to fall again just before dawn. Smith woke up and leaned over in bed. Whitton was breathing lightly next to him. She seemed peaceful and Smith was sure she was smiling in her sleep. He got up and quietly made his way to the bathroom. He examined his face in the mirror. His reflection appeared odd to him - he was older somehow. Grey hairs had sprouted out from his ears and he had more wrinkles than before. More grey hair had appeared on his head. The hair was growing quickly. He looked more closely in the mirror and realised that he was growing old before his sunken eyes. The eyes seemed to droop, and huge bags appeared. He splashed some water on his face but all he achieved was a blurring of the grotesque image in the mirror. He watched as the grey hair became longer - it reached his shoulders and kept growing. His face suddenly started to crack and then turned to ash.
"Jesus Christ," Smith woke up in bed.
Sweat was pouring off his face. Whitton was leaning over him.
"I've been trying to wake you for ages," she said. "That must have been some dream."
"Do I seem older to you? I had two dreams again. I thought I'd woken up and then I must have had another dream."
"You're still as old as you were last night, are you alright?"
She wiped the sweat from his forehead.
"You're burning up," she said.
"These dreams are starting to freak me out. I dreamt I woke up, went to the bathroom and watched myself grow old in the mirror. It seemed

so real. My eyes popped out and my whole face turned to ash."

"I told you, you should think about seeing someone about it, there's obviously something bothering you."

"It's nothing you can't help me with," he pulled Whitton on top of him and kissed her on the lips.

"Dream therapy," he pulled her closer. "Replacing the bad thoughts with good ones."

An hour later, Smith, Whitton and Bridge sat in the canteen at the station. Smith was staring out of the window contemplating the grey snow clouds that were circling in from the west.

"It's strange not having Thompson around," he said. "He didn't do much but at least he was around."

"I wonder if they'll replace him," Whitton said.

"Thompson's irreplaceable," Smith said.

"He's been dead almost a week now," Whitton said. "I still can't believe he didn't tell anybody he was sick."

"I can. I'm going to check my emails."

Smith sat in his office and switched on his computer. He looked at the two photographs on the wall. Lucy Maclean and his sister, Laura. Both of them killed because of me, Smith thought, am I getting immune to death?

He opened up his emails. There was one from Superintendent Smyth wondering why Smith had not shown any interest in being awarded the top policeman of 2010 award.

Top cop, Smith smiled, what a joke.

He deleted the email. He had no intention of showing up at any award ceremony. The email at the bottom of the list caught his eye. It was from an address he did not recognise L.gravov@outlook.ru. There was no message in the body of the email but there was an attachment.

Smith opened it up. It was a photograph of a young girl. She appeared to be fifteen or sixteen years old. She seemed vaguely familiar. She had long black hair and piercing brown eyes. Smith stared at the photograph for quite some time. He didn't know why someone had sent him a photograph of a mystery girl. He suddenly remembered the other emails he had received from an unknown sender. He clicked on the deleted items icon and scrolled down. The same email address appeared on the screen L.gravov@outlook.ru.

"Anything interesting?" Whitton appeared in the doorway.

"This is odd," Smith said. "Someone has sent me three emails and I have no idea who it is."

Whitton looked at the screen.

"That's from a Russian server," she said. "Dot RU. It's Russian."

"I don't know anybody in Russia."

"Reply to the email," Whitton suggested. "Ask them who they are and what they want."

Smith took Whitton's advice literally. He clicked on the reply icon and wrote seven words, 'Who are you? What do you want?'

He pressed send.

"We've got a meeting in Brownhill's office," Whitton said. "Yang Chu calls it the Groundhog Day briefing."

"Groundhog Day?"

"Like the film, you know the one where the guy wakes up and lives the same day over and over again? I don't think we'll ever catch this woman. We'd better go. We wouldn't want to keep the DI waiting."

The atmosphere in Brownhill's office was gloomier than ever. There was an air of despair in the room. Nobody expected to make any progress anymore - that expectation had died out weeks ago and

Thompson's death had done nothing to help lift their spirits. The team was at its worst.

"Where's Chalmers?" Bridge asked.

Everyone had started to get used to the DCI's presence in their meetings.

"He's been called away for a week," Brownhill said. "Smyth has dragged him off to a conference in Scarborough."

"Lucky bastard," Bridge said.

"Scarborough in January?" Whitton said. "I can't think of anything worse."

"Anyway," Brownhill said. "Let's get started, shall we? I know this whole business is starting to drag on a bit, but we have to keep plodding along. Something will turn up."

"Groundhog Day," Yang Chu said.

"You're not helping things with that attitude. Let's go back to the beginning once more. We have two dead men, neither of which appeared to know the other. Both were killed in exactly the same way and tucked in afterwards. We have no witnesses as such and no evidence that we can use to identify this killer. Once again, does anybody have any suggestions? Did anybody wake up this morning and experience a Eureka moment?"

"What about a new angle?" Smith said.

"Good, can you explain what you're thinking?"

"OK, let's step back and look at this from a different perspective. Every murder case I've ever worked on has had one thing in common. Motive, the motive is the key to the murder. So far, we've been wracking our brains to work out some rational reason why these men are dead. Let's look for an irrational one."

"I think you need to get more sleep, Sarge," Bridge said. "You're talking nonsense."

"No," Brownhill said. "I like it. Go on."

"The very act of murder is irrational," Smith said. "It goes against our very nature. Let's forget about the most common motives - revenge, hatred, love, jealousy and financial gain and look for something else."

"Like what?" Yang Chu said.

"That's why you're all here, that's why we have a team. Spit out the first thing that comes into your head."

"A hatred of sad, lonely middle aged men," Bridge said.

"A deep seated fear of beer bellies," Yang Chu chipped in.

"That's enough," Brownhill said.

"I think, in this woman's head, she felt that she had to kill," Smith said. "And there was nothing she could do to stop it."

"What do you mean?" Bridge said.

"Look at the evidence. Both men were rendered unconscious first. They felt no pain. That indicates a certain amount of compassion. They were then killed and made comfortable in their beds."

"It's almost as if she felt sorry for them afterwards," Whitton said.

"That's right," Smith said.

"Remorseful even," Brownhill added.

"Why did she kill them though?" Yang Chu said. "Why kill them in the first place."

"Don't think about why, the very act of killing them is why."

"I don't understand," Yang Chu said.

"Are you saying we're looking for a complete wacko?" Bridge said.

"One of those loonies who hear voices in their heads?"

"I don't think so. Both of the murders were well planned. The chloroform and the way the murders were carried out indicates meticulous planning - it wasn't a spur of the moment act of madness. She watched them beforehand and timed the whole thing to the last second."

"Do you think she'll kill again?" Yang Chu asked.

"I don't know. Part of me wishes she will. Maybe she'll slip up somewhere along the line."

"Then we'll have another serial killer on our hands," Bridge said.

"Three murders. That's what classes a serial killer."

"Only in America," Brownhill said. "If Smith is right here then I think we're going to need some help."

"What kind of help?" Yang Chu said.

"A psychiatrist," Smith said.

"A head shrinker?" Bridge said. "How the hell is that going to help us?"

"To bring a new perspective on the whole thing," Smith said. "I hate to admit it, but I think the DI is right. Do you have anybody in mind?"

"As a matter of fact I do," Brownhill said. "A woman by the name of Jessica Blakemore. We used her once or twice to great effect in Leeds. Her insight into the human psyche is incredible."

"A shrink?" Bridge still couldn't believe what Brownhill was suggesting. "How's a shrink going to help."

"What harm can it do?" Smith said. "I don't mind admitting it - we've hit a brick wall here. How soon can you get her here?"

"She can be here by this afternoon. In the meantime, does anybody have any other suggestions?"

Nobody said a word.

"OK, we'll meet back here again at three this afternoon."

"What are we supposed to do until then?" Bridge looked at his watch.

"Go home for a few hours. I'm giving you a direct order to bugger off home. Do whatever you like. Get some sleep - spend some time with your families. Absolutely no drinking though."

## CHAPTER THIRTY EIGHT

"Do you feel like going shopping?" Smith said to Whitton outside the station, "I'm going to look for a new guitar."

"I think I'll pass," Whitton said. "I've spent so much time at your place recently, I've almost forgotten where I live."

"OK, I think I'll see if there are any guitars worth looking at and then take Theakston for a walk. The poor thing's getting unfit."

"He's always been unfit. I'll see you back here at three."

She kissed him on the cheek and walked to her car. Smith watched her go. He still couldn't believe what was happening to them. It didn't seem real somehow.

Maybe this is just another of my weird dreams, he thought, maybe I'll suddenly wake up and none of this will have happened.

Smith arrived home without a new guitar an hour later. There had been nothing that really jumped out at him at the music shop. He had tried out a Mexican Fender, but the action had been far too high, and the tone wasn't what he had been looking for. He missed his old beaten up Fender. It'd been destroyed with everything else when his house had burned down the year before. He turned the key in the lock and opened the door. Theakston was waiting for him as usual in the hallway.

"Do you feel like a walk, boy?" Smith said.

Theakston eyed him suspiciously. It had been a long time since Smith had taken the dog for a walk and he seemed unsure as to whether he'd heard correctly. Smith fetched the collar and lead from the kitchen cupboard and put them on Theakston's neck. The collar barely fitted anymore - the dog had got so fat.

"You need to go on a diet," Smith said. "We'll go down to the park. It should be quiet this time of the year."

The walk down to the park usually took ten minutes but with a twenty five kilogram Bull Terrier pulling him along, he made it in less than five. Smith almost had to run to keep up. He was grateful when they reached the park and found it was deserted. He removed the lead and Theakston shot off in search of the ducks near the small lake. Smith sat on one of the benches overlooking the lake. The snow had stopped but the ominous grey clouds overhead promised more snow very soon. He watched as Theakston darted in and out of the trees and stopped by the lake. A thin layer of ice had formed on the top and the dog appeared to be trying to decide if he could walk across or not. Don't do it, Smith thought, there's no way I'm going swimming in there today.

Theakston turned around, ran up to the bench where Smith was sitting and collapsed at his feet.

"You definitely need more exercise," Smith said. "You used to run this park flat when you were younger."

Smith looked across the lake. The ducks were nowhere to be seen He wondered where they went in the winter months. He thought it strange that when April finally arrived, there was always a new group of ducks with their offspring swimming behind them. He thought about the meeting with Brownhill's psychiatrist. He still had four hours to kill before the meeting.

Jessica Blakemore, he thought, she doesn't sound like a shrink.

He wondered if they were ever going to get to the bottom of the investigation. In all his years as a detective he had never experienced a case like this one. Two murders without any apparent motive. Two faceless, lonely men killed for no reason whatsoever. A motiveless

murder was the hardest murder to solve. The whole thing was baffling. His thoughts turned once again to the disturbing dreams he'd been having. They were becoming more and more frequent.
Maybe everything's connected, he thought, maybe the dreams are a result of the frustration at not being able to fathom out this case. Maybe I ought to take Whitton's advice and see someone about it. Perhaps I should ask this head doctor.

Theakston was starting to snore loudly at Smith's feet. The first snowflakes were settling on the dog's head.
"I think that's our cue to leave," Smith stood up.
Theakston stirred and got to his feet. The walk home took considerably longer than the walk down to the park - Theakston was exhausted and he was worried he might actually have to carry the poor dog home. By the time Smith opened the door to his house, both he and Theakston were drenched from the snow. He went inside and fetched a towel to dry the dog off. He filled the dog bowl with food and Theakston finished it in less than two minutes.
"You're such a pig," Smith said.
His phone started to ring in his pocket. He took it out and answered it. It was Whitton.
"Missing me already?" Smith said.
"Are you anywhere near a computer?" Whitton said.
"I'm at home. We've just got back from a walk to the park."
"Turn on your computer, I've found something interesting."
Smith walked through to the living room and turned on his computer.
"What's this all about?" He said.
"Google the name Jessica Blakemore, and you'll see what it's about."
"Hold on, this computer of mine is so slow. I think I need to get another one. Why did you Google the shrink?"

"I was bored, I didn't have a mental case detective sergeant to entertain me. I was curious to know what this woman's like."

"You've really got a problem with women haven't you?"

"I have not," Whitton said. "I just like to know a bit about people before I meet them."

"OK, it's finally booted up."

He typed in Blakemore's name into the search engine.

"What's so interesting?" He said read the information on the screen.

"Thirty five years old. I see she has a whole load of qualifications. She's only been practicing for eight years. What am I looking for?"

"Look at the photo of her."

Smith scrolled down, and a black and white photograph appeared on the screen.

"Not bad, I don't really like black hair though. She doesn't look like a head doctor."

"Doesn't she remind you of someone?"

"She looks a bit like Baldwin," Smith said. "An older version. What's this all about?"

"The photofit the guy from the pub came up with," Whitton said. "It's the spitting image of our psychiatrist."

"Come on, Whitton, are you honestly telling me you think the shrink Brownhill is bringing in to help is actually our murderer?"

"Look at the photo."

"The guy in the pub was blotto."

"I'm just telling you what I think."

"I think you need more sleep."

"Think about it," Whitton said. "How many times have you read about murderers who get close to the investigations in one way or another?"

"What do you suggest we do? Tell Brownhill that the expert she's brought in is our murder suspect. Do we take her fingerprints and a hair sample as soon as she gets to the station or do we hear what she has to say first?"

"Don't be sarcastic," Whitton said.

"I'm not, it's just a bit ridiculous."

"I'll see you at work," Whitton said and hung up.

Smith stared at the blank screen on his phone. He thought about phoning Whitton back but decided against it.

This investigation is messing with our heads, he thought, I'll be glad when it's all over.

Smith turned off the computer, sat down on the couch and closed his eyes. He drifted off to sleep and was woken a few minutes later by his phone ringing.

It's Whitton calling to admit she was wrong, he thought.

He answered the phone.

"Smith," He said.

There was silence on the other end.

"Who is this?"

"A friend," a man's voice said. "I know who your killer is."

"Who is this?"

The line went dead. Smith leaned further back in his chair. A strange sensation came over him. It felt like there was somebody else in the room with him. He could hear someone breathing nearby. He felt a hand over his mouth and a pungent smell filled his nostrils. He was starting to feel dizzy. He struggled but the hand over his mouth wouldn't budge. He managed to twist his body and raised his hand up to his face. He felt a sharp pain in the palm of his hand and when he raised it up he realised it was covered in blood. There was a gaping wound in his hand. He screamed.

"Holy Crap," Smith woke up.

Theakston was barking at him.

I'm losing my mind, Smith thought.

He went through to the kitchen and turned on the tap. He splashed some water on his face and dried it off with his shirt. He turned on the kettle and made the strongest cup of coffee he could. He sat down on the kitchen table and lit a cigarette. He looked at the clock - the meeting with the psychiatrist was due to begin in just over an hour.

## CHAPTER THIRTY NINE

DI Brownhill had decided that it would be best if the four members of the investigative team and herself met with Jessica Blakemore in the privacy of her office for the first briefing. Whitton and Yang Chu were already seated when Smith walked in.

"Am I late?" He said.

"No," Whitton said. "Bridge isn't here yet. He's going to have to watch his step. Brownhill won't put up with his behaviour for much longer."

"He's probably with that mystery woman of his," Yang Chu said. "Does anybody know who she is?"

"I've got no idea," Smith said.

Brownhill entered the room with a tall thin woman. Smith recognised her from the photograph on the internet.

"Good afternoon," Brownhill said. "This is Jessica Blakemore. I'm sure she will prove to be very helpful in this investigation."

Yang Chu stood up and shook Blakemore's hand. Smith did the same. Whitton merely nodded and averted her gaze. Smith couldn't help but stare at this incredibly striking woman. Whitton had been right - she did bear an uncanny resemblance to PC Baldwin and the photofit the man in the pub had come up with. She had long black hair and thick eyebrows of a similar hue. Her eyes were intense. Smith had never seen eyes like them before - they seemed to be warm and welcoming yet slightly intimidating at the same time. Smith wondered if she used them in her profession to hypnotise her patients.

"Where's Bridge?" Brownhill asked.

"He'll be here in a few minutes," Smith said. "It's not yet three."

"What's going on with him? He never used to be late for meetings."

Right on cue, Bridge burst through the door. He was red in the face. He looked like he had been running.

"Sorry I'm late," he said. "I fell asleep."

He stared at Jessica Blakemore and smiled.

"You must be the famous head doctor. I'm DC Bridge. It's a pleasure to meet you."

He held out his hand. Blakemore nodded at him.

"OK," Brownhill said. "Seeing as though we have everybody here we might as well make a start. We have a lot to get through. Jessica has kindly agreed to give up her time to offer us some assistance. We're hoping she can bring a fresh approach to the investigation. Smith, would you like to go through everything that has happened for her benefit?"

Smith spent the next twenty minutes filling Jessica Blakemore in on every aspect of the case so far. Blakemore listened intently, never once taking her eyes off Smith.

"So, there you have it," Brownhill said when Smith was finished. "As I explained to you on the phone, we've hit a brick wall. We're no closer to closing in on whoever did this than we were over a month ago when Christopher Riley was killed."

"Right," Blakemore said.

She had a very unusual voice. It was warm but there was something in the way she said that one word that Smith found intriguing. He couldn't wait to listen to her further.

"Firstly," she said. "I don't want you have any illusions about my being here. I am not going to magically pull a name out of a hat for you - I'm not a miracle worker and I don't want you to be disappointed if my assistance bears no fruit."

She smiled at Smith.

"What do you think?" she said.

"Think?" Smith said.

"Two men are dead. Tell me what you think about it."

"I don't know," Smith wasn't prepared for this. "Both Christopher Riley and Arnold Mather were lonely, single, middle aged men. They were both quite drunk when they were killed. I'd say they were carefully selected."

"Why?"

"Because of what they were. They had no friends - no family to speak of. I just think it's easier to get away with killing someone that nobody is going to miss for a while."

"What else?"

"I thought you were going to tell us."

"What else?" Blakemore ignored him.

"I don't think this woman really enjoyed killing them."

"Why do you say that?" Blakemore took out a notepad and wrote something down in it.

"It's just a feeling I get. I've investigated murders before and the majority of the perpetrators gain some kind of thrill out of it. I don't think this woman does. Like I say, it's just a feeling I get. I could be wrong."

"He seldom is," Brownhill said.

"I see," Blakemore said. "Intuitive sort, are you?"

"It's a curse I was born with."

He didn't notice that Whitton's face was getting redder and redder by the second. It was clear she didn't like this woman.

"I'm inclined to agree with you," Blakemore said. "The chloroform and the very way these men were left after they were killed support your theory. It suggests a certain amount of remorse."

"Can I say something?" Whitton said.

"I was hoping you would."

"We already know all of this. We've gone over this again and again for weeks now. I thought you were here to give us something new."

"I'm trying to establish all the factors of the equation," Blakemore said.

"The DI said you've helped her out before," Whitton said. "Excuse me if I sound rude but how did that work out? Were you at all helpful then?"

"Mrs Blakemore was extremely useful," Brownhill wasn't happy. "But, like she said, we can't expect miracles from her."

"OK," Blakemore said. "You all seem pretty sure that you're looking for a woman here and even without the witness accounts, I must admit I'm inclined to agree. I would suggest that she charmed these men into letting her into their homes, knocked them out with the chloroform and then killed them. Do you know what my initial feeling is?"

"The suspense is killing us," Whitton said.

"I believe she underwent four phases," Blakemore ignored Whitton's sarcasm. "Four distinct phases. Phase one is the preparation period - she observes her victim for a while beforehand. She knows exactly when to strike. She has procured the chloroform and the knife, and she's completely prepared. Phase two is where she puts this meticulous planning into action. She manages to gain the trust of the victim and gains access to where they feel the safest - in their own homes. She knocks them out with the chloroform and all the time she will appear perfectly calm. These men didn't stand a chance. They will have had no inkling of what was going to happen. The third phase is the most disturbing one. Her whole personality will change. She slices open the throat of her victim. Slitting somebody's throat is not easy - it requires a determination to kill and there are many other ways to kill someone - less drastic ways."

"Do you think the way they were killed is significant?" Smith said.

"Definitely, I'm sure I'm only stating what you've all been thinking. Why slit their throats when they're completely helpless? Why not just poison them? Why does it have to be so violent?"

"What's phase four?" Whitton said. "Have you forgotten about the fourth phase?"

"She calms down again," Blakemore said. "Her blood pressure most certainly drops, and she realises what she's done. She knows she had to kill them, but she starts to feel remorse. That's why she tucks them up in bed. Then she leaves."

"Are you saying we're looking for a lunatic?" Yang Chu said. "A mad woman?"

"Madness is complicated, and I'll be the first to admit that psychiatry is not an exact science. The human brain is an enigma but yes, the person you're looking for is definitely unbalanced. I wouldn't rule out schizophrenia but please don't quote me on that."

"Do you have any suggestions as to why she's doing this?" Brownhill said.

"Not yet, without knowing more about her - her childhood for instance, it's impossible to say."

"This is a waste of time," Whitton said. "I thought you were here to help us."

"Detective?"

"Whitton," Whitton said.

"Detective Whitton, this isn't the movies. This is real life. If you expected me to come in here for a few hours and put together a profile picture that points out your killer, you're not living in the real world."
"Speaking of pictures," Whitton said. "Where were you on Christmas Day?"
"Whitton," Brownhill said. "That's enough. I think we'll take a break for half an hour."
Everybody stood up.
"Whitton," Brownhill said. "Could I have a word before you go?"

## CHAPTER FORTY

"What the hell was all that about?" Brownhill said to Whitton when they were alone in the office.
"What was what about?" Whitton said.
"Your whole attitude. Jessica is here to help. I'd appreciate it if you'd show her a bit of common courtesy, not to mention respect. She's very accomplished in her field."
"I don't like her. There's something not quite right about her."
"No doubt she thinks the same of you. Take a break. When we resume I expect you to behave like a police detective."
Whitton left the office and headed for the canteen. Smith, Bridge and Yang Chu were sitting by the window talking to Jessica Blakemore. Whitton sat down next to Smith.
"I hope I didn't get you into trouble back there," Blakemore said.
"I'm sorry if I was a bit rude," Whitton managed to force the words out.
"Rude?" Blakemore said. "I don't think you were rude at all. I wish more people were as open as you are. It would make my job a whole lot easier - yours too I imagine. I think that was a very productive session. I didn't want you to hold back; I wanted you to say exactly what was on your mind."
"Are you married?" Bridge said. "I'm just saying what's on my mind."
Everybody laughed. Even Whitton managed a smile.
"Yes," Blakemore said. "I'm married. He's an architect. He's a southerner but he's alright. That brings me to your question."
She looked at Whitton.
"Question?"

"Christmas Day. You asked me where I was on Christmas Day. I was in London with my husband's family."

"We're just frustrated," Smith said. "We've been slogging away for weeks and we've got absolutely nothing. We were hoping you would be able to give us something new."

"Let me sleep on it," Blakemore said. "It's amazing what the human brain can come up with when you least expect it. Let me process all of this and I'll get back to you tomorrow."

"What about the rest of the meeting?" Bridge seemed disappointed.

"I'd say we've accomplished more in here in five minutes than we did in two hours in there."

She stood up.

"I'll see you in the morning," she said. "That's if you still want me to try and help you."

"Of course we do," Smith turned to Whitton.

"We do," Whitton said. "This one is getting to us, that's all."

"Let it get to you - that's how you're going to crack it. That's a bit of free advice. Anything more and I'm going to have to start charging you by the hour and I'm not cheap."

She walked out of the canteen.

"What do you make of her?" Smith said when Blakemore was gone.

"I like her," Bridge said.

"Me too," Yang Chu added.

"She's not as bad as I thought she would be," Whitton admitted.

"At least we have a bit more to go on now," Smith said.

"Do we?" Whitton said.

"We now know for sure that Riley and Mather were not connected - they were chosen at random. At least now we can stop wasting our time on finding a link."

"What do you suggest we waste our time on now then?" Yang Chu said.

Smith looked at his watch.

"Ourselves," he said.

Everybody stared at him.

"What's happened to you?" Bridge said. "You used to be obsessed about solving a case. You wouldn't sleep until you'd got to the bottom of it."

"Look where that got me. I almost lost my mind a few times when there were things I couldn't figure out."

He stood up.

"Where are you going?" Whitton said.

"To speak to Brownhill. To tell her we're calling it a day. Do you feel like seeing a band tonight?"

"A band?"

"The Sweaty Pigs are playing at The Fringe tonight," Smith said.

"The Sweaty Pigs?"

"They're a bit rough and ready, but they play the best raw blues I've heard in a long time."

"Sounds great," Whitton said, "I think."

"I'll pick you up at seven."

He walked out of the canteen.

　　Brownhill was still in her office when Smith went in. She was talking to Jessica Blakemore. They seemed to be sharing a joke.

"Excuse me," Smith said. "The team and I have decided to call it a day if that's alright with you."

"So I've gathered," Brownhill said. "Jessica was just giving me her professional opinion on all of you,"

"I don't want to know. I'll see you in the morning."

"I'll walk with you," Blakemore said.

She stood up and left the room with Smith.

"I've heard all about you, DS Smith," Blakemore said as they walked down the corridor towards the front desk. "I could devote an entire psychological dissertation to somebody like you."

"I'm just a bit unlucky."

"Unlucky?" Blakemore stopped by the door that led to the front desk. "Unlucky?" She said again. "I'd say you're more than unlucky. Your father commits suicide when you're a kid and your sister disappears the very next year. You're sent to York to stay with your Gran and a few years later she dies too. You join the police force and things really start to happen. You find your girlfriend dead in your bathroom and a few months later your sister is pulled out of the river. Your house gets blown up and your friend dies when his car explodes. That's more than unlucky."

Smith nodded.

"That's about it," he said.

"Not to mention how many times you've almost died yourself. What is it? Three or four times?"

"More like six," Smith said. "If you count the time I spent in Talinn looking for my sister."

"I'm surprised you're still in one piece. Mentally that is. Anybody else would be in an institution by now banging their heads against the wall all day."

"The dreams probably help," Smith said.

"OK, now we're talking. Dreams - the most uncharted of territories. I imagine it's nightmares you're talking about?"

"Sort of," Smith didn't know why he was telling this stranger all of this. There was something about her that made her easy to talk to.

"Whitton calls them double dreams," he said. "Something like that anyway. Lucid dreams."

"Double awakenings," Blakemore's intense eyes seemed to brighten. "You've been having lucid double awakenings?"

"I wake up, or at least I think I've woken up. I'm in complete control of the dream. It's like I'm really awake and then I wake up for real."

"That's extremely rare," Blakemore said.

"I'd better go. I'll see you in the morning. Are you staying in York tonight?"

"I'll be here for the whole week. Bryony has kindly offered to put me up."

"See you tomorrow then," Smith said.

He started to walk away and felt a hand on his shoulder. It seemed to send a shockwave throughout his whole body.

"Detective," Blakemore said.

Smith turned around. Blakemore's eyes bored into his.

"If you want to talk about those dreams of yours," she said. "I'd be happy to listen. No charge of course. I'd be very interested to hear about them."

"I'll think about it."

"They're only going to get worse."

"I'll be fine," Smith walked past Baldwin's desk and out of the station.

## CHAPTER FORTY ONE

The Fringe Club was a small intimate venue just outside the city centre. It was one of those so called alternative night spots frequented by students and wannabe hipsters keen to escape the drudgery of their nine to five existences. Smith and Whitton had arrived at half past seven and by eight the place was slowly filling up. Smith had chosen a table in the middle of the room - not too far away from the stage but not to close that the close proximity to the band would leave him half deaf for the next few days.
"Look at them," he said to Whitton. "York's finest. Top ten percent. We're all doomed if they're the future of this country."
Scores of young student types were propped up at the bar frantically drinking to make sure they took full advantage of the mid-week booze specials.
"You're so cynical," Whitton knocked back half of the beer in her glass. "They're not that bad. I was a student once you know."
"Me too, that's how come I know so much about them. I'm going to get a few drinks in before the band come on. And before that rabble drink the place dry."
He walked towards the bar and pushed his way through the aliens with their peculiar hairstyles and obscure attire. He was suddenly aware that he was being observed. He'd experienced the feeling before. It was as if the pair of eyes that were watching him were burning through his skin. He turned round but he couldn't see anybody who appeared to be out of place.
"Four pints of Theakstons," he said to a sweaty bull of a man with long greasy hair. "The beer's not watered down is it?"
The barman glared at him.

"Of course it isn't," he said.

"These student bastards wouldn't even notice, but I would. It's illegal you know."

"What are you?" The barman poured the beers. "The beer police?"

*Something like that,* Smith thought but decided to hold his tongue.

Smith took the drinks back to the table. The feeling that he was being watched was still with him.

"About time," Whitton took a long drink from the glass. "What time are the Greasy Pigs on?"

"Sweaty Pigs," Smith said. "Their first set is at nine. I think someone's watching me."

"Watching you?" Whitton looked around the club. "Everybody's watching you. You're not exactly dressed like the rest of the elite clientele in here. You stick out like a sore thumb."

Whitton's words instantly made Smith feel depressed.

"What's wrong with the way I'm dressed? Anyway, I used to rock in clubs like this one. You've seen me play."

"That was a long time ago," Whitton said. "You've grown up since then."

"What a terrible thing to say. You're making me feel old."

"Not old, just more mature."

"That's even worse."

Smith thought back to the many times he had stood on the stage of The Deep Blues club and played off the top of his head.

I'm buying myself another guitar, he thought, as soon as this awful investigation is over.

"I'm going to the ladies," Whitton stood up. "Keep my seat."

"OK," Smith said. "Unless someone better comes along. Maybe someone who likes old men like me."

Whitton shook her head and headed for the toilets.

While Smith was waiting for Whitton to come back he scanned the room. It was a habit he had acquired when he had joined the police. Young men and women wearing T shirts depicting bands Smith had never heard of were smiling and talking about how they were going to change the world.

Idealists, Smith thought, they'll soon realise how shitty this world is when their dreams are smashed.

It was while Smith was looking around the room that he saw him - a man in his thirties who didn't seem to belong there. For a split second, their eyes met, and the man quickly looked away. Smith wracked his brain. He didn't recognise the man. He was tall with dark hair and an unfortunately large nose. He appeared to be on his own. Whitton returned to the table.

"Three of the students have already thrown up in the ladies," she said.

"Oh, the simple joys of youth."

"Look over there," Smith said. "Between the pillar and the jukebox. There's a man on his own with dark hair. He's the one who's been watching me."

Whitton looked over.

"I can't see anyone like that," she said.

Smith tried to locate the man again, but he appeared to have vanished.

"You're imagining things. Here, this'll cheer you up."

She put her hand in her coat pocket and pulled out a small silver hip flask. She handed it to Smith.

"Jack Daniel's," she said. "That's what blues guys drink isn't it? We used to smuggle booze in all the time when I was a student."

Smith smiled and took a long swig from the flask.

"These mangy hogs had better be good," Whitton said.

Two hours later, Smith and Whitton stood outside The Fringe Club waiting in a line of inebriated academics for a taxi. An altercation could be heard further down the queue but it soon evaporated and loud laughter could be heard.

"They weren't bad," Whitton admitted. "Not really my kind of thing but I wouldn't mind seeing them again."

"They were brilliant," Smith said.

He was feeling very drunk.

"Country Joe and the Fish, Grateful Dead, Zappa - all the classics. Their version of Good Vibrations was pure genius."

"I prefer the original," Whitton said.

"You would. I mean, anyone who thinks Meatloaf is music would. Hold on."

He had spotted something across the road from the taxi rank.

"It's that bloke again," he said. "He's just walked off down the road."

Before Whitton could say anything, Smith had set off across the road. He was almost run down by an approaching taxi. The driver hooted as it drove past. Smith half walked, half ran in the direction he had seen the man go. He came to the shop on the corner and looked around. The street was deserted. He felt a hand on his shoulder and braced himself for an attack.

"We've lost our place in the queue," Whitton said. "What's going on?"

"It was him," Smith said. "That bloke who was watching me inside the club. I'm sure of it."

"Let's walk, it's not that far. The fresh air will do us good."

She took his hand and they set off in the direction of the city centre.

"Do you have any of that Jack Daniel's left?" Smith said as they passed the off license around the corner from his house.

"We drank it all. I mean you drank it all."

"It's alright, I have plenty of the stuff at home. The walk has sobered me up a bit."

They reached Smith's house and he fumbled with the key in the lock.

"After you," Smith opened the door.

Whitton went in first and Smith closed the door behind them. Neither of them noticed the tall man with the dark hair. He'd been watching them from behind a wall on the other side of the street.

# CHAPTER FORTY TWO

### *Wednesday 1 February 2011*

Smith woke from a dreamless sleep to find he was alone. Whitton was gone. He got up and went downstairs. She had left a note on the kitchen table to inform him she'd gone home to change her clothes before work. Theakston wasn't begging to be fed so he assumed Whitton had already fed him. The dog sat by the front door waiting to be let out. Smith turned on the kettle, picked up his cigarettes and opened the back door. A blast of cold air blew into the kitchen. Smith went outside, a blanket of fresh snow had covered the entire back garden - it had obviously snowed heavily during the night. He lit a cigarette and shivered. His head felt remarkably clear considering the amount of alcohol he had consumed the night before. It must have been watered down beer, he thought. He finished the cigarette and threw it into the snow. The butt made a quiet hiss as it made contact with the snow.

Smith went back inside the house and made some coffee. He decided he would do something he hadn't done in a very long time. He turned on the radio, tuned into the local station and listened. A song he had not heard in years was playing. It was a song Smith used to love. Something about being happy and having sunshine. He smiled but when the song ended, and the DJ announced that The Gorillaz' 'Clint Eastwood' was ten years old it made Smith feel slightly depressed. I am getting old, he thought. The news started, and Smith flinched as the announcer began talking about the two murders. Apparently, the York Police Department were no closer to bringing a close to the investigation. They had no new leads and no more witnesses had come forward.

"This is exactly why I don't listen to the radio," Smith said to Theakston. "Where do they get their information from?"

The weather report warned of more heavy snowfall and Baltic temperatures in the north of the country for the coming week. A huge cold front was moving in from the Arctic and the announcer suggested that people should stay indoors whenever possible.

Great, Smith thought, why the hell did I ever move here?

He picked up his phone. There were no new messages. He opened up the phone browser and googled the weather in Perth. Thirty degrees and clear blue skies. For the first time since Smith had come to York he contemplated going back to Australia.

At least for a short while, he thought, they don't have snow and Baltic weather there - only warm seas and sunshine.

    A noise woke Smith from his thoughts. The morning mail had landed on the doormat with a dull thud. He finished his coffee and went to see what bills had dropped on his carpet today. He smiled when all he saw on the doormat was the February issue of 'Guitar Monthly'.

Punctual as always, he thought, it's a sign - I need to buy myself a new guitar.

He picked up the magazine and was about to take it to the kitchen when he noticed there was a letter underneath it. He picked it up. His name was written on the front of the envelope but nothing else. It had been handwritten. He took it to the kitchen and made another cup of coffee. He opened up the guitar magazine and went straight to the back to the classifieds. He scanned through the guitars for sale and something caught his eye. It was a 1982 Gibson Les Paul gold top.

From the photograph, the guitar appeared to be immaculate. The price was four thousand pounds, but Smith knew he would be able to knock it down a bit. Times were hard, and people needed the cash. He tore out the advertisement and stuck it on the front of the fridge.
"When this is all over," he looked at the photograph of the guitar. "You're mine."
1982, he thought, the year I was born. It's a sign.

Smith took a sip of coffee and opened up the envelope. Inside was a small piece of paper folded in half. He opened it up and read.
'I can help you,' he read. 'I have some answers. I'll be in touch.'
That was all it said - thirteen simple words. There was nothing to suggest who wrote the note - no name at the bottom and no contact details, nothing at all to say what the letter was all about. Smith read the words again.
"Who the hell are you?" he said.
It has to be the same person who's been sending me the emails, he thought.
He made a mental note to bring the matter up at the investigation meeting later that day.

For once, Bridge was the first to arrive at the station. He was drinking from a bottle of water when Smith walked in.
"You're early," Smith sat opposite him. "No big date last night then?"
"No," Bridge said. "Her kid was ill, and I didn't feel like looking after a sick child all night."
"Kid?" Smith said. "Exactly how old is this woman?"
"Old enough to teach me a few things, if you know what I mean."
"Who is this mystery female?"
"I told you," Bridge smiled. "Trade secret. How was the band last night?"

"Brilliant. Completely wasted on those low life students though."
"Why do you hate students so much?"
"I don't know, I can't explain it. It all started when I wasn't one anymore."
Yang Chu and Whitton walked in. Whitton went straight over to Smith and kissed him on the cheek.
"Can you two just get a room?" Yang Chu said. "You're embarrassing."
"How's this weather?" Bridge said. "My windscreen was frozen over this morning."
"There's a bastard of a cold front coming in from the north," Smith said. "I'll be glad when this winter is over. Has anybody seen Brownhill this morning?"
"She was already here when I got in," Bridge said. "Her and that hot shrink."
"You're terrible," Whitton said. "Do you ever think about anything else?"
"What else is there to think about? And I'm not terrible, I'm single."
"What about the grandmother you've shacked up with?" Yang Chu said.
"Jealousy doesn't suit you."

Brownhill walked in and sat down next to Smith. Smith thought she looked different, she seemed to be happy - her face was animated somehow.
"Morning, boss," he said. "You look fresh this morning. What time do you want us in your office?"
"Slight change of plan. We'll be having the meeting in here today. The heating in my office is on the blink and Jessica agrees that we'll probably be more productive in this informal environment."
"She's the expert," Bridge said. "Where is she anyway?"

"She had to make a few phone calls. She'll be along shortly."

They sat in silence for a while. Each of them appeared to be lost in their own personal thoughts.

*These are my only friends,* Smith looked at the faces gathered around the table. *We live and die together.*

His thoughts suddenly turned to Thompson. He felt sad that Thompson's name had hardly been mentioned since his death.

Oh well, he thought, maybe that's how it is - maybe it's for the best to concentrate on the living.

"Sorry to keep you all waiting," Jessica Blakemore hurried into the room. "I had a number of tedious matters to sort out. Being a shrink is never plain sailing. Why all the contemplative expressions?"

Blakemore's cheery disposition seemed to wake everybody up.

"OK," she looked at Whitton. "Don't leave anything out. Tell me about your childhood."

Whitton burst out laughing. Bridge followed suit. Soon, the whole canteen was filled with raucous laughter. A PC in uniform walked in and looked at them as if they had gone mad. He looked exhausted - he had obviously just finished a night shift.

"The canteen's closed," Brownhill said. "Go home and get some sleep."

The policeman looked at her with bleary eyes and left the canteen.

"I'll put a note on the door," Bridge said.

He stood up, tore a piece of paper out of his notebook and stuck it on the door. Smith watched as Bridge smiled and wrote something on the paper.

"That should do the trick," Bridge sat down again.

"What did you write?" Smith said.

"Canteen closed due to snow, that'll confuse the hell out of everybody."

"Right," Brownhill said. "I can see we're all unusually sharp witted this morning. I've got a feeling a breakthrough is on the cards sometime soon. Who wants to start?"

"There's something I think I need to share," Smith said. "I didn't think much of it before and it may or may not be important, but I've been getting strange emails and letters."

He told them about the emails he had received from the anonymous sender.

"Beware the full moon?" Bridge said. "What on earth does that mean?"

"Maybe our killer is a werewolf," Yang Chu suggested.

Brownhill gave him a look of disapproval.

"What about the map of Romania?" Brownhill said. "What does that imply?"

"I have no idea," Smith said. "And this morning I got a letter through my door from someone claiming to be able to help me."

"You say this person knows who our murderer is?" Brownhill said. "Do you still have the photograph of the young girl this person sent you?"

"It's on my PC. It's all very strange. Last night I'm sure someone was watching me, I think I'm being followed and I think it's the same guy."

"What exactly did the letter you received this morning say?" Blakemore said.

She seemed quite agitated somehow.

"It said I can help you, and I have some answers. He said he'd be in touch."

"And you have no idea who this person is?" Blakemore said.

"No."

"Probably some whack job," Blakemore said. "There's plenty of them out there. I ought to know."

"I think it's worth looking into anyway," Brownhill said.

"You're wasting your time," Blakemore insisted. "I think we've got much more important things on the agenda."

Brownhill looked confused.

"Jessica, it's been over a month now since we've had anything to go on. Finally, we have a lead and I'm not going to ignore it, Bridge?"

"Yes, Ma'am," Bridge said.

"You're pretty clued up with computers, aren't you?"

"I keep up to date."

"See if you can find out where these emails came from. Get some technical help if need be. Smith, I need that map and the letter that arrived this morning. Webber can go over them with a fine-tooth comb."

"I'm afraid the map was pretty much chewed up by my dog," Smith said. "He gets destructive when he doesn't get his own way sometimes, but I have the letter at home."

"Get the map and the letter to forensics, I think we might be finally starting to get somewhere."

"I still think you're wasting your time here," Blakemore said again. "We should be going through other things. I may have come up with a realistic profile of the woman we're looking for."

"We'll look at that later," Brownhill said.

"I thought you said this profiling thing was bullshit," Bridge said. "You said they only did that in the movies."

"There is some truth in it," Blakemore said. "They tend to exaggerate it in the films."

"We'll hear what you have to say later," Brownhill said. "Right now, we're going to concentrate on the concrete evidence we have."

"But I spent all night coming up with this."

"Later," Brownhill was adamant. "Whitton, you and Yang Chu find out everything you can about Romania. If our killer is from Romania, she must have come into the country somehow. Find out when and where."

"The top part of the map was highlighted," Smith said.

"Get onto it. We need to find this person. If he knows who this woman is, we need to find him as soon as possible. Oh, and Bridge."

"Ma'am?"

"Take the note off the door. This meeting is over."

## CHAPTER FORTY THREE

It took Smith less than half an hour to go home and then drive to the forensics building. The snow was starting to melt, and thick layers of slush had covered the side of the road. Grant Webber was in an unusually good mood when Smith went inside his office. Smith was instantly on his guard - he much preferred Webber when he was irritable and rude.

"Morning," Webber smiled. "It looks like the weather's finally going to clear up. The weather guys got it wrong again. What can I do for you this morning?"

"I don't know," Smith took out the letter and the box containing the reassembled map of Romania. "Brownhill asked me to bring these over for you to have a look at. They were delivered to my house anonymously."

"What am I supposed to do with them?"

"We need to establish where they came from."

Webber picked up the envelope, removed the letter by the corner and read it.

"I can help you," he read. "I have some answers. I'll be in touch."

"Do you think you'll be able to get any prints off it?"

"I doubt it, this type of paper doesn't really reveal prints, but stranger things have happened. Is this to do with the murder investigation?"

"Yes, I don't know if this person is for real, but he's sent me a couple of emails too and the other night I'm sure he was following me."

"What have you got in there?" Webber pointed to the small box.

"A map of Romania. It was also dropped off at my house. It's pretty ripped up, but I managed to piece it back together."

"The map is useless," Webber said. "Your prints will be all over it, but I'll have a good look at the box it came in. How are things going anyway?"

"With the investigation? Badly. This is the most frustrating case I've ever worked on."

"Not the investigation," Webber said. "With you, how are things going between you and Whitton? I believe you two have finally hooked up. It took you long enough."

"It's early days," was as much as Smith felt like divulging to Webber. "Leave this lot with me. I'll get back to you in due course if I find anything useful."

When Smith got back to the station and walked through the front door an overwhelming feeling of anti-climax washed over him. The upbeat mood from the meeting earlier had rapidly descended into melancholy. Webber had been right - they didn't expect to find out much from the letter and the map. Smith realised he didn't know what to do. As he stood by the front desk, he felt impotent - helpless and hopeless at the same time.

"Penny for them," Baldwin said.

"Sorry?" Smith said.

"You're miles away there. Are things alright between you and Whitton?"

"Why can't everybody just mind their own bloody business?" Smith said. "I knew this was a bad idea."

He walked down the corridor towards his office.

Bridge and a man Smith didn't recognise were sitting behind Smith's computer in the office. The stranger was typing frantically on the keyboard of a laptop computer. Smith cleared his throat to announce his presence and Bridge turned round.

"We've found him," Bridge said. "At least we know who he is."
Smith's mood suddenly lifted. It was good news for once.
"Luka Gravov," Bridge said. "Thirty three years old, lives in Moscow. Born in a small village just across the border from Romania. Luzhany - it's now in the Ukraine."
"Romania?" Smith said.
"That's right," Bridge said.
"Therein lies the rub," the man with the laptop stopped typing and looked at Bridge.
"Sorry," Bridge said. "This is DS Smith. Smith this is John Milton. What he doesn't know about computers isn't worth knowing."
"Pleased to meet you," Smith shook Milton's hand.
"John Milton," Milton looked at Smith as if he were expecting a different reaction.
"John Milton," Smith repeated. "I got it the first time."
"Like the poet," Milton said. "Paradise Lost, Paradise Regained? I usually get some kind of comment."
"Never heard of him," Smith said. "Good work anyway."
"It was a piece of cake," Milton seemed offended. "I don't like to undervalue my expertise but, in this instance, a ten year old with a server could have figured it out."
"I couldn't," Smith admitted.
"Let me show you then," Milton opened up his lap top. "If you don't mind, your system is older and slower than God's dog."
Smith watched as he typed the email address into the search engine. A whole list of similar emails appeared on the screen.
"Did you know there are over two hundred million email addresses in Russia?" Milton said.
He clicked on one of the links.

"This narrows it down to around two thousand," he carried on clicking and clicking at an alarming rate. "And then there was one. Luka Gravov, thirty three years old. Around six two with dark hair and brown eyes. Listens to Barbara Streisand and Barry Manilow while he's not watching repeats of the X Files and working as a teller at a bank in Moscow."

Smith was amazed.

"You can find out all of this from a single email address?" He said.

"Not quite," Milton scratched his nose. "I used the most sophisticated free spy tool ever invented. Facebook."

"Facebook?"

"Do you have a Facebook account?" Milton said.

"No."

"Probably for the best. You must have heard of Big Brother? Well, Facebook is the Big Brother of the twenty first century. Governments spend billions on fancy surveillance technology when they can do most of it for free on Facebook. Let me show you what your stalker looks like."

He opened up the Facebook page and typed in Luka Gravov's name. A whole list of men with the same name appeared.

"With a bit of insight into how the system works and a bit of investigative savvy, it's quite easy to find almost anybody on here. You should really consider using it in the future."

A profile page for Luka Gravov appeared on the screen. Smith took a closer look. A photograph of a man slightly older than Smith was shown in the top left hand corner.

"This is your phantom email sender," Milton smiled proudly. "Not only do we know what he looks like - we also know where he is."

He scrolled down the timeline to one of Gravov's posts.

"That's the Minster in the background," Smith said.

"Correct," Milton said. "For the past week Gravov has been on holiday in York. Nice time of the year to visit although the weather here is probably a lot warmer than it is in Moscow right now."

"This is amazing."

"No," Milton said. "This is the invasion of personal privacy at its worst. God knows where it'll all end. Did you know that the FBI and the CIA have been using Facebook to track down terrorists for years now? The creators of social media didn't realise what a monster they were to create when they started."

"How can we find him?" Smith said.

"That's your department," Milton stood up. "I have an online game of chess scheduled for two this afternoon and I prefer to go to war in the comfort of my own flat. Gentlemen."

Milton picked up his laptop and left the office.

"Quite a character, isn't he?" Bridge said.

"Where did you find him?"

"He was one of my roommates when I was at University believe it or not. His brain works like nobody else's."

"Right," Smith said. "I intend to find this man before he finds me. If he's been in York for a week he must be staying somewhere, and he must have come in from somewhere. Check all the arrivals for Luka Gravov for the last week."

"That's if he used his real name."

"I think he will have done. I don't know much about computers, but he didn't exactly try to hide his identity in cyberspace, did he?"

"Why don't you just wait for him? He said he was going to contact you."

"Because I want to catch him unawares. He's been messing us around. I want him to know he doesn't have the upper hand anymore. That way we'll probably get more out of him. Get onto it. I'm going to see what Whitton and Yang Chu have come up with."

## CHAPTER FORTY FOUR

Smith found Whitton and Yang Chu in the canteen. They appeared to be taking a break. A pile of papers lay on the table in front of them.
"We've found out who my mystery stalker is," Smith sat down next to Whitton. "Luka Gravov. He was born in a small village in the Ukraine just across the border from Romania."
"The highlighted part of the map," Whitton said. "Northern Romania borders on the Ukraine."
"That's where we concentrate on then. I'm positive that our killer comes from somewhere around there."
He told them what Bridge's computer expert friend had found out.
"Facebook?" Yang Chu said. "I always knew that thing was dangerous."
"Dangerous yes, but extremely useful. This Milton guy found out in one hour what would have probably taken us weeks. What do we know about Northern Romania?"
"Not much," Yang Chu sighed. "It's pretty backward. The Carpathian Mountains form the border between Romania and Ukraine. It's mostly small farming villages. The people there don't appear to have evolved in hundreds of years."
"Sounds idyllic," Smith said. "This woman is from there. I can feel it. What I don't know is why the hell she's killing people in York of all places. We need to find this Luka Gravov as soon as possible."
"Didn't he say he'd be in touch? Why not just wait for him?"
"Because I'm tired of waiting. This whole investigation has been about waiting - waiting for leads, waiting for witnesses to come forward, waiting for evidence to be analysed. Christ, we're even waiting for

another poor bastard to be found with his throat sliced open. I'm sick and tired of this whole thing to be honest."

"We didn't know what we were supposed to be looking for," Whitton said. "Nothing much happens in Northern Romania. They're simple people who lead simple lives. That's it."

"Where's the shrink?" Smith said.

"Probably sulking," Whitton said. "Did you see how she reacted when Brownhill shot her down about her profiling?"

"It was a bit over the top," Smith admitted. "Anyway, let's go and find her. See what she has to say. Bridge is trying to find the whereabouts of this Gravov bloke, Webber is looking into the stuff that got delivered to my house, we've got nothing better to do."

Jessica Blakemore was nowhere to be seen. According to Baldwin, she had been cooped up in Brownhill's office all morning but when Smith knocked on the door there was no answer. They found her in the small conference room. She was sitting by herself in the corner, staring at the blank overhead projector screen."

"Hello," Smith said. "Can we come in?"

Blakemore jumped and stood up.

"Hi," she said. "Sorry, I was miles away there. It's funny isn't it that sometimes it's when we concentrate on nothing that the most profound inspiration comes along. It's like staring at the moon - it gives you a certain perspective on things."

"Sorry about earlier," Smith said. "Brownhill's frustration is getting to her. We'd like to hear about that profile you talked about if that's alright."

Blakemore looked at Whitton then Yang Chu and finally back at Smith. She sat down again.

"Take a seat then," she said.

Everybody sat down.

"This is what I've come up with," Blakemore began. "From the information I've been given so far. I haven't been given much time, but this is how I see it. Firstly, a female murderer is extremely rare if you take statistics into consideration. Primevally, a woman's role is to nurture - to preserve life, not to destroy it. A woman who kills once can be rationalized - they could be protecting somebody or frightened for their own life, but this woman is rather exceptional that she has taken the lives of two men for no apparent reason whatsoever."
She stopped and gazed at the blank screen again.

"Secondly," she seemed to wake up. "These murders appear to have been planned very carefully. They weren't some kneejerk reaction to an outside stimulus. This suggests a certain cold heartedness which brings me to my third point: the paradox."

"Paradox?" Yang Chu said.

"Contrary behaviour. First, she plans the murder methodically and carries it out. Then she wraps her victims up warmly as if reverting back to her nurturing role. This would suggest a certain psychosis and, in my experience, these tendencies are not present from birth - they develop somewhere along the line due to some kind of trauma or other."

"Tell me about your childhood," Whitton said.

Blakemore smiled.

"Exactly," she said. "In my opinion something happened to this woman early on in her life that has now materialised into homicidal behaviour."

"Do you think she'll kill again?" Smith said.

"Unfortunately, yes, she needs to be stopped. This woman is extremely sick."

"Childhood," Smith thought out loud.

"Sorry?" Blakemore said.

"Nothing, just thinking about childhood."

"Studies have shown," Blakemore said. "For what it's worth, that the first sixteen years of our lives are instrumental in moulding us into what we are today. There are exceptions of course but look at all the documented serial killers. Almost all of them suffered severe trauma in their childhood."

"Thank you," Smith said. "You've given us something to think about anyway. Whitton, do you feel like a drink? I need to talk to you about something. It's already dark outside. Let's call it a day."

The Hog's Head was packed to the brim when Smith and Whitton went inside. Smith couldn't understand why. A Tuesday night in the middle of winter was not normally when business boomed in the pub trade. He pushed his way through the crowds to the bar. Marge was frantically pouring drinks for the mostly elderly men behind the counter.

"Jason," she caught Smith's eye. "I'll be with you in a moment. Two pints of Theakstons?"

She smiled at Whitton.

"Thanks, Marge," Smith said. "Why's it so busy in here tonight?"

"Bright idea of the breweries," Marge said. "Tuesday half price pensioner's night. They're like a bunch of animals. Don't worry though, this place will be empty again come eight o clock."

She placed two pints of beer on the counter.

"Hey you," a man with an impressive handlebar moustache shouted over to Smith. "You're not a bloody pensioner."

"Good genes," Smith said. "I keep myself in shape."

He picked up the beers and took them to the only free table in the pub.

"Cheers," he took a long swig of beer. "Here's to pensioner's half price beer."

"What did you want to talk to me about?" Whitton sounded serious.

"Do you think we're doing the right thing?"

"What do you mean? Are you having second thoughts?"

"I don't know, everything seems to be getting to me at the moment. This investigation, the dreams, everybody poking their noses into our business."

An altercation seemed to be breaking out by the bar. A tall skinny man who was obviously very drunk was having an argument with a much shorter man."

"Come on then," the tall man started to roll up his shirt sleeves. "I used to box for the RAF. I still have a few moves."

"RAF?" The smaller man scoffed. "Public school pansies. You lot used to hit each other with your handbags."

Both men squared up for a fight. Smith was finding the whole spectacle quite amusing. The two men started circling one another, neither one of them daring to throw the first punch.

"You two," Marge screamed from behind the bar. "That's enough. Pack it in or I'll throw you both out."

The men eyed one another and returned to their seats.

"That was entertaining," Smith said.

Whitton appeared lost in thought.

"Are you saying we should end this?" She said. "Break up?"

"I don't know, let's get out of here. I've got plenty to drink at home. Let's get out of here before the geriatric pugilists start up again."

Smith and Whitton didn't say one word to each other on the drive back to Smith's house. Smith parked outside, and they got out.
"Beer?" Smith said to Whitton in the kitchen.
"Thanks, I've got a feeling I'm going to need it."
Smith took two beers out of the fridge, opened them both and handed one to Whitton. He opened the back door and went outside to the garden for a cigarette. Whitton followed him out and sat on the bench.
"I wish people would stop poking their noses into our lives," Smith took a long drag of the cigarette and held it in his lungs for as long as possible.
"They're just curious. It's human nature. Anyway, most people are happy for us."
"Are you happy?"
"I thought I was, until you started with all this analysing shit."
"I feel like such a hypocrite," Smith said. "How many years have I gone on and on about relationships at work never working? And yet, here we are."
"Here we are," Whitton sighed.
"Are you hungry?"
"No."
"Me neither," Smith threw his cigarette butt into his neighbour's dead rose bushes.

"What is it you want exactly?" Whitton said two hours and eight beers later in Smith's living room.
"The same as everybody else I suppose. To be happy and live a normal life."
"Bollocks," Whitton started to laugh. "You're not destined to live a normal life. You can still be happy though."

"Whitton," Smith finished the rest of his beer. "I'm damaged goods. I'm not normal. People who get close to me always seem to suffer. Do you want to take that risk?"

"I've always wanted to take that risk. For a shit hot detective, you're pretty dumb sometimes."

Smith smiled and kissed her on the lips.

"Shall we risk a drop of Jack Daniel's?" he said. "I've got a whole bottle in there."

He pointed to the sideboard.

## CHAPTER FORTY FIVE

*Wednesday 2 February 2011*

A good friend of Smith's, the late Paul 'The Ghoul' Johnson had a theory that Smith had always agreed with. If you hit a brick wall in a murder investigation, finding another dead body is always a bonus. More evidence will come to light and there is a chance that the killer will have slipped up. The Ghoul also maintained that the best way to ensure the appearance of another cadaver is to drink eight beers and a bottle of whiskey. Thus, when Smith's phone started to ring on his bedside table at one-fifteen in the morning, Smith had been asleep for less than half an hour and was still as intoxicated as he had been when he drifted off to sleep.
"Smith," he groaned into the phone.
The room around him was spinning.
"Sarge," it was Bridge.
"What time is it?" Smith said.
"Quarter past one."
"What the hell do you want?"
"We've found this Luka Gravov bloke," Bridge said.
Smith's senses were slowly coming back.
"Where is he?" He said.
"I traced him to a hotel just outside the city centre. I organised a couple of uniform officers to bring him in."
"Couldn't this wait until tomorrow? I'll speak to him first thing in the morning."
"I don't think he's going to be able to tell you much," Bridge said.
"He's dead. He's had his throat sliced open."

"Christ, Bridge," Smith sat up in bed. "What's the name of the hotel?"
"The Beacon," Bridge said. "It's just off the old Foss Road."

Whitton stirred in the bed next to Smith, but she didn't wake up. Smith got out of bed, got dressed and went downstairs. He made the strongest cup of coffee he could stomach and sipped it slowly. He realised he was in no fit state to drive but he didn't feel like the rigmarole of organising a taxi to come and pick him up.
"What's going on?" Whitton appeared in the doorway.
She stretched her arms and yawned.
"Our star witness is dead. Bridge tracked him down to a hotel, but it appears we were too late. She beat us to it."
"Do you want me to go with you?"
"Go back to bed," Smith said. "There's no point in both of us feeling like zombies tomorrow. Today, I mean."
He finished his coffee and picked up his phone and car keys. He hugged Whitton tightly and left the house.

Smith drove under twenty miles per hour the whole way to the Beacon Hotel. He had all the windows in the car wide open to let in as much fresh air as possible. He was thankful that the roads were deserted. He knew he was taking a huge risk driving in his condition, but he didn't bump into any police cars along the way.
This is becoming a habit, he thought as he drove, I'm becoming a serial drunk driver.
He parked outside the hotel and stopped the engine. Three police cars and an ambulance were already on the scene. Webber's car was also there as usual. Smith realised he didn't have his police ID with him when he walked through the doors of the hotel and up to the reception desk. PC Jarvis was standing talking to a thin woman behind the reception counter.

"Morning, Sarge," Jarvis said. "Room twenty nine. Not a pretty sight."
Smith walked past him to the lift, changed his mind and took the stairs instead.

Two officers in uniform were standing outside room twenty nine. Smith started to panic - he didn't recognise either of them.
"Move along please, sir," one of them said as Smith approached.
"DS Smith," Smith said as clearly as he could.
The PC recoiled as he smelled the alcohol on Smith's breath.
"Sir," he said. "Go back to your room please."
"Let him in," a gruff voice was heard from inside the room.
It was Webber. Smith pushed his way inside and looked at the mess in the room. The man assumed to be Luka Gravov was lying on his back on the floor. His throat had been sliced open and blood had dried on his neck and shirt. There was more blood on the wall behind him and on the bed. The mirror on the wall was also covered in blood and it had been smashed.
"You stink," Webber said. "I think you ought to go home. You're still drunk."
"Bridge phoned me. I'd only just gone to sleep. What have we got?"
"What does it look like? Hit and run? Dead tourist by the looks of things. His passport was in the drawer. Ukrainian national. Luka Gravov. God only knows what the hell he was doing in York at this time of the year."
"He was looking for me," Smith said. "The same knife was used wasn't it?"
"Looks like it, but this one's different. I doubt if the chloroform was used."
"Why?"
"Look at his hands," Webber said.

Smith looked closer and saw that both of Gravov's hands had deep lacerations in them.

"Defence wounds," Webber explained. "He tried to protect himself. I've got nothing more for you right now. Go home and get some sleep. You look terrible. Bridge has organised for a few officers to speak to the other guests in the hotel. You're in no fit state to do anything right now."

Smith was about to argue but he realised that Webber was right. He could be in big trouble if he was found on duty with so much alcohol in his system. Besides, all he wanted to do was curl up in bed for a very long time. Days, maybe.

Whitton was fast asleep when Smith finally collapsed next to her in the bed. She was breathing heavily. Smith smiled and looked at the clock on the bedside table. It was three in the morning. He had four hours of sleep to look forward to. He closed his eyes and an image of Luka Gravov filled his head. He was lying on the floor in the hotel room covered in blood.

*What does this mean?* Smith thought but that thought and any other he may have had soon disappeared as he drifted into the darkness.

## CHAPTER FORTY SIX

"Wake up, sleepy head," Smith was aware of Whitton's voice and the smell of coffee in the room. He opened his eyes and winced. Whitton had opened the curtains and bright light was burning into the back of his skull.
"What time is it?" he said.
"Half eight, it's a beautiful day too. A perfect crisp, clear winter's day."
Half past eight, Smith thought.
He suddenly wondered if what had happened in the night had just been a dream he had just woken up from. Bridge's phone call - the trip to the Hotel, maybe he had dreamed the whole lot.
"Luka Gravov is dead," he said.
"I know," Whitton said.
It hadn't been a dream.
"Why did you let me sleep so late?" Smith sat up in the bed and his vision went black.
"I was told to. Brownhill phoned early this morning. Apparently, she was following Webber's advice."
Smith finished the coffee and got out of bed.
"I feel like shit," he said.
"I'm not surprised," Whitton said. "Eight beers and the best part of a bottle of Jack Daniel's tends to do that to you."
"We're back to square one," Smith held his head in his hands.
"Whatever Luka Gravov had to tell us died with him in that hotel room last night."
"Maybe not, Brownhill hinted that Webber might have found something. Something important."

"I suppose we should get going then. I need a cold shower first though."

Smith felt marginally better when he sat opposite Brownhill in the small conference room half an hour later. Whitton, Bridge, Yang Chu, Webber and the two officers in uniform who had discovered Gravov's body were also there.

"Right," Brownhill said. "Let's get moving on this. Luka Gravov, a Ukrainian national was found in his hotel room just after midnight last night. His throat was sliced open. Early indications point to the weapon being the same as the one used on Christopher Riley and Arnold Mather. This time the MO was slightly different. No traces of chloroform were found and Gravov had deep defence wounds on both hands."

"She didn't go there with the intention of killing him," Smith said. Everybody stared at him. Grant Webber nodded in agreement.

"I came to the same conclusion," Webber said. "The room was in a bit of a mess. The mirror was smashed, and it appears that quite a struggle took place. I'd say this was a spur of the moment killing."

"OK," Brownhill said. "What exactly does this mean to the investigation?"

The room fell silent.

"My brain hurts," Smith said eventually. "But even so, I have a theory."

"Let's have it then."

"This Luka Gravov bloke contacted me on more than one occasion. He claimed to know quite a lot about our murderer. He wanted to help me and now he's dead."

"And that's your theory?" Yang Chu said.

"I haven't finished," Smith said. "If this man knew who our killer was he also probably knew where she was. He may have tracked her down. I reckon he made contact with her and she killed him."

"I don't buy it," Bridge said. "Are you saying they met in her hotel room and she just walked in and killed him?"

"Bridge, I'm the one who got bugger all sleep last night. Think. I'm saying that I don't think she had any intention of killing him when she entered that hotel room. Haven't you been listening?"

"Now you're contradicting yourself," Bridge said.

Smith sighed deeply.

"I think it was only after they started talking in the room, and she realised what he knew that she killed him. He put up quite a fight."

"You could be right," Brownhill said. "But it still doesn't leave us with much. Our only witness is dead and according to the statements we received from the hotel staff, nobody can recall seeing a woman with Gravov last night."

"What about the other guests? Have we spoken to them?"

"All three of them," Bridge said. "This isn't exactly the tourist season. None of them saw a thing."

Smith remembered something that Whitton had said that morning - something about Webber finding something important.

"Webber," he said. "You found something didn't you? Something you didn't find at the other murder scenes?"

"It may or may not be important," Webber said. "But the dead man had traces of skin and blood under the fingernails on his right hand. I'd say he managed to take a chunk out of whoever did this before he died."

"How does that help us?" Smith said. "We've already got this woman's DNA from the other murders but she's not on any of the databases."

"No, but whoever did this will have quite a wound to cover up. We also found more black hair and a footprint in the blood on the carpet. It's too small to have come from Gravov."

"So, we have some evidence for once, but it's still worthless without someone to compare it with."

"That's your job," Webber said. "I'm just telling you what I found."

"Sorry, Webber. Nice work."

"I haven't finished. We also found fingerprints on the wall and a complete handprint on the broken mirror. A beautiful handprint. This was definitely a spur of the moment thing. Before, she was careful not to leave much for us to find but this time she just lost it."

"Where do you suggest we go from here then?" Brownhill said.

"Romania," Smith said. "I don't know where the hell it is, but I think I should take a trip to Romania."

"Why?" Brownhill said. "The woman may or may not come from Romania but surely that's irrelevant now."

"I don't think it is. I want to see if I can find out more about her. Something is bugging me, and I want to get to the bottom of it."

"Definitely not," Brownhill said. "I'm not going to authorise an expensive trip to Romania because something is bugging you."

"Then I want to request some leave. I have quite a few days owing to me. I'll lose them if I don't take them soon."

"I said no," Brownhill was adamant. "And you're definitely not going to be allowed to take leave while a murder investigation is in full swing."

"I'll speak to the Super," Smith stood up. "Surely the top cop of 2010 has the right to take leave when he wants to?"

"I'll block it. We need you here. Now sit back down please."

Smith smiled and sat down. Brownhill didn't notice him winking at Whitton.

# CHAPTER FORTY SEVEN

**Cluj Napoca, Romania**

When the doors of the plane opened at Cluj Napoca Airport in central Romania, Smith didn't know quite what to expect. A six hour delay in Bucharest due to heavy snowfall after the four hour flight from Manchester meant he'd been in transit for almost thirteen hours. It was already dark outside when he got off the plane and was hit with what felt like a wall of ice. The cold seemed to creep inside his clothing and cling to his skin. He shivered and drew his coat tighter around him. The terminal consisted of a building half the size of the police station Smith worked in. He'd taken Whitton's advice and taken only hand luggage with him to avoid the queue at baggage retrieval. Brownhill had been furious when she found out he had gone over her head to arrange his leave, but she'd left him no choice - he was certain the heart of the investigation lay in this Godforsaken place.

Smith suddenly realised he was in a different world. All of the signs and notices appeared to be in Romanian - there was not a trace of English anywhere. He walked up to what he assumed was an information desk of sorts and stood in front of a stern looking man who appeared to be asleep. He coughed to get the man's attention and the man opened one eye and glared at him.
"Excuse me," Smith said. "Do you speak English?"
"Of course," the man said and closed his eyes again.
"I need to go North," Smith said. "Up to the Maramures."
Smith had done a fair bit of homework before he left. He wanted to know exactly where he should start looking. The man opened his eyes again.

"I need to get to the Maramures," Smith said again.

"What for?" The man asked.

His curtness took Smith by surprise.

Webber would appreciate this guy, he thought.

"I'm meeting an old friend."

The man eyed him suspiciously.

"My brother can take you."

"Great," Smith said.

"But not tonight," the man added. "And it's not going to be for free. I'll let him know."

"Great," Smith said again. "Is there somewhere near here where I can spend the night? Can you recommend somewhere?"

"The Oscar is the best," the man said.

"How do I get there?"

"It's closed. It's winter for the sake of Christ. You could try The Biscuit."

"Biscuit?" Smith said.

"Biscuit," the man repeated in a tone that suggested Smith was a complete idiot. "It's a five minute walk from here. There's only one road out of the airport. Follow it for a few hundred metres and turn right. The Biscuit is on the corner. You're going to freeze in those clothes."

He eyed Smith up and down again and then closed his eyes to indicate their conversation was over.

As Smith walked away from the airport terminal he decided he would add Romania to a list of the worst places anyone could visit. The people were miserable, and the weather was terrible. By the time he reached the hotel he could barely feel any of his limbs. He went inside. The whole place was in darkness apart from a small fluorescent light

that flickered on and off over the reception desk. Smith approached and pressed the bell on the counter. A few seconds later a woman in her twenties emerged from the darkness and sat behind the desk.
"Good evening," she said in English. "Are you lost?"
"No," Smith said. "I need a room for tonight and something to eat if it's not too much trouble."
"Passport."
Smith took out his passport and handed it to the woman. She opened it and looked Smith in the eyes.
"Australia?" She said. "Are you on holiday?"
"Yes," Smith said without thinking.
"The room will be two hundred Leu. The kitchen's closed - its winter but I can make you a sandwich."
Smith paid and received the key to his room.
"First floor, down the corridor to the left. I'll bring the sandwich to your room in twenty minutes."
"Thank you," Smith said.

When Smith went inside his room it wasn't at all what he'd expected it to be like. He was ready to be pounced upon by cockroaches and all other nature of evils, but the room was quite neat and tidy. It was very small but clean. The bed took up most of the space but there was room for a small cupboard and a counter for making coffee and tea. A small television set hung in one corner. There was a separate bathroom next to the door. Smith went inside and splashed some water on his face. He looked at his reflection in the mirror.
I'm growing old, he thought. I'm aging before my eyes, growing old in some Godforsaken country I'd never heard of before. What kind of dreams am I going to have in a place like this?

Smith left the bathroom and lay down on the bed. It was surprisingly comfortable. He worked out how to switch the television set, but a football game was showing so he switched it straight off again. There was a knock on the door and he jumped. He remembered the sandwich the receptionist had promised. He opened the door, the woman handed him the sandwich on a plastic plate and turned to leave.

"Wait," he said. "Can I ask you something?"

She nodded.

"Hold on," Smith opened his bag and took out the map of Romania. He showed her the highlighted part of the map.

"What's up here?" He pointed to the map.

"Snow," she said. "In summer it's very beautiful but now..."

She shook her head.

"That's where I'm headed," Smith said.

He took a bite of the sandwich and winced. The filling was some kind of meat paste that had obviously seen better days.

"I'm looking for somebody," he added. "From just across the border with Ukraine."

"I've got work to do," the woman turned and walked off down the corridor.

Smith left the rest of the sandwich well alone and lay on the bed. He closed his eyes and did a bit of mental arithmetic. The room had cost him less than thirty pounds. He listened to the sound of the Romanian evening. The only sound he could hear was the water pipes contracting in the cold. He turned the television back on. The football game was finished and from what he could gather, some kind of weather forecast was on. He couldn't understand what was being said but from the figures on the screen he realised that tomorrow was going to be very cold - minus fifteen degrees Celsius. He shivered and crept under the covers fully clothed. He turned off the television and was asleep in seconds.

## CHAPTER FORTY EIGHT

*Saturday 5 February 2011*

Smith woke to an incessant whining noise. It was coming from the table next to the bed. He sat up and tried to find the source of the annoying sound. A black digital alarm clock of the type popular in the eighties was flashing 07.00 before his eyes. He pressed the button on the top, but nothing happened. Eventually, after pressing every button he could find, he opened up the back and removed the batteries. The noise stopped but he could still hear it ringing in his ears. He got out of bed, opened the curtains and looked outside. It was still dark, but the sun was promising to come up over the mountains in the distance. Smith washed his face, brushed his teeth and wondered if breakfast was going to be too much to ask for. He rarely had the time for breakfast, but his stomach was growling, and he realised he hadn't eaten anything besides the bite from the rancid sandwich since he left York. He packed everything he had into his bag and scanned the room to check he had not left anything behind. He wouldn't be coming back here in a hurry.

Smith was surprised when he reached the reception area - quite a few people were up and about. There was a different woman behind the reception desk. Smith waited until she had finished dealing with an extremely round faced man and asked her where he could find some breakfast. Her reply was to point a long bony finger to a room to the right where five or six people were already queuing up waiting to go inside. He joined the back of the queue and waited for the doors to open.

Smith was halfway through a breakfast of cheese, ham and bread with coffee when a tall man with thick black hair entered the dining room. From the look on his face, Smith knew at once that he was looking for someone. They made eye contact and the man approached Smith's table.

"You need to go north," the man sat down opposite Smith. "You want to go to the Maramures."

Smith realised he must be the brother of the surly airport attendant. "Yes," he said. "I'm Jason Smith."

He held out his hand, but the man made no attempt to shake it. "My name is Alin," he said. "Alin Nicolescu. Alex is my younger brother. I'm the serious one I'm afraid. Alex is much more light hearted."

*Light hearted?* Smith thought.

"The price will be five hundred Leu," Alin said. "Let's go."

He stood up and Smith had no choice but to cut his breakfast short and follow him out of the dining room, past the reception desk and out of the hotel. They emerged into the half-light of a new Romanian day. The cold was worse than it had been the day before. Alin led Smith to an old brown Datsun with snow chains on the tyres. Smith got in the passenger side and shivered. Alin started the engine and drove up the road.

They drove in silence for the first twenty miles. Smith was grateful - he didn't feel like talking to this strange man. He watched the white countryside whizz past as they drove. He could see the mountains far away in the distance - clouds had settled on the higher peaks.

"Where do you need to go?" Alin asked suddenly as if he realised how rude he had been.

"I don't know exactly," Smith said. "I'm looking for someone. Someone who used to live just across the border from Luzhany in Ukraine."

Alin thought hard for a moment. It appeared to Smith as if the effect of the thought process was actually painful to him. His face tensed up and his eyes closed slightly.

"Borsa," Alin said. "Borsa is the closest town to Luzhany."

"What's in Borsa?"

"Nothing. Farms and a few churches. It's pretty in the summer but right now it's very bleak. Who are you looking for?"

"I don't know," Smith said and realised how ridiculous he sounded.

Alin shook his head and turned right onto a road that looked like it was rarely used.

"Do you speak Romanian?" he asked.

"No."

"What about Russian?"

"No, English is all I can manage."

"I thought so. It's not going to be easy then. The people in the north are very simple people. They haven't changed much in hundreds of years. Strange things go on up there if you believe the tales."

"What strange things?"

"Ah," Alin said. "Just superstitious nonsense. We're almost there."

Smith marvelled at the approaching mountain range covered in snow. He'd never seen anything like it before - it was like something you only saw on picture postcards. They drove past a few houses, a farm stall, a place that looked like a bar and an old wooden church. Alin stopped the car.

"Why are we stopping?" Smith asked.

"Borsa," Alin smiled. "We've just driven through it. If you blink, you might miss most of the town. If we carry on any further on this road, we'll end up in Ukraine."

Smith thought for a moment. He suddenly realised that he didn't have any idea what he hoped to find here.

"Will you help me?" He said to Alin. "I'll pay you of course."

"I've told you the price. I said I'd help you and I will. But let's have a drink first."

He reversed back and stopped outside on old stone building with boarded up windows. They got out of the car and Alin led Smith up a gravel path to a door. He knocked hard on the door and shortly afterwards a small elderly man opened it up. Alin said something to him in Romanian and the old man stepped to the side.

"Come in and get warm," Alin said to Smith.

Smith headed straight for a table next to an open fire. The only other patrons were two huge men who were sipping coffee and playing dominoes in the corner of the room. They didn't even look up when Smith and Alin walked in.

Alin placed two cups of coffee and two glasses containing a brown liquid on the table.

"Drink this first," he picked up one of the glasses. "Welcome to Romania."

He raised the glass to his lips and waited for Smith to do the same. Smith eyed the contents of the glass suspiciously, shrugged and drained the glass in one go. The burning sensation that followed was something he would never forget. It started in his throat, continued down to his stomach and seemed to spread out to his chest, arms and legs. When Smith was certain he couldn't take it anymore, the heat calmed down and he felt a strange warming sensation spread throughout his whole body. Alin Smiled.

"Now drink some coffee," he said.

"What was that stuff?" Smith gasped.

"Tuica. It's made from plums. It'll turn you insane if you drink too much but not many people can manage more than a glass or two. I can see you can handle your drink."

"I've had a bit of practice," Smith took a sip of the coffee.

It was much stronger than he was used to, but it tasted delicious after the Tuica.

"OK," Alin said. "Here we are in Borsa. Tell me who you're looking for."

Smith didn't know how to tell a complete stranger that he was looking for someone who had killed three men in the space of a couple of months.

"I'm trying to find a woman," he said. "Someone who may have lived here fifteen to twenty years ago."

"I see," Alin's face turned serious. "Can I ask you a question first?"

"Of course."

"Why didn't you tell me straight away that you were a policeman?"

"Is it that obvious?"

"Not at all," Alin said. "You look nothing like any police I've come across, but my brother saw it straight away. He spent ten years as a policeman. He says there's something in the way a policeman talks that will always give them away."

"Sorry," Smith said. "Detective Sergeant Jason Smith. That's who I am."

"Detective? Then it must be serious. I'm going to order us two more Tuicas and if you're still capable of talking after that, you can tell me everything. From the beginning.

## CHAPTER FORTY NINE

**YORK**

Whitton and Yang Chu sat in Brownhill's office waiting for the DI to finish her phone conversation.

"Yes," Brownhill said. "We do believe that there is a connection between the three murders. No, we're still working on the connection. If anything comes to light, you lot will be the first to know. Goodbye."

She slammed down the phone so hard that the whole desk shook.

"Reporters?" Whitton said.

"The worst of them all," Brownhill said. "Yorkshire Post. I don't even know how that vulture managed to get hold of my number."

"I wonder how Smith is getting on," Yang Chu said. "It must be freezing over there at the moment."

"It's not that warm over here," Brownhill said. "And Smith is going to find it even colder when he gets back and faces the consequences of going over my head. What was he thinking?"

"There's another front on its way," Yang Chu changed the subject. "It's moving in across the Atlantic. I wonder when it's ever going to end."

"Where's Blakemore?" Whitton said. "I haven't seen her around for a few days. Is she finished helping us?"

"She's sick. I think she's caught this flu bug that's been going around."

"Do we know anything else about this Gravov guy?" Yang Chu said.

"Nothing, apart from the fact he was a bank clerk living in Moscow. They've finished with the autopsy - his family are arriving on Monday to make the necessary arrangements."

"I wonder what he wanted to tell Smith," Whitton said.

"Whatever it was, it was so important that it cost him his life. This has to be the most frustrating investigation I've ever worked on. It seems like every time we feel like we're getting somewhere, we end up back to square one."

"I don't think we're ever going to get to the bottom of this mess," Whitton sighed."

"Smith will bring something back with him," Yang Chu said. "He always does, doesn't he?"

"He better come back with something," Brownhill said. "We'll solve this one sooner or later."

"I don't know," Whitton said. "This case is different to any other. It's like you said - it's frustrating. It's as if this woman is some kind of ghost. Nobody saw her at the hotel Gravov was staying at. Nobody knows anything about her. She appears and then disappears like a phantom."

"We need to stay positive. Where's Bridge? Isn't he supposed to be on duty today?"

"He is," Whitton said. "But I swapped my day off with him. Bridge asked if he could swap - he's got a date with that mystery woman of his. They've gone ice skating."

"Ice skating in this weather?"

"Apparently Bridge's girlfriend has a young kid," Whitton said. "I never thought Bridge would hook up with a woman with a kid."

"We all have to grow up some time," Brownhill mused. "Even Bridge."

Grant Webber entered the room. He seemed very agitated.

"There's trouble at the front desk," he said. "Baldwin's trying to fob off a bunch of journos. They're not exactly behaving themselves."

Yang Chu stood up.

"I'll go and sort them out," he said.

"No," Brownhill said. "Let's give them what they want."

"What do you mean?"

"I'm going to arrange a press conference for this afternoon."

"Do you think that's a good idea?" Whitton asked.

"It can't be helped. Those parasites are going to write about these murders anyway. At least this way we'll have a bit of control over what they write. Speculation can be very damaging to our public image."

"Bryony's right," Webber said. "Give them a bit of info to be going along with. It'll prevent the kind of panic we had with that Harlequin mess."

Baldwin was fighting off six or seven journalists by the front desk when Brownhill appeared. She appeared to be taking some strain.

"Quiet everybody," Brownhill boomed.

Everybody shut up and stared at her.

"I understand you wanting to know what's going on," Brownhill said. "But this is not the way to go about things."

"Three men have been killed in York in a couple of months," a young woman with a voice louder than Brownhill's said. "Do we have another serial killer at large?"

"I've decided to give a press conference," Brownhill said. "Four this afternoon. Your questions will be answered then and only then. I seem to remember a time when there was such a thing as journalistic etiquette."

"Journalistic etiquette?" A balding man in his fifties started to laugh. "I love it. That's my new favourite oxymoron. That's even better than police intelligence."

"Four o' clock sharp," Brownhill ignored him. "Now would you please get out of here and leave us to do our jobs?"

"Journalistic etiquette," the bald man sniggered to himself.

He walked towards the door. The other members of the press followed after him.

"Didn't you hear me?" Brownhill said to a tall thin man with a goatee beard. "The press conference will be at four."

"I'm not a reporter," the man said. "the name's Ian. Ian Blakemore."

"Blakemore?"

"I'm Jessica's husband," he said.

"What seems to be the problem, Mr Blakemore?"

"Call me Ian," he said.

"OK, Ian. What can I do for you?"

"Not here, can we talk somewhere private?"

Whitton and Yang Chu were still sitting in Brownhill's office when she returned with Ian Blakemore.

"This is Jessica Blakemore's husband," Brownhill said. "Can you leave us in peace please?"

Ian Blakemore smiled at Whitton, but Whitton sensed immediately that something was not right.

"Come on," she said to Yang Chu. "I'm dying for a cup of coffee. You can buy me one."

Yang Chu stood up.

"Nice to meet you," he said to Ian Blakemore and left the room.

Brownhill closed the door.

"Please take a seat," she said.

"It's Jess," Ian sat down. "I'm really worried about her."

"She's got a bit of flu, I'm sure she'll be fine."

"Flu?" Ian seemed confused. "She hasn't got the flu."

"I spoke to her on Wednesday morning. She said she'd be off for a few days with flu."

"I saw her on Wednesday, and she most certainly didn't have flu."

"Maybe I heard wrong, what's going on here?"

"She came home on Wednesday afternoon," Ian said. "I was surprised to see her, and she was even more surprised to see me. I'd been working from home on a new project. I got the distinct impression she wasn't too happy to see me."

"I'm sorry, but what has this got to do with me?"

"I'm worried about her. She didn't seem herself."

"How do you mean?"

"She was acting weird, like something was bothering her."

"This investigation is taking its toll on all of us. We're all a bit on edge at the moment."

"She had a nasty scratch on her face," Ian said. "Naturally I asked her about it and she completely lost it."

"What did she do?"

"She told me not to pretend that I even cared where she got it. I was very upset. Of course, I care. Anyway, she finally told me that your cat scratched her when she was staying with you. 'Brownhill's fucking cat' were the words she used if you'll excuse my language."

"But," Brownhill suddenly felt sick. "I don't have a cat. I hate cats."

Ian looked confused.

"Why would she lie about something like that?"

"I don't know," Brownhill said, "where is Jessica now?"

"That's why I'm here. I haven't seen her since. She stormed out on Wednesday and she hasn't come back. I thought she might have come back here."

"No, I last saw her on Tuesday. She phoned on Wednesday to say she wouldn't be coming in for a few days."

"I've tried phoning her, but it looks like she's switched her phone off. I don't know what to do."

"I'm sure there's a perfectly reasonable explanation," Brownhill said although she could hear the doubt in her own voice.

## CHAPTER FIFTY

**BORSA, ROMANIA**

"So," Alin said, "you think this Femme Fatale of yours is Romanian?" Smith stared at the six empty glasses on the table in front of him. His head was pounding, and the room was starting to spin. He'd just finished telling Alin about the investigation.

"I'm sure about it," Smith said. "Luka Gravov, the man who was killed, wanted to tell me something before he died. He sent me a map of Romania and a photo of a young girl. He knew who she is, I'm certain he knew who she is."

"And you think by coming here you'll find answers?" Alin said. "Just like that?"

He tried to snap his fingers together, but nothing happened.

"It's better than sitting back in York going crazy. We've hit a dead end."

"So, you have the photograph with you?"

"Of course," Smith opened up his bag and took out the copy of the photograph.

"Pretty girl," Alin looked at the photograph. "Unusual eyes."

"Do you know who she is?"

"Never seen her before."

"Maybe if we start showing it around someone might recognise her."

"Maybe," Alin agreed. "But take a piece of advice first. You start to show this photograph around and say you're looking for a murderer you'll be met with such a silence that you'll end up going crazy."

"What do you suggest then?

Alin scratched his head and took a drink from one of the glasses on the table. He didn't notice that it was already empty.

"OK," he said. "You do this. You're not a policeman - you're a friend of the woman's and you're here to try and find her family. That's where we'll start."

"Why couldn't she just come back herself to find them?"

"Because she doesn't know you're looking for them. Do you have any better suggestions?"

Smith realised he didn't have a better suggestion.

"Where do we start then?" He said.

"I'm going to sleep for a while. I need to sleep off six glasses of tuica. I've never managed six before. I suggest you do the same."

Three hours later, Smith woke from a dream about guitars and realised he was alone. The log fire was still burning but the bar was empty. His mouth felt incredibly dry and he could feel a headache coming. The old man appeared as if from nowhere and placed a jug of water and two glasses on the table. Alin was nowhere to be seen. The old man walked off without saying a word. Smith filled one of the glasses and drank it in one go. It tasted of lemons. Alin pulled up his chair and sat down.

"I needed the bathroom," he said. "How's your head?"

"Not too bad," Smith lied.

"Then you're a much better drinker than me. I never thought I'd ever say that to anyone. I've spoken to the man who owns this place - he knows everybody around here and he told me something very interesting."

Smith rubbed his eyes and poured himself another glass of water.

"Let's go," Alin stood up. "There's a small village to the south of here where we might find some answers."

Smith and Alin drove out of Borsa and headed south towards a vast expanse of fields and open land. The snow was thick on the ground and Smith wasn't sure if they were actually on the road or not. He was grateful for the chains on the tyres. Alin stopped the car next to an old farm house. Smoke was rising straight up from the stone chimney - there wasn't a breath of wind in the air.

"Give me the photograph," Alin ordered. "And stay in the car. These people can be very suspicious of strangers."

Smith took the photograph of the young girl out of his bag and handed it to Alin. Alin opened the car door and the cold air rushed in. Smith watched as Alin walked up to the old house and knocked on the wooden door. It was opened soon after and Alin started to speak. Smith couldn't see who was behind the door. He watched as Alin handed the photograph to the mystery person behind the door and then nodded. He then offered his hand and received the photograph instead of a handshake. The door was promptly slammed in his face. Alin returned to the car and got in. He started the engine and drove towards a dense forest in the distance.

"Problems?" Smith asked.

"Not at all, I think I may have found the person you're looking for - or at least I have a place to begin."

Smith could feel the blood soaring through his veins.

This could be it, he thought, this could be the breakthrough they needed.

Alin drove for a further two or three miles through the countryside and stopped outside a house standing on its own in the middle of a huge field. A large barn stood a hundred metres away from it. The whole place appeared to be deserted.

"This is the place," Alin said.

He got out of the car. Smith also got out. He took out a packet of cigarettes, lit one and offered the pack to Alin.

"You don't strike me as the smoking type," he took a cigarette and let Smith light the end.

"I'm not," Smith said. "It helps me to think. That moonshine back there almost fried my brain."

Alin laughed.

"It keeps you warm at night. We need to tread very carefully here. If what the old woman in that house back there told me is correct, the girl in the photograph used to live here."

He threw the cigarette in the snow and walked up to the house. Smith followed behind him. The front door was in a state of disrepair - the panels had obviously been repaired one too many times. The word 'Lupei' was carved in the wood on the door.

Alin banged on the door so hard Smith was worried the panels would break. Moments later it was opened with a creaking sound and a large man in his late fifties stood in the doorway. He looked Smith and Alin up and down then said something in Romanian. Alin replied to him and took out the photograph of the young girl. The man looked carefully at the black and white photograph and his whole demeanour changed - he seemed to shrink to half his size. Tears started to flow from the corner of his eyes and he had to hold onto the doorframe to prevent himself from falling over.

"Selene," he sobbed. "Selene."

# CHAPTER FIFTY ONE

**YORK**

At four on the dot an eerie hush descended on the large conference room at York police station. Fortunately, Superintendent Smyth had been called away at the last minute to attend to some administrative business and DI Brownhill was left in peace to run the press conference. Chalmers entered the room and made his way to the front where Brownhill was going through some last minute notes.
"Smyth should be out of action for a good few hours," Chalmers said. "I've made sure of it."
"Thanks, sir," Brownhill said. "How did you manage that?"
"That's neither here nor there," Chalmers smiled. "He's out of our way. He only buggers things up for us. Let's get this out of the way, shall we?"
Brownhill stood up.
"Ladies and gentlemen," she began. "Thank you for your patience. Let's get started. Most of you know the drill by now. For any of you who don't, I'll start with what we've got so far, and I'll be happy to answer any questions you may have afterwards. Is that clear?"
A low murmuring was heard in the room. Brownhill scanned her audience. The room was packed to the brim. Ian Blakemore was sitting at the very back. Brownhill offered him a sympathetic smile, but he wasn't looking in her direction. He seemed distracted.

"Firstly," Brownhill said. "I assure you all that we intend to get to the bottom of this investigation. Three men have been murdered in York in a little over two months. So far, we believe there is no connection between them - they didn't appear to know one another.

However, the evidence that we have would suggest the same killer was responsible for all three murders."

A fat man with a repulsive wart on his cheekbone stood up.

"Sorry," he said. "I know I'm going against protocol and all that. Kenny Young, Mail on Sunday. Could you please cut out the ambiguous crap? Phrases like 'we believe', 'it appears' and 'we think' don't exactly fill us with confidence. In fact, they're phrases that would suggest you don't know any more about what's going on than my Aunt Fanny's dead dog. Could you perhaps give us something you know for a fact?"

He sat down again. Brownhill didn't know what to say. She hadn't expected this.

"We know that three men are dead," she stressed the word 'know'. "And we know that two of them were rendered unconscious before they had their throats sliced open with a very unusual knife. We also know we are looking for a woman with black hair - traces of hair were found at all three murder scenes but what we don't know at this moment is who this woman is and why she's doing this. Why is she killing men in this city?"

Kenny Young stood up again.

"You know bugger all then," he said.

The whole room erupted.

"At this moment," Brownhill raised her voice. "I have to admit that we've reached a bit of a deadlock. This is one of the most baffling cases I've ever worked on but we're carrying on regardless. We won't give up until whoever is responsible for these crimes is brought to justice. Now, are there any questions?"

"You said two of the men were rendered unconscious before they were killed," a woman with a slight lisp said.

"That's right," Brownhill said.

"Why do you think the last victim wasn't?"

"We don't know, this man's murder is still a mystery."

"He was Russian I believe?"

"He was Ukrainian," Brownhill corrected her. "He worked in Russia."

"What was he doing in York?"

"We don't know," Brownhill said.

She decided to leave out the fact that Luka Gravov may have had some information about the woman they were looking for.

"Any other questions?" She said.

A young man with shoulder length brown hair stood up.

"Gavin Lightfoot," he said. "Evening Post. I'm the new guy. Do you think there's any significance to the fact that the first two men were killed during the full moon?"

Brownhill looked at Chalmers. Chalmers shrugged his shoulders.

"I doubt it," Brownhill said. "It's probably just a coincidence. There wasn't a full moon when Luka Gravov was killed. Next question."

She wanted the ground to swallow her up. Why had they not made the connection with the full moon?

"Where's the famous DS Smith?" a tall woman with bright red hair asked. "I don't see him here today. Has he been suspended again?"

"No, he hasn't been suspended. He's taken a bit of leave that's all."

"In the middle of a murder investigation? I find that very hard to believe. Has he lost his touch? Where is he?"

"He's in Romania," Brownhill said without thinking. "Like I said, he's taking a bit of time off."

"Romania?" The woman wasn't going to give up. "At this time of year? I'm starting to think you're not telling us everything."

"I've given you all the information at my disposal."

"Ukraine," the woman said. "Romania? Is there a connection there? Has this got something to do with illegal immigrants? Is DS Smith in Romania as part of the investigation?"

"No comment," Brownhill looked to Chalmers for some support. Chalmers stood up.

"That's all we have for you at this time," he said. "The DI has given you more than enough to satisfy your sordid thirsts for now. Please leave in an orderly fashion. I'm sure you all have deadlines to meet." He nodded to Brownhill.

"Come on," he said. "Let's get the hell out of here. Just being in the presence of these scumbags makes me sick to the stomach."

Brownhill sipped her coffee in the canteen. Her hands were shaking.

"I'm sorry," she said to Chalmers. "I really messed that one up, didn't I?"

"It could've gone better, but don't worry about it - you can never tell what that lot are going to chuck at you."

"I don't know if I'm cut out for this anymore."

"Get a grip," Chalmers said. "You should know by now, you can't let a bunch of parasites get to you."

"Everything's getting to me. It's been over two months now and we're still no closer to working this mess out."

"Something will turn up. Have you heard anything from Smith?"

"That's a bit of a sore point. He went straight over my head and cleared his leave with the Super."

"Bryony," the sound of Chalmers using her first name made her sit up in the chair. "I've known Smith for a good few years. He can be a right royal pain in the arse but he's one of the best detectives I've ever met, if not the best. If Smith went over your head to make sure he got to

Romania I can promise you he had a bloody good reason for it. His stubborn refusal to follow rules has got us results plenty of times in the past."

"What do you think about that full moon stuff?" Brownhill said. "I can't believe we didn't figure that out."

"Because it's probably not important. Two murders during a full moon is hardly anything more than a coincidence."

"Do you think I made it worse by mentioning Smith's trip to Romania?"

"No, not at all. I know those bastards - they'll concentrate on the gory parts. Romania will be the last thing on their minds."

# CHAPTER FIFTY TWO

**BORSA, ROMANIA**

Smith had to duck to fit under the low doorframe and enter the house. The large man led him and Alin through a dark hallway into a small kitchen. A log fire was burning in the corner. A woman roughly the same age as Smith was drinking tea at the table with an older man. The woman bore a striking resemblance to the girl in the photograph. Smith could feel their eyes on him the whole time. The big man said something to Alin in Romanian.
"Please sit down," Alin said.
Smith sat opposite the woman.
"Would you like some tea?" The woman asked him in perfect English.
"That would be great," Smith smiled at her.
Her eyes were the same as the girl's in the photograph. While the woman made the tea, the big man said something to the other man. Smith couldn't understand what was being said but from the tone of the conversation he knew it wasn't just pleasantries.
"Have you found Selene?" The woman placed a pot of tea on the table and poured Smith and Alin a cup.
Smith nodded.
"We think so," he said.
He didn't know how he was going to begin.
How can I tell these people that a member of their family is a suspect in a triple murder investigation? he thought.
"My name is Natasha," the woman said. "Selene is my sister. This is my husband Cristian and my father Eduard. Do you know where Selene is?"

"We don't know," Smith realised how ridiculous he sounded. "We might do. When was the last time you saw your sister?"

"Twenty five years ago. She disappeared one night, and we haven't seen her since. My mother was so distraught that she died six months later. I think her heart broke and couldn't be mended."

"Do you know what happened to her?" Smith took a sip of the strange looking tea.

It tasted very bitter.

Natasha looked at her husband. He shook his head.

"She just disappeared," Natasha said.

"Where is she?" Cristian asked.

"In York," Smith said. "In the north of England or at least we think she's there. Do you know a man by the name of Luka Gravov? He's from Ukraine."

"No," Cristian said. "What's this all about? Selene disappeared twenty five years ago, and you come here now. Who are you anyway?"

Smith decided to be straight with them.

"My name is Jason Smith," he said. "I'm a detective sergeant with the York police department. Three men are dead, and we believe Selene may be involved somehow."

"Why?" Cristian stood up and looked out the small window.

Smith started from the beginning. He told them everything. Alin translated for Eduard as Smith spoke. Smith told them about the murders of Christopher Riley and Arnold Mather and about the strange Ukrainian. He left nothing out.

When Smith was finished, the room fell silent. Eduard sat at the table with his head in his hands.

"You've made a mistake," Natasha said. "Selene wouldn't do these things."

"Like I said," Smith said. "We're not sure yet but everything we've got seems to lead to her."

"I think you should leave now," Cristian stood up, "I'll walk you out."

"Thanks for the tea," Smith said.

He stood up and followed Cristian towards the front door. Alin walked behind him.

"Thank you for your time," Smith said to Cristian in the doorway.

"There's more," Cristian walked outside and closed the door. "But we can't talk here. Take the road out of here and drive a few hundred metres until you reach an old abandoned church. I'll meet you there in twenty minutes."

"What's going on here?" Smith said.

"Not here, I'll meet you at the church in twenty minutes."

He went back inside the house and slammed the door behind him.

## CHAPTER FIFTY THREE

YORK

Sunday 6 February 2011

Chalmers' words were still fresh in DI Brownhill's ears when the Sunday papers landed on her doormat. The Sunday Mail was staring at her from the carpet. On the front page the headline read: 'Serial killer still at large. Police suspect Romanian immigrants.
Brownhill had to read it twice to make sure she wasn't dreaming. What have I done? She thought.
Her phone started to ring in the hallway. She ignored it. The ringing stopped, and the ringtone of her mobile could be heard from the kitchen. She walked though and looked at the screen. It was Grant Webber.
"Grant," she answered it.
"Are you alright?" Webber said. "Have you seen the Sunday papers yet?"
"Only the headline. I haven't had chance to read the article yet."
"Don't, it's all nonsense. There's some pretty nasty stuff in there. Do you want me to come over?"
"I'll be fine, you know what newspapers are like - it'll all be forgotten about in a few days."
She rang off. The phone started to ring again. She put the phone down and went upstairs. She turned on the shower and undressed. She stood underneath and felt the warm jets blasting onto her shoulders. For a moment she forgot all about the murder investigation. Her thoughts turned to a time when she was a child on a sailing holiday in Wales with her family. She remembered how her father would make

her and her brother check the anchor chain and rope before they set off. Her father had drummed it into them that every link in the chain had to be checked for defects. She remembered his exact words. 'One buggered link will render the whole thing useless'.
Sometimes it was hours before they could weigh anchor and set the sails. Her brother used to find the whole thing tedious and it was not long before he would make up any excuse not to go sailing with them but, as Brownhill thought about it again, she realised it was all part of the whole experience. Checking the anchoring system became part of a ritual that she actually came to enjoy.

Brownhill turned off the shower and dried herself. She could hear that both her landline and mobile phone were ringing downstairs.
This isn't going to be a quiet Sunday, she thought.
The steam from the shower disappeared and she looked at her face in the mirror. Hair was starting to sprout from her upper lip again. She shook her head and brushed her teeth.
*Let it grow,* she thought.
She went downstairs and made some coffee. She picked up her mobile phone and saw that she had sixteen missed calls. She switched the phone off and sighed. She walked through to the hallway, unplugged the landline from the wall and sat down to read the paper. The murder investigation was the main story. Brownhill read the article from start to finish and then read it again. It began with an outline of the murders of Christopher Riley and Arnold Mather and then changed tack completely. When the article reached the part about a Ukrainian national being killed it turned into an immigration issue with Romanian immigrants believed to be the main suspects. She was thankful there was no mention of the full moon.

Brownhill finished her coffee and slumped down in her chair. She realised that the backlash from the newspapers would be enormous. The immigration issue was already a tender one and this would only make matters worse. She stood up, picked up her car keys and left the house. She drove away from the city and headed for nowhere in particular. She just wanted to drive - to get away from everything for a while. The sky was clear, and the snow had given up the ghost for the time being. She turned onto the A19 and headed north.
I'll drive to Scotland if I have to, she thought.
She pressed her foot down on the accelerator and increased her speed. There were very few cars on the road on this winter Sunday morning. She increased the pressure on the accelerator further, but the old Citroen failed to respond. It appeared to be slowing down. It came to an abrupt stop on the side of the road. Brownhill looked at the dashboard. The red light that had been flashing for the past half an hour was now glaring at her. She'd run out of petrol. Brownhill started to laugh. She didn't know where it came from, but she couldn't stop herself. The laughter continued until her eyes filled with tears. She managed to contain herself and reached inside her coat pocket for her mobile phone. It wasn't there – she'd left it switched off at home.

A car approached, slowed down but didn't stop. Brownhill got out of the car and shivered. She realised she didn't even know where she was. She saw a truck approaching in the opposite direction. She watched as it slowed down and came to a halt on the other side of the road. A thin man with a beard jumped down and crossed the road.
"Broken down?" He said.
"This is so embarrassing," Brownhill said. "I seem to have run out of petrol."

"It happens to the best of us. You don't see many of them on the roads these days."

He pointed to Brownhill's old Citroen.

"I've got some petrol in the back," he walked back to his truck and returned with a jerry can.

He found the petrol cap, unscrewed it and emptied the contents of the jerry can into the car.

"That ought to be enough to get you to the nearest petrol station," he said. "York's the closest I think."

"Thank you," Brownhill said. "How much do I owe you?"

"Owe me?"

"For the petrol."

"Don't be daft, I can't charge a damsel in distress, now can I?"

Without waiting for an answer, he crossed the road and got back in his truck. Brownhill watched as he drove away. She got back in her car, started the engine and drove to the next exit. She re-joined the A19 south and headed off back to York.

The incident with the truck driver had lifted her spirits somewhat and by the time Brownhill parked outside her house she was feeling much more positive. She went inside and switched on her mobile phone. She listened to her messages. Most of them were from journalists. How they had found her mobile number, Brownhill could only guess. The last message was from Smith. Brownhill listened to it three times.

"Boss," he said. "I've got a name. I'm almost certain that the woman we're looking for is a thirty six year old Romanian. Her name is Selene Lupei."

# CHAPTER FIFTY FOUR

**BORSA**

Smith closed the door of the old church behind him and shivered. He rubbed his hands together, but it didn't seem to help. The church smelled musty and damp. The cloth on the wooden benches was worn through - the church had obviously not been used for a very long time. The door opened, and Cristian walked in. He looked extremely anxious. He closed the door behind him and sat down on one of the benches.
"I shouldn't be here," he said. "But we have to stop this."
"Stop what?" Smith sat down next to him.
"The sacrifices - I thought it was all over. It'll never be over will it?" Smith was confused.
"What are you talking about? What sacrifices? What has this got to do with Selene?"
Cristian looked around the room as though he was frightened there may be somebody listening in.
"Twenty five years ago," he said. "Selene did a very foolish thing. She must have heard about it from the rumours going around and, being curious of nature she decided to see it for herself."
"See what?" Smith was still not sure what this man was talking about.
"For centuries things have stood still in Borsa," Cristian said. "The winter turns to spring and the planting starts. The full moon shines and then dies. There are people here who haven't changed in hundreds of years. They are simple people and superstitions are still strong."
"Superstitions?"

Alin shook his head as a hint to Smith to keep quiet.

"People will always believe in God," Cristian continued. "A god in some form or other - some higher force of nature that gives them hope. I myself find it difficult to comprehend the existence of such a deity - an all seeing, all knowing force that determines our fate. But I used to. I was young then and enthralled by the stories I used to hear. Have you ever heard of pagan rituals?"

He looked Smith in the eyes.

"Of course," Smith said. "The druids and other weirdoes like them. It's all nonsense."

"Plenty of people believe in it. I used to be one of them. I know exactly what happened to Selene that night."

Smith felt a shiver run down his spine. He knew he was getting closer to the truth.

"I was there that night," Cristian continued. "I remember it like it was yesterday. I was eighteen years old and it was only my second sacrifice."

Smith was about to say something but changed his mind.

"He was a farmer," Cristian said. "A man from my own village. The full moon appeared, and the ceremony got under way. When it was all over we heard a noise from a rocky crag overlooking the valley. It was Selene - she had seen the whole thing. Hidden from view, she had seen what she shouldn't have seen. I didn't know her, but I knew what was going to happen to her."

"Sorry," Smith said. "I'm finding all this difficult to take in. Are you telling me that people used to be put forward as human sacrifices when the full moon came out?"

"Not people," Cristian said. "Men. Only men. We believed in the power of the full moon. We believed if we made an offering we would have prosperity. Our crops would thrive, and nature would reward us. A sacrifice was made under the full moon to appease some kind of spirit."

"A man was murdered once a month?" Smith couldn't believe what he was hearing.

"Not murdered - these men volunteered. They believed it was an honour. They were not murdered."

"And you say Selene saw this?"

"Grigore was very angry," Cristian said.

"Grigore?"

"The high priest if you like," Cristian said. "The one who used to call up the spirits and make the sacrifice."

"How were these men killed?"

"With a knife. With a knife so sharp they wouldn't even feel it. The blood would drain out of them in seconds. They felt no pain."

"What happened when Selene was discovered?" Smith's head was starting to throb with all this information.

"She ran away of course," Cristian said. "And we ran after her. She had seen something somebody who wasn't one of us shouldn't have seen and she had to be stopped."

"But she escaped?"

"No, Grigore caught her. He was half spirit himself. Everybody was terrified of him."

"I don't understand. If he caught her why didn't he kill her?'

"Only men can be sacrificed, that was the way it was."

"What did he do to her?" Smith said. "This high priest maniac."

"He kept her hidden away. For five years he locked her away from the world and schooled her in his ways."

"What happened then?"

"When she was sixteen, she was allowed to participate in the sacrifice. Grigore considered her ready."

"I thought you said it was only men allowed."

"Only men can be offered up as sacrifices, but we had plenty of women in our midst. Selene managed to slip away during the ceremony and nobody has seen her since."

"These rituals," Smith said. "Do they still go on?"

"They did," Cristian said. "Until very recently. Grigore died last year and the whole thing seemed to die out. I suppose people finally gave in to reason."

"I still don't see what's made this woman suddenly decide to kill men," Smith said. "After all these years."

"Grigore died three days before Christmas last year. Three days before the full moon. When was your first victim killed?"

Smith thought hard and realised that Cristian was right. Christopher Riley was killed on Christmas Day under a full moon and Arnold Mather was also killed during a full moon.

"But why?" He said. "If she escaped all those years ago, why did she suddenly start the sacrifices again."

"I don't know, maybe she heard about Grigore's death and something snapped inside her - something that had been lying dormant for over twenty years. You have to understand that Selene was very young when she was taken. Her innocent mind was manipulated for five years between the ages of eleven and sixteen. The most impressionable years of a girl's life."

"And you think she thinks she has a duty to carry on Grigore's work now he's dead?"

"That's up to you to decide. I've said enough. I have to go now. My wife knows nothing of this and I'd prefer it to stay that way."

"You have my word," Smith said. "My colleagues are going to think I've gone crazy when I tell them all this."

"We live in a crazy world," Cristian stood up, opened the door and left the church.

## CHAPTER FIFTY FIVE

**YORK**

"Selene Lupei," Brownhill said. "Thirty six years old. Romanian national."
"Whitton, Bridge and Yang Chu were sitting opposite her in her office. Brownhill had called them in after hearing Smith's message.
"When's Smith due back?" Yang Chu said.
"Tomorrow morning. He tried to get an earlier flight but travel out of Romania isn't that easy at this time of the year."
"Are we sure this is our killer?" Whitton said.
"No, but Smith seems to be pretty convinced and that's good enough for me."
"Does that mean he's forgiven?" Whitton said. "For going over your head and everything?"
"The Jury's still out on that. All I know is we've got to start looking for this Selene Lupei woman."
"She sounds like a character from an old horror film," Yang Chu said.
"One of those ones with Bela Lugosi in it."
"Where do we start looking?" Bridge said.
"We'll know more when Smith gets back. I just wanted to give you all a heads up on what Smith discovered. I'm afraid you're going to have to brace yourselves for a hell of a lot of work this week. I suggest you go home and get some rest - you're going to need it. We'll meet back here tomorrow at seven thirty."
"Any word from the shrink?" Bridge said.
Brownhill glared at him.

"Jessica will turn up," she said. "I'm sure there's no cause for concern there."

"Did you read the papers this morning?" Yang Chu said. "They reckon all this is about Romanian immigrants. The Sunday Mail reckons there'll be riots and everything. Bloody immigrants."

"The Sunday Mail would say that," Brownhill said. "As it's mostly the lower intelligence proportion of the population who read it, I don't think we've got anything to worry about."

"It's those types of people who are most likely to riot," Yang Chu said. "They have that kind of mentality."

"There's not going to be any rioting."

"They rioted at the circus grounds," Yang Chu wasn't giving up.

"Go home, and I'll hear no more talk of riots."

When Brownhill was alone in her office she closed the door and picked up the telephone. She dialled Jessica Blakemore's mobile number and was surprised when it was answered on the third ring.

"Bryony," Blakemore said. "Sorry to disappear like that. How are you?"

"We might be getting somewhere on the murder investigation," Brownhill said. "Are you alright?"

"I'm fine," Blakemore said.

"Your husband was really worried about you."

"He's always worried about me. He tends to overreact sometimes. I forgot to renew my prescription and went for a couple of days without my pills but I'm fine now. They say a doctor makes the worst patient."

"Can we meet?"

"Sounds great," Blakemore said. "How about lunch?"

"Meet me at the Keys Hotel in an hour. Does your husband know you're alright?"

"I talked to him last night. Everything's fine."

Just over an hour later, Brownhill and Jessica Blakemore sat in the conservatory at the Keys Hotel next to the river. Brownhill couldn't help but stare at the scratch on Blakemore's cheek.

"That looks nasty," Brownhill said. "That must have been some cat."

"Sorry about that," Blakemore said. "I said that to stop my dear husband from fretting. It was the medication again. I'm a bit freaked out about it myself. It's actually self-inflicted."

"You did that to yourself?"

"Not on purpose. When I don't take the pills, I get nightmares. I fell asleep with my face on my hand, woke up abruptly from a nightmare and scraped my cheek on my nails. The cat story was all I could come up with on the spur of the moment."

"What medication are you on? Are you ill?"

Blakemore started to laugh. A tall waiter approached their table and Brownhill ordered a bottle of Chardonnay.

"I'm bipolar," Blakemore said. "It's more embarrassing than anything else to be honest. I mean, come on, have you ever heard anything more absurd? A psychiatrist with bipolar disorder?"

Brownhill didn't know what to say.

"I'm not completely cuckoo, and it's completely controllable if I remember to take the pills. I forget sometimes that's all."

"I'm sorry," Brownhill said. "I had no idea."

"I don't need sympathy, and you'd be surprised how popular being bipolar is these days. Everybody's doing it - models, film stars. It's the yuppie flu of the twenty first century. Can we talk about something else now?"

The waiter returned with the bottle of Chardonnay and two glasses. Brownhill poured them each a glass and took a long swig from hers.

"Any news on the investigation?" Blakemore asked. "I read about the Ukrainian guy. This woman isn't going to stop, is she?"

"Smith found out something interesting in Romania."

"Romania?" Blakemore seemed shocked.

"I really don't know how he does it," Brownhill finished the remaining wine in her glass and poured herself another one.

Blakemore had hardly touched hers.

"He has this unbelievable sixth sense," Brownhill said. "He reckons he's found out who this woman is."

"In Romania? That's amazing. Who is she?"

"Smith should be back tomorrow, we'll hear all about it then."

For some reason, Brownhill's instinct told her not to reveal too much about what Smith had found.

The waiter appeared to take their order. Brownhill suddenly realised she wasn't very hungry any more. She scanned the menu and ordered a small chef's salad. Blakemore ordered the same.

"Do you think you'll catch her?" Blakemore said when the waiter was gone.

"We'll catch her. This case has been the most frustrating one any of us have ever worked on. We'll catch her sooner or later."

"Shall I order another bottle of wine?" Blakemore pointed to the empty Chardonnay bottle on the table. "I see you really enjoyed the first one."

"Why not? I must admit it's going down rather well."

"Do you still need my help?"

"I don't know, I'm not sure how you can help us anymore."

"Well, I'm here if you need me."

The salads arrived, and they ate in silence for a while. Brownhill spent most of the time pushing the food around the plate. She really wasn't hungry.

"How are you and Grant getting on?" Blakemore said.

"Great, he's so different to Malcolm, my ex-husband. Grant is the most direct man I've ever met - there's no pretence about him. I like that."

"Good for you," Blakemore finally took a sip from her glass.

Her phone started to ring inside her handbag. She took it out and looked at the screen.

"Sorry, do you mind if I take this?"

Brownhill nodded. The waiter appeared and looked at the food on Brownhill's plate.

"Could we get another bottle of that please?" Brownhill pointed to the empty wine bottle.

Blakemore had disappeared from sight. When she came back she had an anxious look on her face.

"Sorry about that," she sat back down. "One of my patients was having a rather disturbing anxiety episode. I managed to calm him down again."

The waiter put a new bottle of wine on the table.

"Is everything alright with the food?" He asked Brownhill.

"Yes," Brownhill said. "It looks great. I'm just not that hungry."

The waiter nodded and walked back inside the kitchen.

"I'm afraid I have to go," Blakemore said. "I promised Ian we'd have a little heart to heart. Let me know if you need my help."

She stood up, placed some banknotes on the table and walked out of the room.

## CHAPTER FIFTY SIX

Smith was surprised to see that the lights were still on inside his house when he parked his car outside. Whitton had agreed to stay there while he was away to look after Theakston, but he thought they'd both be asleep by now. It was almost midnight. He was exhausted - all the travelling had taken its toll. All he wanted was a hot shower and a warm bed to pass out in. He opened the door and went inside the house. He'd never felt so happy to be home before. He could hear the sound of the television coming from the living room. Whitton and Theakston were nowhere to be seen. He hung up his coat, threw his bag on the carpet and went into the living room. Whitton was fast asleep on the sofa. Theakston was snoring next to her. Smith smiled.
"Some guard dog you are," he whispered.
He kissed Whitton on the top of her head and she woke up.
"You didn't have to wait up for me," Smith said.
"What time is it?" Whitton rubbed her eyes.
"Around midnight."
"How was Romania?"
"Miserable," Smith said. "Weird people and terrible weather. I'm so glad to be home again."
"Do you want some coffee?" Whitton sat up straighter on the sofa.
"I'll make it. You go to bed if you're tired. We can talk more in the morning."
He walked to the kitchen. Whitton followed after him and sat down at the table while he made the coffee."
"You didn't miss much while you were away," Whitton said. "A God awful press conference is about it. Brownhill really messed that one up."

"I believe so," Smith said. "I read some of the Sunday papers on the plane."

He placed two mugs of coffee on the table.

"Yang Chu reckons that people are going to go crazy again," Whitton said. "They're going to target the immigrants for the murders."

"I don't think it'll amount to that."

"So, tell me what you found out."

Theakston strolled in, looked at the empty dog bowl in disgust and banged his head against the back door. Smith opened it and let him out.

"Thanks for looking after him," he said.

"He's no trouble. All he does is eat and sleep. He's got really bad wind though. Tell me what you found out."

"You wouldn't believe me if I told you," Smith sat down at the table.

"Try me."

"The first two men died when there was a full moon."

"I know," Whitton said. "One of the young press guys pointed that out. We didn't think it was important. Chalmers says it's probably just a coincidence. Luka Gravov wasn't killed during a full moon."

"The full moon is the key to all of this. I spoke to this woman's brother in law and he told me everything. This whole thing revolves around some kind of ancient pagan ritual."

"Pagan ritual?"

"Selene Lupei was ten years old when it started. She was caught spying on a sacrifice. She wasn't supposed to be there, and they locked her up for six years. By the time she managed to escape it was too late. She'd been brainwashed into believing what these people thought. She thought it was normal. She was only sixteen when she managed to escape but, like I said, by then it was too late."

"I still don't understand. What's this sacrifice you're talking about?"

"Human sacrifice," Smith said.

Whitton shuddered.

"Once a month, when the full moon was at its brightest, a man was sacrificed in the mountains of Northern Romania. His throat was sliced open and his blood was shed onto the earth. These maniacs believed they would appease some kind of pagan spirit and the crops would prosper."

"Does this sort of thing still go on?" Whitton couldn't believe what she was hearing.

"It did, until very recently. The leader of these people - their high priest if you want to call it that, died three days before Christmas Day last year. I believe this Selene woman found out about it and something snapped inside her. I think she really believed she had to carry on these sacrifices."

"You realise that nobody is going to believe you, don't you?" Whitton said. "Do you know how ridiculous this all sounds?"

"I know, I'm afraid I'm going to have a hard time convincing anybody about any of this. Jessica Blakemore said something a few days ago that made me think. She mentioned something about traumatic events in childhood can have severe consequences later in life. I think the five years that Selene spent with these fanatics has finally burst out of her in a terrible way."

"I need a drink," Whitton stood up and walked to the back door.

"I've got just the thing," Smith went to fetch his bag from the hallway. He took it back to the kitchen, opened it and took out the bottle of Tuica. He had managed to smuggle one back with him.

"What on earth is that?" Whitton pointed to the unusual looking bottle.

"Fire water. Romanian moonshine. I managed to get my hands on a bottle before I left."

He took out two shot glasses and poured two small measures.

"It's advisable to down it in one go," he said. "Otherwise you'll never manage it."

Whitton picked up the glass and took a tentative sniff.

"It doesn't smell too bad."

"Cheers," Smith raised the glass to his lips and drank.

Whitton did the same. Her eyes were soon watering profusely, and she let out a small cough.

"That's bloody awful," she said.

"I know. Do you want another one?"

"Yes please."

After two more shots of Tuica, Smith and Whitton faced each other across the table.

"Nobody is going to believe you," Whitton said again. "They'll think you've lost your mind."

"I didn't believe it at first, but you should see the place where this Selene woman grew up. They're still in the Dark Ages there. Anything's possible in a place like that."

"What do we do now?"

Smith eyed the bottle of Tuica on the table and shivered.

"We go to bed," he said. "And try not to think of what's going to happen tomorrow."

## CHAPTER FIFTY SEVEN

Monday 7 February 2011

When Smith woke up, Whitton wasn't lying in the bed next to him. He looked around the room. A thin sliver of sunlight was shining in through a gap in the curtains. He patted the bed where Whitton usually slept. It was cold.
She's obviously been up for a while, he thought.
Theakston was also nowhere to be seen. Smith got out of bed, stretched and walked through to the bathroom. The door was ajar and the light inside was on.
"Whitton," he said.
He suddenly realised that it was about time he started to use her first name when they were not at work.
"Erica," he said. "Are you in there? I'm dying for a pee."
There was no sound from inside. Smith pushed the door open and looked inside. Whitton was lying naked on the tiles next to the shower. Her eyes were open, and she had a gaping wound in her neck. Blood had covered her bare chest. Smith tried to scream but the sound wouldn't come out. He rested his shoulder against the door frame. He felt his legs give way and fell to the ground next to the sink. A knife with a peculiar rounded blade lay inches from his face. He screamed again and this time the noise echoed around the bathroom.

Smith shot up in bed and lashed out with his arms. He knocked the clock on the bedside table flying and it smashed against the wall on the far side of the room. Whitton woke up and looked at him.
"Another nightmare?" She said.

"Worst one yet," Smith realised his heart was pumping dangerously fast. "You weren't in bed and I found you in the bathroom. You were lying on the floor with your throat sliced open. It was just like..."
"Like Lucy?"
"It was so real," Smith lay back in the bed. "I think I might be close to losing it. I don't know how much more of this I can take."
"Calm down," Whitton stroked his forehead. "I told you, I think you should speak to somebody about it. Speak to Jessica Blakemore."
"I thought you didn't like her."
"She's not that bad."
"I'll think about it. She did say she'd be interested in hearing about the dreams. What time is it? I seem to have demolished my clock."
Whitton took her phone off the table next to her and looked at the screen.
"It's half eight, I suppose we ought to get going."

By the time Smith and Whitton arrived at the station, the rest of the team had already been there for over two hours. Everybody was sitting in the small conference room waiting for them. Brownhill, Webber, Bridge, Yang Chu and Jessica Blakemore were waiting in anticipation to hear what Smith had found out in Romania. Smith sat down next to Brownhill and looked around the room. The absence of Thompson was noticeable for the first time since his death.
"Morning," Smith tried to sound as cheerful as possible. "Have you been waiting long?"
"Long enough," Brownhill said. "I hope that little holiday of yours was worth it."
"I think so. The woman we're looking for is a Selene Lupei. She's a Romanian who was last seen in the Ukraine twenty years ago."

He stopped there. He didn't know how he was going to word what he was about to say next.

"Before I begin," he said. "I would ask you to listen with open minds. Most of this is difficult to comprehend - I didn't believe it at first but I've had it confirmed by a few people and it seems to make sense now. All of this was actually happening in Northern Romania."

He proceeded to tell them about the sacrifices, the full moon rituals and how Selene was captured when she was a small girl and forced to endure the teachings of a fanatical so-called priest. When he was finished everybody in the room looked at him as though he had lost his mind. Smith had not expected anything different from his rational colleagues.

"That's the biggest load of nonsense I've ever heard," Grant Webber said eventually. "Do you actually expect us to believe all of this?"

"I agree," Brownhill said. "I must say I didn't take you for the gullible type."

"I didn't believe it at first either," Smith said. "But when you think about it, it all fits together. This high priest dies and three days later a lonely man is sacrificed here in York under the light of the full moon. Another man dies when the full moon appears again less than a month later. The weapon they used to use in the sacrifice is the same one that Webber came up with from the forensics reports. Luka Gravov knew what was going on and he wanted us to stop it, but he was killed before he could get to us."

"I think you need more sleep," Bridge said. "Or you need to see a shrink or something."

"I believe him," Jessica Blakemore said.

Everybody stared at her.

"I agree it's all a bit far-fetched," she said. "But I agree with him. This woman was ten years old when she was abducted. She was then put through six years of psychological trauma. This trauma was bound to show its ugly face in one way or another."

"But human sacrifices?" Yang Chu decided to join in the debate. "Surely that kind of thing doesn't happen anymore. People don't believe in that sort of stuff these days."

"Yes, they do," Blakemore said. "What about the Muslims - the extreme terrorists, the suicide bombers. These people are willing to sacrifice their own lives for a higher purpose. Whether we believe it to be right or not is immaterial - there are still plenty of people who think that through the ultimate sacrifice, they will reap the ultimate reward."

"It sounds as if you believe in this full moon crap yourself," Bridge said.

Blakemore suddenly turned very pale.

"Whatever you decide to believe," Smith said. "The fact of the matter is this: people are dying when the full moon appears. I've checked, and we have eleven days before the next full moon. Eleven days to find this woman before she kills somebody else."

## CHAPTER FIFTY EIGHT

An hour later they gathered again in the same room. Everybody had had a chance to mull over what Smith had told them. From the expressions on their faces, Smith could see that they still didn't believe what he had told them.

"Time is running out," Smith said. "A thirty six year old woman by the name of Selene Lupei is going to kill another man in eleven days' time. Does anybody have any suggestions on what to do about this?"

"We could send out a press release," Yang Chu suggested. "We can tell all the sad, lonely men out there to stay indoors and lock their doors during the full moon."

Smith glared at him.

"Any constructive suggestions?" he said.

"I'm still trying to get my head round all of this," Whitton said. "But we need to start looking for this woman. We know her name now and we know where she came from."

"But we don't know when she entered the country," Brownhill pointed out. "She could have been here for twenty years or she could have been here three months. We just don't know."

"I have an idea," Bridge said.

"Let's hear it then," Brownhill said.

"The photograph of the young girl - why don't we use the photograph?"

"It was taken twenty years ago Bridge," Smith said. "People can change a lot in twenty years - they can make themselves change."

"It's just a suggestion," Bridge said. "But there's this computer program - it's more for fun than anything else but there's an app that can be used to show what people will look like when they're older. I

have it on my phone although you don't want to know what I'm going to look like when I'm old."
"Get onto it," Smith said. "We know she has black hair. I also have a photograph of her younger sister - she's a few years younger than Selene but she looks just like the girl in the photograph."
Bridge stood up and left the room.
"What else?" Brownhill asked.
"How does a Romanian enter the country?" Yang Chu said. "I know that recently most of the immigrants have arrived via France."
"Check the records," Brownhill said.
"If I'm not mistaken," Whitton said. "The records are pretty sketchy. Plenty of them get under the radar and aren't even documented."
The room was silent for a few seconds.

"Go back," Smith said eventually. "We go back to the time just after she escaped from those lunatics. She was last seen in The Ukraine in ninety one. Where did she go from there?"
"You're not going to the Ukraine," Brownhill said. "I have to put my foot down on this one."
"I have no intention of leaving York for a very long time. I have a strong feeling that she came straight here."
"Why do you say that?"
"I don't know, one of those nasty feelings I get every now and then."
"How does a sixteen year old girl make her way to England on her own?" Yang Chu said. "Are you suggesting she did it by herself?"
"I don't know. I don't know how she got here but I know one thing, I've seen where she grew up. I very much doubt she had a passport. I suggest we look back to ninety one and ninety two and find out if anybody matching her age and description arrived here as a refugee.

It shouldn't be too hard to find out - there wasn't the same influx of immigrants into the country back then."

Brownhill realised she was nodding her head unconsciously. Jessica Blakemore hadn't said a word throughout the meeting. She had a vague smile on her face.

"Let's get onto it then," Brownhill said. "Smith, you and Whitton find out from the immigration people if someone matching Selene Lupei's description has entered the country. Find out if her fingerprints were taken when she was processed. We need those fingerprints. Yang Chu, I'm going to educate you in the art of damage control. We're going to help Baldwin with the barrage of phone calls we're going to get today from people worried about what they've read in the papers. Baldwin won't be able to handle it on her own."

Everybody stood up.

"Grant," Brownhill said to Webber. "I'm afraid I'm not going to be able to make it for dinner tonight. I've got a feeling it's going to be a very long day."

"I'm going to be in the lab all day and night anyway," Webber said. "I'm going to go through everything I've got again. I'm sure I must have overlooked something. We've never hit a brick wall like this before."

Brownhill nodded even though she knew that Webber never overlooked anything.

"Smith," Brownhill said as Smith was about to leave. "I've managed to stall the Super for as long as I can but, about that bloody award."

"I don't want it," Smith insisted.

"Smyth is adamant. Please just humour him and get him off my back. He can be a real pain when he gets a bee in his bonnet."

"I'll see what I can do."

## CHAPTER FIFTY NINE

Smith and Whitton were sitting in the canteen drinking coffee when Jessica Blakemore walked in. She looked utterly dejected. Smith thought she resembled a lost little girl.

"Do you mind if I join you?" Blakemore asked.

"Of course not," Whitton said.

Blakemore sat down.

"I feel like a loose wheel," she said. "I thought I'd come here to help but nobody seems to need my help anymore. I think it's time I moved on."

Smith didn't know what to say to her.

"I came here with such enthusiasm," Blakemore continued. "I thought I could use my expertise to help you crack this. It all started so well but now I just feel drained."

"We all do," Smith said. "This investigation has taken it out of all of us."

"I think I've worn out my welcome," Blakemore stood up. "It's been very interesting working with you. I'll see you around maybe."

Whitton nudged Smith.

Blakemore headed for the door. Whitton nudged Smith again.

"What?" He said.

"The dreams," Whitton whispered. "You said you would talk to her about your dreams."

"Hold on," Smith said.

Blakemore turned around.

"There is something you can help with," Smith said.

Blakemore's eyes widened.

"I'm still having those disturbing dreams," Smith continued. "The nightmares. The double awakenings - the ones where I wake up but I'm still dreaming. It feels so real. What did you call them? Lurid dreams?"

"Lucid," Blakemore laughed.

Her eyes were sparkling.

"Anyway, can you help me to stop them?"

"I can try."

"I don't want to lie back on a couch though. I don't want to tell you all about my childhood and all that crap."

"How about a drink then?" Blakemore suggested.

Smith looked at Whitton. Her eyes should have told him she didn't like the idea, but Smith didn't appear to notice.

"A drink sounds great," Smith said. "I know just the place. It's quiet and we can talk in peace. The Hog's Head. I'll meet you there at seven."

"I'll look forward to it," Blakemore smiled and walked out of the canteen.

"We'd better get to work," Smith finished the rest of the coffee in his cup.

It tasted different - it wasn't as repulsive as it usually was.

They must have changed the brand, he thought.

"You're the boss," Whitton stood up and walked out of the canteen without him.

"Are you alright?" Smith turned on the computer in his office and waited for it to boot up.

"I'm fine, everything's just fine."

Smith typed in his password and a picture of Theakston filled the screen.

"Where do we start?" Smith said.

"How about a drink?" Whitton said in a nasal whine. "A drink sounds great."

"What? What's wrong?"

"Nothing's wrong," Whitton said. "Apart from the fact that you're going on a date with that psycho woman."

"It's not a date. She's going to help me with my dreams. Christ, it was your idea in the first place."

"I didn't mean you had to take her out on a date. Get into the system mainframe and look for the immigration records."

Smith was about to say something but changed his mind.

I'll never understand women, he thought.

He found the records for all the people who had entered the country in ninety one and ninety two. Over eighteen thousand people had decided to remain permanently in the UK in those two years.

"This is going to take some time, more than eighteen thousand people came here in two years."

"That's nothing," Whitton said. "Look at this."

She pointed to the most recent immigration figures.

"Last year, over a quarter of a million people came here. The whole country is going to burst at the seams if this carries on. We need to narrow it down a bit."

She scrolled down a list on the screen and clicked on 'Romania'. There were still six hundred names on the list for the two years.

"OK," she said. "Age group sixteen to seventeen."

Eighty eight names appeared.

"Female."

They were left with eight names. Selene Lupei's wasn't one of them.

"Crap," Smith said. "Maybe she didn't arrive here then. I was sure of it."

The next four hours were spent going through every single person of Selene's age who had arrived in the country since nineteen ninety one. As the years went by, the search became more and more tedious. When they had reached the point where the records stopped, and Smith and Whitton had found out how many Romanians had entered the country, Selene Lupei's name was still not there.

"I need a smoke," Smith said.

"I'm going to get some coffee," Whitton said. "I'll see you back here in twenty minutes."

Smith put his hand on her shoulder, but she brushed it away.

Chalmers was standing in the car park smoking a cigarette when Smith went outside.

"Great minds think alike," Chalmers said. "Smoke?"

He handed Smith his packet of cigarettes

"No thanks, boss," Smith said. "Try one of these instead."

He took out a red, white and blue box.

"Assos?" Chalmers said. "Never heard of them. Where the hell did you get them from?"

"I brought two cartons back with me from Romania. Five quid a carton."

Chalmers took out a cigarette and eyed it suspiciously. He put it in his mouth and lit the end.

"Not too bad," he took a long drag.

Smith lit one of his own and stared at the sky. More snow clouds were forming overhead.

"Is this winter ever going to end?"

"They say it's going to drag on way into March," Chalmers said. "It's still nowhere near as bad as the winter of seventy six. How's it going with the investigation?"

"I thought we had her, now it seems like the trip to Romania was a complete waste of time. Me and Whitton have just spent four hours going through the immigration lists. We've gone through everyone who's entered the country from Romania since ninety one and we found nothing."

"Maybe she came in under a false name," Chalmers said.

"Do you know how many Romanians have come here to live in the past twenty years? Over eighty thousand. We don't know when she arrived. Do you know how long it'll take to go through every woman on the list?"

"What's your initial feeling? What does your gut tell you?"

"I think she came here shortly after she left Romania. She was last seen in the Ukraine in ninety one. I think she headed for the UK then. Something about the way these murders were carried out suggests she hasn't just arrived here - she's been here a very long time. She appears to be very familiar with the place."

He threw his cigarette butt into the distance and lit another one. He offered the pack to Chalmers.

"No thanks," Chalmers said. "One of those is enough for me. Go with that gut of yours. Dig a bit deeper into ninety one and ninety two."

"We have done, there were eight young women aged sixteen or seventeen who arrived during that time."

"Check them out. Like I said, maybe she used a false name. She probably had no passport. How's it going with you and Whitton by the way?"

"Women," Smith said. "I don't think I'll ever understand women. Whitton told me to do something and when I did it she got all sulky."

"You probably didn't do it the way she wanted you to do it. Never, ever try to understand the way a woman's brain works - it'll drive you to the brink of insanity. I've been married to Mrs Chalmers for over thirty years and I gave up trying to understand her after ten. That's the secret to a happy marriage. I'd better get going. Old Smyth will be snapping at my feet soon."

"Thanks, boss," Smith said.

"For what?"

"I don't know," Smith said.

Chalmers shook his head and went back inside the station.

## CHAPTER SIXTY

Whitton was already waiting in Smith's office when he went back inside.

"Where've you been?" She said. "I thought you said twenty minutes."

"Relax," Smith said. "I was talking to Chalmers. What's wrong with you today?"

"With me? I'm fine. I'm not the one who has a date with a hot head doctor."

"I'll cancel it then, I'll phone and say I can't make it."

"I'm starting to think you were right all along, about relationships at work never working out."

"What's brought this on all of a sudden?"

"Nothing. Let's get back to work."

"Chalmers reckons I should go with my gut," Smith said. "Selene Lupei came into the country in ninety one or ninety two. I'm pretty sure of it. Let's concentrate on the eight Romanian girls who arrived during that time."

He clicked on the list of young women and printed out a list. Whitton took the piece of paper, folded it in half and tore off four of the names."

"What are you doing?" Smith said.

"I think it would be best if we take four names each. I'll work better in my own office. If that's alright with you, Sarge?"

She emphasized the word 'Sarge'.

"No problem," Smith shrugged.

"Enjoy your date," Whitton said and left the office.

   Smith took a deep breath and got to work on the four names on the list. Whitton's behaviour had confused him – he'd never seen her act like that before. The first name on the list was Adriana Constantin. There was no information about her on the screen apart from her name and age. Smith thought about contacting the relevant immigration department to find out more about her, but he knew that could take weeks and they were running out of time. He remembered something Bridge's computer geek friend had said about Facebook being a great spy tool and decided to give it a try. He opened up the Facebook page but realised he didn't have an account with them. He picked up the phone and dialled the number for the front desk. Baldwin answered immediately. She sounded very stressed.

"Baldwin," Smith said. "Are you alright?"

"I'm knackered, sir," Baldwin said. "I've been taking phone calls from irate citizens all day. This immigrant thing is getting way out of hand."

"I need to open a Facebook account."

"You need to do what?"

"Open a Facebook account, how do I do it? I have the page open in front of me now."

"Sir," Baldwin said. "Is this really the time to start looking for old friends?"

"I don't have any old friends. How do I open a Facebook account?"

"It's easy, there's a place where it says, 'Sign up now'. Enter your email address and a password and you're ready to go."

"Thanks, Baldwin," Smith hung up the phone.

He did as Baldwin had instructed and was informed that an email had been sent for him to confirm his details and to activate his account. He clicked on the link on the email and was redirected to the Facebook page. He typed in 'Theakston' as his password and his profile page opened up.

Smith ignored all the questions on the screen asking him to add a profile picture and more information and tried to remember exactly what Bridge's friend had done. He found the search bar and typed in Adriana Constantin. There were six possible results. Smith could tell from their photographs that none of them could possibly be Selene Lupei. He repeated the process for the three remaining names on the list. The last woman on the list, a woman by the name of Emilia Dragos was not on Facebook, but Smith could definitely rule out the first three. He closed down Facebook and typed in Emilia Dragos in the Google search bar. He scrolled down until he found a possible match. Emilia Dragos was a lecturer in Eastern European studies at the University of Manchester. She was thirty five years old and had been in the country since nineteen ninety two. Smith opened up the link and sighed - even if she lost fifty kilograms and wore a black wig, she still would bear little resemblance to the eye witness accounts of Selene Lupei.

Smith felt drained. He looked at his watch. It was six thirty. He'd been digging away for over eight hours and had still come up with nothing. He wondered if Whitton had found anything. He closed down his computer and switched off the light in his office. He was about to go and check in on Whitton but changed his mind - he wasn't in the mood for any more of Whitton's mood swings. He was due to meet Jessica Blakemore in half an hour.

I'll leave Whitton to calm down a bit, he thought, I need a drink.

## CHAPTER SIXTY ONE

Jessica Blakemore was already at the Hog's head when Smith walked in. She was sitting at the bar drinking a glass of white wine. There were three other people in the pub - an old man sitting at the bar by himself and a young couple sitting at one of the tables. They were laughing at something on a mobile phone. Smith walked up to the bar. Marge was nowhere to be seen.
"Sorry I'm late," Smith said to Blakemore. "Can I buy you a drink?"
"I've got one," Blakemore said. "You're not late. I was early. I've had a rough day."
"That makes two of us."
He nodded to the stranger behind the bar.
"Pint of Theakstons," he said.
The barman poured the beer and placed it on the counter.
"Let's sit at a table," Blakemore suggested. "Somewhere away from prying ears."
Smith picked up his beer and walked over to his usual table by the fire. He pulled out a chair for Blakemore and she sat down.
"That's something you don't see very often these days," she said. "A gentleman as well. Is there any limit to your talents?"
She had a playful glint in her eyes.
"It's one of my few good traits," Smith said. "My Gran brought me up well."
He took a long swig of his beer and felt instantly relaxed.
"Your girlfriend is not happy about us meeting like this. I was actually surprised when you showed up. I thought she might have tried to talk you out of it."
"It was her idea, I don't understand women sometimes."

"Don't even try."

"You're the second person to tell me that today," Smith finished his beer. "Can I get you another drink?"

"Not at the moment," Blakemore said.

Smith went to the bar and returned with two pints of beer.

"Saves me getting up again," he smiled. "Where do you want me to start?"

"How did the digging go today? Did you find anything?"

"Nothing, I'm getting this close to giving up on this altogether."

"But you never give up do you?" Blakemore took a tiny sip of wine. "When did the dreams start?"

"A few years ago," Smith said. "I had this recurring dream about my sister."

Blakemore nodded for him to continue.

"In the dreams, I'm always under the water. I'm sinking down and running out of air. I see my sister and try to swim down to her. My lungs feel like they're going to explode. Sometimes in the dream I can reach out and touch my sister, but I can never quite manage to pull her to the surface. My lungs are about to burst, and this is when I always wake up."

"What happened to your sister?"

"She disappeared. I was sixteen at the time. We'd bunked school and I'd taken her surfing. I got distracted and I left her by the shore. When I looked back at her, she was gone."

"And you blamed yourself?"

"Of course I did - it was my fault. If I hadn't taken her surfing that day she'd still be with us and I wouldn't even be here talking to you today."

He finished one of the beers in one go.

"Did your parents blame you too?"

"It was only my mother," Smith said. "My father was dead. It was my mother who sent me here to live with my Gran."

"I see," Blakemore seemed to stop and think about what Smith had just told her. "Your father killed himself, didn't he?"

"I thought you were going to help me get to the bottom of my nightmares."

"I am, but I need to know where they stem from - what triggers them off."

"I was the one who found him. My father I mean, he was hanging from a tree in the back garden."

"Why do you think he killed himself?"

"I don't know. Something to do with his time in Vietnam I think. Maybe he was weak. I don't know."

"Your sister drowned, didn't she? She was pulled out of the river."

"She was trying to help a young boy," Smith said. "So, they killed her."

"Who killed her?"

"Wolfie did, or at least his people did."

Smith didn't know what was happening to him. He was talking to a virtual stranger about things he had hardly spoken about before.

"Have I been hypnotised?" He said. "Have you put me under without me even realising it?"

"Not at all, I do this for a living remember. This is what I do - I help people to work through traumatic events in their lives. Let's go to the most recent dreams shall we. The double awakenings. When did the lucid dreams start?"

"A few months ago," Smith said. "The first one really freaked me out. I woke up and everything appeared to be normal. I went about my normal morning stuff and then I woke up again."

"What about the most recent one?"

"They just keep getting more and more real. I had one just this morning. I woke up and I was alone in the bed. Whitton was nowhere to be seen. The sun was shining through the curtains. I walked down the hallway and saw that the light was on in the bathroom. I called out to her, but she didn't answer. I opened the bathroom door and Whitton was lying on the floor next to the shower. Her throat had been slashed open. I tried to scream but nothing came out. My legs gave way and I fell to the ground. I saw a knife with a curved blade only inches from my face and screamed. That's when I woke up for real."

Smith drained his glass and stood up.

"I need something stronger," he said.

Smith returned with two large measures of Jack Daniel's.

"I insist you have a drink with me," he pushed one of the glasses closer to Blakemore, lifted the other one to his lips and waited for her to pick up the glass.

Blakemore smiled, raised her glass and drank it down in one go. Smith did the same.

"How did you get that scratch on your face?" Smith asked her.

He was starting to feel quite drunk.

"Stupid accident, I woke up with a start and scratched my own face. You don't have the monopoly on bad dreams you know."

"Why am I having these dreams?"

"Dreams are an enigma. They're a grey area in psychology. There has been plenty of research done on the subject but we're still years away from finding anything conclusive as to the cause of dreams. A popular belief is that dreams are a way of processing thoughts in our subconscious - thoughts that the defence mechanisms in our brains

have pushed to one side in order for us to cope without going insane. Did you ever have nightmares when you were a child?"
"I don't think so. I could never remember the dreams I had when I was younger."
"That makes them even more unusual, and it makes it even harder to try and fathom out what's going on in your head now. Nightmares normally start during childhood. It's seen as a sign of an active imagination. The dreams you're having are obviously caused by something else. What are you afraid of?"
"I don't know," Smith said. "Not much."
"Everybody is afraid of something. It could be dying, heights, snakes, flying, anything. Without fear we wouldn't survive for long. What are you afraid of most?"
"I used to have this thing about the ocean. I used to freeze when I saw the vast expanse of water in front of me but that stopped a while ago. I suppose what I'm afraid of most is seeing people I care about getting hurt. People close to me seem to end up dead. My dad, my sister, my Gran, Lucy."
Smith appeared to drift off for a moment.
"I'm not even thirty," he said. "And I've seen so much death. Am I going crazy?"
"No. Far from it. You have one of the strongest defence mechanisms I've ever come across."
"I'll take that as a compliment. What about the dreams?"
"The dreams are part of that defence mechanism."
"Will they ever stop?"
"No, I don't think they'll stop but they should get easier to understand. I want you to try an exercise for me."
"Hold that thought," Smith stood up and went to the bar.

He came back with a bottle of Jack Daniel's.

"This bottle is going to cost me a fortune," he said. "But I've got a feeling it's going to be worth it. Go on. What did you mean about trying an exercise?"

He poured them both a large measure of whiskey.

"I want you to try this," Blakemore said. "The next time you have one of the dreams - when you realise you're in control of everything that's happening in it, try to direct it."

"I don't understand."

"Control it. You dictate how the dream unfolds. For example, the dream you had this morning. Whitton doesn't have to end up dead, you can make it that she ends up flying over the rooftops of York holding your hand."

"Can I do that?"

"You can learn to do it. You have a very rare gift if I can call it that. Fewer than one percent of people can actually control what happens in their dreams. People have tried to train themselves but very few actually manage to pull it off. Don't let the dreams control you - get in first."

Smith took a long drink from the glass and smiled. He felt more relaxed than he had done in weeks. He realised that he was also extremely hungry.

"Are you hungry?" he said. "Let me buy you supper. It's the least I can do."

"I could eat a Chinese," Blakemore said.

"Chinese it is then."

## CHAPTER SIXTY TWO

"Take us to the nearest Chinese restaurant," Smith said to the driver of the taxi Blakemore and he had just got into.
"I know just the place," the driver drove out of the car park and headed for the city centre.
Smith looked out of the window as the taxi drove through the deserted streets. Snow was starting to fall again. Thick flakes brushed against the windows as they drove. The driver turned left onto a side street and parked outside a familiar building. The sign for the Big Wok restaurant lit up the street.
"They do the best chow mein in York," the driver said. "That'll be six quid please."
Smith paid the driver and opened the door for Jessica Blakemore. The snow was falling heavier now. They rushed inside the restaurant. Smith shivered when he looked up at the flat on the top floor above the restaurant. It was in darkness. He wondered if the large Chinese man had managed to find somebody else to rent it after what had happened to Christopher Riley there a few months ago.

The Big Wok was quiet when Smith and Blakemore went inside. Mr Yin, the obese proprietor was indulging in a healthy portion of noodles at a table in the back of the restaurant. He glanced over at Smith and smiled.
"Mr Smith," he said. "What can I do for you?"
"Are you still open?" Smith said.
He looked at a strange clock on the wall. It was almost ten.
"If doors are open then we're open," Yin said. "Please take a seat. Who's your friend?"
He looked Blakemore up and down.

"She's a colleague of mine."

Yin nodded. Smith and Blakemore sat at the table behind Yin.

"The chef is almost finished for the night," Yin said. "Would it be ok if you order soon? Would you like something to drink?"

"Two beers please, and two chicken chow meins."

"Billy," Yin shouted in his high pitched voice.

A skinny waiter appeared from the back room, looked at Smith and Blakemore and bowed his head.

"Billy, two chicken chow meins and two Tsing Taos."

The waiter backed into the kitchen with his head still bowed.

"Mr Smith," Yin said. "Why don't you catch that man who killed my tenant? It's over two months now."

"We'll find whoever did this, and we'll lock them up for a very long time. Have you managed to find another tenant?"

"What do you think? Who wants to rent a flat where someone got murdered? No, this has cost me plenty of money."

The waiter arrived with two large bottles of Chinese beer. Smith eyed the bottles suspiciously.

"Very good beer," Yin said. "I don't drink but this is good beer. Made from rice - keeps you very regular."

The waiter poured the beers and left. Yin pushed his chair back and with great effort managed to lift his considerable bulk into a standing position.

"If you'll excuse me," he said. "I have to cash up now. Enjoy the food."

He wobbled off to his office. He reminded Smith of a silverback gorilla.

"I didn't know this place was where the first guy died," Blakemore said when they were alone.

"Christopher Riley," Smith said. "He rented the flat above the restaurant."

"It's quite creepy actually. I mean, we're sitting here about to eat a meal a few metres from where a man was brutally killed."

"I didn't know the taxi driver was going to bring us here. Besides, I never had you pegged for someone who freaked out easily."

"I'm not. It's just weird that's all - weird that we find ourselves back where it all started."

She took a sip of her beer and winced.

"This stuff tastes awful," she said.

The waiter returned and placed two plates of chicken chow mein on the table in front of them.

"Enjoy your food," he said. "I'm supposed to be finished now but I can wait around if you need anything else."

"It's fine," Smith said. "We'll just eat and run. You can bring the bill if you like."

"On the house," the waiter said. "Mr Yin seems to like you."

He disappeared to the back of the restaurant again.

Smith and Blakemore ate in silence for a while. Neither of them touched the beer.

"That taxi driver was right," Smith said. "I don't usually eat Chinese food but this chow mein is delicious."

He finished eating and placed his knife and fork on the plate.

"I'm stuffed," he sighed.

Yin emerged from the back room and smiled at the empty plates. He handed Smith and Blakemore each a plate with a strange looking biscuit on it.

"Fortune cookies," he said.

"I thought that was an American thing," Smith said.

"It is, but the tourists seem to like them. No peeking though. Fortune only comes true if you keep it a secret."

Blakemore opened hers first. On a small piece of paper were six words, 'You're very close to your dream'.
"Read yours," Blakemore said. "It's just a bit of a laugh."
Smith shook his head and opened up the fortune cookie. He read the words on the piece of paper.
'Be very careful of wolf dressed as sheep'.
He smiled, crumpled up the piece of paper and put it in his pocket.
"Just a bit of fun," Yin winked at Smith.
"I think we've kept you here for long enough," Smith stood up. "Thank you so much, Mr Yin - that was delicious. Are you sure I can't pay for it?"
"No need, Mr Smith, on the house. Besides, I've already cashed up for the day. I'm tired now. I need my sleep."
"What did your fortune cookie say?" Blakemore asked Smith outside the restaurant.
"Something about getting plenty of sleep," Smith lied. "What about yours?"
"I've forgotten already. What now? Shall we call for a taxi?"
"I feel like a walk. I need to walk off all that food. My house is only about a mile from here. I can phone a taxi for you if you want."
"I'll walk with you, if that's alright?"
"Let's go then," Smith said.
He was overcome by a sudden unease - he felt like he was crossing some kind of imaginary line.
I'll phone Whitton as soon as I get home, he thought, as soon as Jessica Blakemore has gone, I'll phone her and tell her everything is going to be alright.
"This is my house here," Smith said. "Thanks for walking with me. Do you want me to phone for a taxi now?'

"I'm freezing," Blakemore said. "Can I wait inside?"

Smith opened the front door and they went inside. Theakston was waiting in the hallway. His tail stopped wagging the instant he saw Jessica Blakemore standing there. He started to growl at her.

"That's enough," Smith said. "That's just rude. Where are your manners?"

He smiled at Blakemore.

"Sorry, he's not used to strangers. I have the number of that taxi company around here somewhere. Where are you staying tonight? Still with Brownhill?"

"I was," Blakemore said. "But I thought I'd give her and Webber a bit of privacy. They haven't been getting on so well recently. I know this is a big ask but would you mind if I stayed here tonight? I'll sleep on the sofa"

"I don't know, I don't think that's such a good idea."

"You're right. Of course, you're right. What was I thinking? I'll check into a hotel for the night. Do you have the number of that taxi firm?"

Smith thought hard for a second.

"You can sleep on the sofa," he said and instantly regretted it.

He felt an unpleasant burning sensation in his stomach.

"Are you sure?" Blakemore shook off her shoes before Smith had a chance to answer.

"Of course, do you want some coffee?"

"Love some."

# CHAPTER SIXTY THREE

### *Tuesday 8 February 2011*

Smith woke to the sound of his mobile phone ringing on the table next to the bed. He rubbed his eyes and answered it. It was Whitton.
"Hey," Whitton said. "Did I wake you?"
"No," Smith said. "I mean yes. I was almost awake anyway."
"Are you at home?"
"Of course, I'm at home."
"I'm turning into your road now. Don't worry, I come in peace. I've brought you breakfast."
She rang off.
Smith shot up in bed.
"Shit," he remembered that Jessica Blakemore had slept on his sofa.
He quickly got dressed and went downstairs. He heard the sound of a car door closing outside and started to panic.
Think, he thought, I did nothing wrong, she just spent the night on the sofa.
There was a knock on the door. Jessica Blakemore was nowhere to be seen. Smith opened the door. Whitton was standing there holding a brown paper bag.
"I'm sorry I was a real cow yesterday," she said. "I should know you better than that by now. I've brought some chocolate donuts. Are you going to let me in?"
"Of course," Smith said. "Come in. I just have to warn you..."
Smith was too late. Jessica Blakemore emerged from the living room. She was wearing a T shirt and nothing else. She stood behind Smith and smiled at Whitton.

"Morning," Blakemore said to Whitton. "I'll put the kettle on."
"What the hell is going on?" Whitton dropped the bag of donuts on the step and two of them fell out.
"It's not what it looks like," Smith said and wished he had said something else.
"I can see what it looks like."
She turned around and walked back to her car.
"Erica," Smith called after her. "Come back. I can explain."
It was no use. Whitton got in her car, started the engine and sped off down the street.
"Damn it," Smith said.
Theakston had discovered the donuts and managed to eat two of them before Smith could stop him. Smith picked up the bag and an incredible sadness washed over him. He closed the front door and walked through to the kitchen. Theakston followed closely behind - the promise of more chocolate donuts was too good an opportunity to pass up on.

Smith sat at the kitchen table with his head in his hands.
"Sorry," Blakemore said. "I messed things up a bit there didn't I?"
Smith didn't say anything.
What was I thinking? he thought. Letting this woman sleep here last night? It was only going to end badly.
"I think you'd better leave," he said.
"I'm supposed to be helping you out today."
"Ask Brownhill if she can pick you up. I don't think it's a good idea for us to be seen arriving at the station together."
"Why? Nothing happened. I slept on your sofa. End of story."
"Are you completely stupid? I'm going for a shower. I don't want you here when I get back downstairs."

He stood up and walked upstairs to the bathroom. He turned on the shower, undressed and stood underneath the jets. He turned up the temperature until the water burned his skin - he wanted to punish himself. He then turned the hot water off completely and stood for as long as he could stand under the freezing cold water. When he felt himself getting numb, he turned off the shower and stood there watching the droplets of water drip off his body. He was covered in gooseflesh. He dried himself off, got dressed and went back downstairs. Jessica Blakemore was gone.

Smith turned on the kettle and made some coffee. The bag of donuts lay on the kitchen table. Theakston was still staring at them. Smith took the coffee outside and sat down on the bench. He lit a cigarette and looked up at the sky. More snow clouds were forming overhead.

When is this winter ever going to end? he thought.

He contemplated phoning Whitton to explain everything, but he knew it wouldn't do any good - it would be better to let her calm down a bit first. He finished the cigarette and lit another one. He heard a commotion from inside the house. He rushed inside and saw that Theakston had succeeded in reaching the donuts on the table – he'd dragged them down to the floor but in doing so the dog had managed to knock over two chairs and he was now trying to escape from the one that landed on top of him. Smith started to laugh. The sight of the poor dog pinned down by the kitchen chair was hilarious. Chocolate was smeared all over his face. Smith managed to contain himself and lifted the chair back up.

"That'll teach you," he said. "That'll teach you for being such a pig. What am I going to do about Whitton? You were here - you know it was all innocent. I wish you could talk sometimes."

Smith went back outside and finished his coffee. He locked the back door, picked up his car keys and left the house. He took the long route to the station. He wasn't in any hurry to get there today. He crossed over the river and turned left. He drove towards the Minster in the distance. As he got closer to it he was aware of a strange noise. He slowed down and stopped. He got out of the car and listened. The noise was still there - a rhythmic thumping sound like a bass drum in an oompha band. Chanting could be heard along with the beat. Smith got back in his car and drove to where he thought the sounds were coming from. He turned right and was met with a wall of people. They were marching slowly through the city. Smith estimated there to be at least three hundred of them. They were chanting and wielding banners with the words 'Immigrants go home' on them.

Suddenly something was thrown through the windscreen of Smith's car. Smith managed to duck just in time. The brick had shattered the windscreen, but it hit the seat behind him. Smith picked it up and placed it on the seat beside him. The crowd of people seemed to be getting closer. He quickly engaged reverse gear and slammed his foot on the accelerator. His red Ford Sierra screamed backwards, turned the corner and crashed into a parked van. Smith put the car into first and sped off in the opposite direction. When he decided he was a safe distance from the crowd of people, he stopped the car and got out to inspect the damage. The wing mirror on the left hand side of the car had been ripped off and there was a huge dent in the door but apart from that the car appeared to be in one piece. He checked to see if his windscreen was still safe - the brick had gone straight through, but Smith knew he could still drive the car. He patted the roof of the car, got back in and drove the most direct route to the station.

By the time Smith parked his car in the car park at the station he was drenched in sweat. The incident with the protestors had unnerved him. He got out of the car and walked inside the station. He ignored Baldwin at the front desk and walked straight down the corridor to Chalmers' office. He went inside without knocking.
"We've got big trouble," he said to Chalmers.
Chalmers was talking on the phone. He waved his hand in the air to tell Smith to be quiet. He finished the call.
"What the hell happened to you?" he said.
"We've got big trouble," Smith said again. "They're marching in the city centre. They're protesting against the immigrants."
"I know. We've had reports of them breaking the windows of foreign owned shops. Nobody seems to have been hurt yet though."
"I nearly was. They threw a brick through my windscreen."
"What were you doing down there? The call only came in a few minutes ago."
"I was driving to work," Smith said. "Taking the scenic route."
"It'll all blow over. Uniform are sorting things out as we speak. This country's gone mad. What's wrong with people these days? You're bleeding by the way."
He pointed to Smith's forehead. A tiny piece of glass had scraped the skin and a thin trickle of blood was seeping out.
"I'll live," Smith said. "I suppose I should get to work. We're still no closer with this Selene Lupei woman."
"Stick to your gut - it's never let you down before."

## CHAPTER SIXTY FOUR

Smith left Chalmers' office and headed straight for the canteen. His heart started to beat faster when he spotted Whitton. She was about to go into the canteen.
"Whitton," he said. "We need to talk."
"There's nothing to talk about."
"Nothing happened. She just slept on the sofa. That's all. She had nowhere else to go."
"I'm not interested."
"Please, let me explain."
Whitton looked Smith in the eyes. Smith thought she looked as if she had been crying. He moved closer and put his hand on her shoulder. She brushed it away.
"Just stay away from me," she turned round and walked down the corridor.

Bridge and yang Chu were standing next to each other when Smith walked in the canteen. They were staring at something out of the window.
"What's going on?" Smith said.
"Look at that," Yang Chu pointed to the snowstorm outside. "I've never seen anything like that before."
Smith moved closer to see what Yang Chu was talking about. A spectacular blizzard was blowing outside. Visibility was virtually nil. A violent squall of snow had obscured the view of the city. Large snowflakes were attacking the windowpane with a vengeance.
"I reckon this is the start of the next ice age," Bridge said. "They say we're about due for another one."

"Rubbish," Smith said. "It's just winter in the north of England."

"You'll see. You've been warned."

"At least it'll keep those morons off the streets," Yang Chu said. "I heard their march was short lived. They were no match for the weather. What's happening between you and Whitton, Sarge?"

Yang Chu looked at Smith.

"Nothing," Smith said.

"She seems upset. I think she's been crying."

"That's none of your business. Haven't you two got any work to do?"

"That app of mine didn't give me much," Bridge said. "I put the old photo of the young girl in and tried all kinds of different combinations but all it spewed out was a combination of Baldwin and that shrink woman. I don't think it's going to give us anything to go on."

"It was worth a try," Smith said.

"Well I wasted the whole of yesterday on those racists," Yang Chu said. "You wouldn't believe how ignorant people are these days. How long is this going to go on for?"

"As of now, I want everybody on the team to concentrate on finding out when this woman entered the country. We know she came from Romania. That's the key to this whole thing. We should be able to piece together where she ended up. It's going to be a lot of work but I'm sure if we all put our heads together we can get to the bottom of it eventually."

"Ten days," Yang Chu mused. "We've got ten days before the next full moon. It's like something out of a bad horror film. We have ten days to save this woman's next victim."

"That's why we need to get cracking," Smith said. "We'll do it systematically. Yang Chu, you and I can concentrate on ninety one and Bridge and Whitton can go over ninety two."

"Are you absolutely sure she came into the UK in those years?" Bridge asked.

"No, but I'm about ninety percent sure. We need to check out every female of Selene Lupei's age who entered the country in those years. One of them has to be her."

Four hours later, the team stopped for a break. They gathered in the canteen. Whitton sat as far away from Smith as possible. Brownhill and Blakemore walked in and sat at a table away from everybody else. Smith sighed. He couldn't remember a time when the team had been as despondent as this. Even during the most frustrating investigations they had found it in themselves to stick together and fight it out.

"This is a waste of time," Yang Chu said. "Four hours of my life wasted. What a complete waste of time."

Every single woman who had entered the country from Romania of Selene Lupei's age at the time had been investigated and discarded from the list. Whitton and Bridge had come close - they believed they had found a likely suspect but when they dug deeper they found out the woman had died a few years earlier.

Brownhill had been watching them from a distance. She noted the despair on the faces of the team and stood up. She walked over to where they were sitting and clapped her hands together.

"Right," she said. "We're going to find this woman. Jessica has come up with an idea and I think it might work."

Whitton snorted.

"Jessica has worked hard on this," Brownhill ignored Whitton. "And I believe it may help. Jessica."

Brownhill beckoned for Blakemore to come and join them. Blakemore stood up and sat on the chair next to the window. She smiled at Whitton, but Whitton turned away.

"This may seem like madness," Blakemore said. "But I'm sure we all agree that there's a very fine distinction between madness and sanity these days."

"You should know," Whitton said.

"I was led to believe, that the people sitting before me are one of the finest if not the finest investigative team in the whole country."

"Is this going to take long?" Whitton said. "We're running out of time here."

"Time," Blakemore said. "Time. That leads me beautifully to my point. You're not going to catch this woman in time."

Everybody stared at her.

"This woman doesn't want you to catch her," Blakemore elaborated. "Almost every documented serial killer, if we can give her that label, has demonstrated some kind of desire to be caught - they secretly want to be stopped but this woman will carry on killing until you outsmart her. She needs to kill."

"How do you suggest we catch her then?" Smith said. "You're wasting our time here. We should be carrying on with the immigration stuff."

"No, that is precisely what you shouldn't be doing. I profess to having a deeper understanding of how the human brain works than you and what I suggest you do right now is stop looking for her."

"That's the most ridiculous thing I've ever heard," Whitton said.

"Isn't it just?" Blakemore smiled at her. "But it just might work. Your brains have reached saturation point - if you carry on like this you won't be able to absorb any more information and you most certainly won't be able to process any of it in any rational order. I suggest you stop what you're doing for a few days and switch off."

"A few days?" Yang Chu said. "We don't have a few days. In ten days' time we're going to have another body to worry about. This woman is going to kill another man in ten days' time."

"Jessica is right," Brownhill said. "I must admit that I was sceptical at first but what she says makes sense. I want you all to go home for a few days. Forget all about the investigation and come back here on Friday morning with fresh brains and fresh ideas."

Nobody made any effort to stand up.

"That's a direct order," Brownhill said. "In case you've all forgotten, I am a detective inspector."

## CHAPTER SIXTY FIVE

"Did I just hear right?" Bridge said. "Did we just receive an order telling us to have a few days off in the middle of a murder investigation?"

"She's got a point though," Yang Chu said. "Our brains are fried. Maybe a few days without having to think about all of this will help. She's the shrink - she seems to know what she's talking about."

"I disagree," Smith said. "I know from experience that my brain works best when it's overloaded. I'm beginning to think she has some kind of ulterior motive."

"Ulterior motive?" Bridge said. "What are you talking about?"

"I don't know. Ever since she's been here she seems intent on distracting us."

"What are you saying?" Bridge said. "Are you suggesting that she's actually our psycho and she's trying to stop us from getting closer to her?"

"Maybe," Smith rubbed his temples. "I don't know. I'm certainly not going to sit on my arse and forget about this investigation for a few days. I can't just switch my brain off like that."

"Well I can," Bridge stood up.

He had a wry smile on his face.

"I'm off to make a certain woman very happy," he added.

"Who is this woman?" Smith said. "I'm starting to think she doesn't even exist - you're making the whole thing up."

"Oh she's very real," Bridge winked at Smith. "Very real indeed."

He swaggered off out of the canteen.

"I'll help you if you want me to," Yang Chu said to Smith. "If you need any help I'm here."

"No, go home. Do what the DI said. I'll see you here on Friday."
Yang Chu looked at Whitton. She was gazing absentmindedly out of the window. The blizzard was still in full force outside.
"See you on Friday," he said and left the canteen.
"I'm sorry," Smith said to Whitton. "You were right. I never should have gone for a drink with Blakemore. Nothing happened, I promise."
"I know," Whitton said. "You have your faults, but dishonesty isn't one of them."
"Theakston says thank you for the donuts. The fat bugger ate the whole lot."
Whitton couldn't help but smile.
"I'm glad they didn't go to waste," she said.
"Are we alright then?"
"I don't know. My head's in a real mess at the moment. I need time to think. This whole business is starting to suffocate me."
"Phone me if you feel like company."
Whitton nodded, took a last look out of the window and walked slowly out of the canteen.

Smith sat by himself for a while. He could hear the wind whistling outside the window. He didn't know what he was going to do. He couldn't just sit back and do nothing while a woman was still a large waiting to plan her next murder.
Ten days, he thought, ten days can go by in the blink of an eye.
He stood up, left the canteen and walked down the corridor towards his office. He turned on the computer and opened up his Facebook page. He typed in 'Jessica Blakemore' on the search bar and fifteen matches appeared on the screen.
"This is crazy," he said out loud. "I'm being paranoid now."

Jessica Blakemore isn't our killer, he thought, the whole idea is preposterous.

He turned off the computer and left his office. He walked through to the front desk. Baldwin was there as usual.

"Where is everybody?" Baldwin said. "The place is deserted. I don't like it."

"Me neither. Blakemore told us all to go home for a few days."

"We're going to be snowed in again. At least it's sent those morons with their placards back indoors. Don't you ever wish you'd stayed in Australia?"

"Not really," Smith said.

He suddenly remembered his smashed windscreen.

"Baldwin, do you have any tape? Something I can use to tape up my windscreen until I get it fixed properly?"

"Duct tape," Baldwin opened her desk and produced a roll of white duct tape. "This stuff can fix anything."

She handed the tape to Smith.

"Thanks Baldwin, I'll replace it."

"No, you won't," Baldwin said.

Smith smiled and walked out into the snow storm.

A thick blanket of snow had settled on the car park when Smith got outside. He ran to his car and groaned. It looked like a disaster area. He had parked into the wind and the hole in the windscreen had let in so much snow he had to spend ten minutes scooping it out with his hands before he could start taping up the windscreen. He took out the tape and covered the hole as best he could. By the time he was finished, his hands were numb with the cold.

I can't drive the car like this, he thought.

He ran back inside the station.

"Baldwin," he said. "Can you do me a huge favour?"

Baldwin sighed.

"Go on," she said.

"Could you arrange for my car to be towed away to the nearest garage? Those fascist idiots threw a brick through my windscreen and I don't think it's safe to drive in this weather. I think my insurance is still up to date. I've got my details here somewhere."

He started to rummage around in his pockets.

"Don't worry, I still have them from the last time. I'll get to go home one of these days."

"Thanks, Baldwin," Smith said. "I owe you one."

Whitton appeared from the corridor. She seemed shocked to see Smith still at the station.

"I thought you'd gone home," Smith said.

"I had to send a few emails."

"Could you give me a lift home?"

"What's wrong with your car?"

"It's a long story," Smith said.

Whitton parked her car outside Smith's house. She left the engine running.

"Are you sure you won't come in?" Smith said.

"Not at the moment."

"Phone me," Smith opened the door and got out.

He watched as Whitton drove off through the blizzard. He ran inside his house and closed the door behind him. He walked through to the kitchen and slumped down on one of the chairs. His clothes were soaked through, but he didn't care. He looked at the advert for the guitar on the fridge.

What the hell, he thought.

He took out his phone and dialled the number on the advert. A woman answered after three rings.

"Hello," Smith said. "I'm phoning about the ad for the guitar. The eighty two Gold Top. Is it still available?"

"It is."

Smith thought hard for a moment.

"Are you still there?" The woman asked.

"Yes, I'm still here. How long have you had the guitar?"

"It was my husbands. He bought it straight out of the box in eighty two."

"Could I speak to your husband? I just want to ask him a few questions."

"He died last year," the woman said. "I need the money. I can't see the point of keeping it. Nobody is going to play it anymore. The price is negotiable."

"I'll take it, and I'll pay the full price. If you could just give me your details and I'll do a transfer and arrange delivery."

The line went silent for a few seconds.

"Are you being serious?" The woman said eventually.

"I want that guitar."

Twenty minutes later the deal was completed. Smith had transferred the money and the guitar was due to be delivered the next day. He sat staring at the photograph on the fridge. Theakston ambled into the kitchen and collapsed on Smith's feet.

"I'm just done something impulsive," Smith said.

Theakston was already snoring.

"I've just spent two months' salary on a guitar."

## CHAPTER SIXTY SIX

### Wednesday 9 February 2011

The guitar arrived the next day just before noon. Smith signed the delivery slip and took the guitar inside. He felt like a child with a new toy. He opened up the case and gasped. The guitar was in immaculate condition. There wasn't a scratch on it. He picked it up and started to play. It was even in tune. The tone was exactly what he had been looking for. He realized he didn't have an amplifier to play it through – he'd forgotten to buy one. He carried on playing.
I need to buy an amp, he thought.
He looked around for his car keys and remembered that his car was in for repairs. He picked up his phone and dialled Bridge's number. It went straight to voice mail. He thought about phoning Whitton but decided against it. He phoned Yang Chu. Yang Chu answered almost straight away.
"Yang Chu," Smith said. "Remember you said you'd help me?"
"Any time, Sarge," Yang Chu said.
"I need a lift into town - my car's in the garage and I've just bought the most amazing instrument and I have no amp to play it through."
"You need a lift to the music shop?"
"It's an emergency."

Yang Chu was outside Smith's house in less than twenty minutes. Smith locked up and climbed in the passenger seat.
"I really appreciate this," he said.
"I was bored at home anyway," Yang Chu set off in the direction of the city centre.

He parked in the short stay car park around the corner from the Minster.

"At least it's stopped snowing," Yang Chu got out of the car. "I'm sick of all this snow."

Smith closed the car door and took a deep breath. The air was crisp and cold. They set off in the direction of the music shop. They passed the McDonalds and were about to carry on when Yang Chu spotted something.

"Hold on," he said, "that's Bridge."

He pointed inside the McDonalds. Bridge was sitting at one of the tables eating a hamburger. A young girl was sitting opposite him. They appeared to be deep in conversation.

"Who's he with?" Smith took a closer look.

"Some kid," Yang Chu said.

"He mentioned something about his new girlfriend having a kid," Smith said.

"Shall we go in and say hello?"

"Why not? Let's go and wind him up a bit."

They went inside the McDonalds and walked up to where Bridge was sitting. Bridge looked up at them and frowned. He was obviously not very pleased to see them.

"Afternoon, Bridge," Smith said. "I never would have pictured you as a fan of McDonalds."

"Afternoon, Sarge," Bridge said. "I'm not. I'm just keeping this little lady company while her mother does a bit of shopping."

"Hello there, "Smith said to the young girl. "I hope Bridge isn't boring you too much."

The girl seemed vaguely familiar.

"He's not in the least bit boring," she said in a tone that surprised Smith.

She sounded much older than she looked.

"Are you going to join us?" She asked.

"No, we just came in to say hello. Wouldn't you rather be shopping than sitting here with an old man?"

"No," she said. "I abhor shopping."

"OK," Smith said. "Goodbye..."

He looked her in the eyes.

"Maggie," she said. "My name's Maggie. Goodbye."

"You know who that was don't you?" Yang Chu said outside the McDonalds.

"Who?"

"The little girl, that's the daughter of the guy who was killed on Christmas Day."

"I thought I recognised her. No wonder Bridge wanted to keep it a secret - he's shacked up with the widow."

"Ex widow," Yang Chu said. "If there is such a thing. She was divorced from Christopher Riley when he died."

"What on earth is Bridge playing at? She has to be at least ten years older than him."

"Maybe he likes that sort of thing."

"It's not right, cosying up to a grieving widow. It's not exactly ethical is it?"

"If I remember right, the mother is quite a looker."

"It's still not right."

They went inside the music shop and Smith studied the guitar amplifiers they had on display. One of them caught his eye immediately. It was an Orange micro twenty amp valve amp.

"Can I help you?" A tall skinny youth with long greasy hair in a ponytail asked.

"I've just got a new guitar," Smith said. "And I need an amp. I was thinking about the Orange."

"What guitar have you got?"

"A Les Paul gold top," Smith said. "Eighty two model."

"The Epiphone one?"

"Gibson," Smith said.

"Bloody hell, do you know what that thing's worth?"

"I have a vague idea," Smith said. "I'll take the Orange."

By the time Smith reached Yang Chu's car he was exhausted. The amplifier wasn't particularly heavy, but it was awkward to carry, and Smith wasn't in the best physical shape.

"I need to get more exercise," he puffed and put the amplifier in the boot of the car. "I used to be quite fit, believe it or not."

"You should try Yoga," Yang Chu suggested.

"I'm not that old yet."

Yang Chu dropped Smith off at home and Smith took the amplifier out of the boot.

"Thanks a lot," Smith said. "Do you want to come in for a beer?"

"No chance. Remember what happened last time? I'll see you on Friday."

Smith watched as he drove away. He went inside the house and headed straight for the living room. He plugged in the guitar, switched on the amp and started to play. The combination of the Orange amplifier and the Les Paul sounded amazing. The tone was perfect - it was the tone he had been waiting years for.

Two hours later, Smith's fingertips were numb. He hadn't played for such a long time that his fingers were much more sensitive than they used to be. He put the guitar back in its case and turned on the television. An advert for McDonalds was playing. Smith walked through to the kitchen and took a beer out of the fridge. He went back to the living room. The news was about to begin. Smith thought about turning the television off but decided to see what was going on in the world. The main news item centered on the immigration issue. A so-called expert on twentieth century mass migration was droning on about the issues causing problems.

"Here we go again," Smith said.

He took a long swig of the beer. The pompous expert was informing the presenter that the main problem these days was not the volume of immigrants streaming into the country to seek better lives for themselves but the alarming number of so called stateless citizens. Thousands of people were flocking in with no papers to indicate where they came from and due to the neo-socialist policies in place, the British government were obliged to offer these stateless citizens some kind of asylum.

At the twentieth mention of stateless citizens, Smith turned off the television and sighed.

That's why I don't watch the news, he thought, nothing but doom and gloom.

He selected a Guthrie Govan DVD, inserted it into the machine and turned up the volume. He fetched another beer from the fridge and sat back to listen to the virtuoso guitar skills of a man who looked like he lived on the streets. Theakston jumped up on the sofa and started to sniff at something on the upholstery. He began scratching frantically.

"What's up, boy?" Smith said.

The dog carried on scratching at the sofa.

"What's got into you?" Smith moved him out of the way.

He wanted to see what the dog was going so crazy about. He lifted the cushion and found what Theakston had been looking for. An elaborate watch had somehow managed to fall down behind the cushion. Smith picked it up and examined it. The screen was scratched but Smith could still make out a mother of pearl moon on the dial. Smaller moons formed an outline on the dial. They appeared to be showing the different phases of the moon throughout the month. A long black hair had been caught in the clasp on the strap.

## CHAPTER SIXTY SEVEN

***Friday 11 February 2011***

The mood in the station seemed somewhat brighter than it had done a few days earlier. Smith and Yang Chu walked up to the front desk. Baldwin was talking on the telephone. She smiled at Smith. Superintendent Smyth appeared, and Smith shook his head.
"Morning," Smyth said cheerfully and walked out of the door.
Smith was relieved.
Maybe he's forgotten all about the top cop award, he thought.
They headed for the canteen and went inside. Whitton and Bridge were sharing a joke at the coffee machine.
"You two are in a good mood," Smith said.
Whitton looked at him and smiled.
"I hate to admit it," she said. "But Blakemore seems to have been right. A few days away from this place is just what the doctor ordered."
"I've bought a new guitar," Smith said.
Whitton shook her head.
"I suppose it's back to reality now," Bridge said.
"How was the McDonalds?" Smith said. "You didn't think you'd be able to keep it a secret forever, did you?"
"I like her," Bridge insisted. "I like her a lot and I like the kid. There's no law against that is there?"
"Ethics, it all boils down to ethics."
DI Brownhill walked in the canteen. She had a very grave expression on her face.
"Something wrong, boss?" Smith said.

"We have a situation," Brownhill said. "My office all of you."

Brownhill closed the door to her office and sat down behind her desk.

"What's going on?" Smith said.

"Jessica Blakemore has disappeared again," Brownhill said.

"Again?"

"I didn't mention it before, I didn't think it was relevant, but you may as well know that Jessica suffers from bipolar."

"Bipolar?" Bridge said. "You're kidding me? Are you saying our shrink is crazy herself?"

"She's not crazy, and if she takes her medication she's able to live a perfectly normal life. Her husband contacted me yesterday evening. He hasn't seen or heard from her since Tuesday. Her phone is switched off."

"Sorry," Smith said. "But what's this got to do with us?"

"I'm coming to that. This isn't the first time this has happened. Jessica seems to go AWOL on a regular basis. She always comes back but her husband told me something very interesting. He's a very practical man and he started to keep a sort of diary to try and find out if something triggers these outbursts of hers."

Brownhill took a piece of paper from her desk drawer.

"Jessica went missing two days before Christmas. She reappeared a few days before New Year. She disappeared again in the middle of January and once more at the beginning of this month."

"I still don't see what it's got to do with us," Smith said.

"It has everything to do with us," Brownhill was getting angry. "The times Jessica went missing all coincide with the dates the three murders were committed."

The room fell silent.

"You've got to be joking," Smith said eventually. "Do you seriously believe Jessica Blakemore is Selene Lupei?"

"I don't want to believe it, but everything is starting to add up. Every time we thought we were getting closer Jessica suddenly suggested we change tack for no reason whatsoever."

"I thought you'd used her in the past," Yang Chu said.

"I did, and she provided results but I'm afraid we can't afford to ignore this. Too much points in her direction. The dates she went missing, the constant changing of our paths of investigation, not to mention the scratch on her face."

"She told me she did that to herself," Smith said.

"She told her husband that my cat scratched her," Brownhill said. "I don't have a cat. Grant found traces of skin under Luka Gravov's fingernails. The next day Jessica appeared with a nasty scratch on her face."

"I think she left a watch at my house," Smith said. "She must have dropped it when she slept on my sofa. The watch shows the phases of the moon. It tells you when the full moon will come out."

"We have to find her," Brownhill said. "That is our main priority at the moment."

"I knew there was something not right about that woman," Whitton said.

"I still don't get it," Smith said. "You brought her in to help - it was your idea wasn't it?"

"That's not quite true," Brownhill stood up and looked out the window. There was not a cloud in the sky.

"We'd kept in touch. We used to talk on the phone sometimes. She phoned me one evening and we got talking about this investigation. She offered help if I needed it."

"This just gets better and better," Smith said. "The press are going to love it. Serial killer shrink helps police in the investigation."

"This must never get out. We bring her in and see what she has to say. For all we know, this might just be a coincidence - she may be totally innocent."

"This is brilliant," Yang Chu said. "No wonder we couldn't catch her. She was with us all the time - watching our every move. She knew exactly what we knew and every time we got a bit closer she would nudge us in another direction. She was probably laughing at us the whole time."

"We've got a week," Smith said. "That is, if she really is the psycho full moon killer. One week. We should be able to find her in a week."

"Where's her husband now?" Bridge said. "We should speak with him."

"He's on his way," Brownhill said. "He should be here any time now."

"I still don't believe it," Smith said. "Something's not right."

"Look at the evidence," Whitton said. "It all points to her. It all makes sense now."

"Let's wait and see what her husband has to say."

## CHAPTER SIXTY EIGHT

Ian Blakemore sat on a chair in the tiny interview room. Smith and Yang Chu were sitting opposite him. Ian looked exhausted. He was very pale with sunken eyes. He'd obviously not had a shave for a few days.

"Ian," Smith said. "It is very important that we find your wife. Do you have any idea where she might be?"

"If I knew that I wouldn't be sitting here talking to you, would I?"

"What about friends?" Smith said. "Family?"

"I've spoken to everybody Jessica knows, nobody's heard from her."

"Let's start at the beginning. When did Jessica's strange behaviour start?"

"She was diagnosed with bipolar a few years ago. It was pure hell at the beginning but when they figured out the correct medication she was my Jessica again."

"What happens when she doesn't take her pills?"

"It depends," Ian started to shake. "One time is never the same as another. She can be depressed one second and high as a kite the other. Then she can freak out altogether. Once, I came home and she was trying to set fire to the curtains. I caught her just in time. That's the scary part, you can never tell which way she'll go."

"You told the DI that Jessica disappeared around Christmas time?" Smith said.

"She was supposed to spend Christmas with my family in London, but she just vanished. It was the most stressful Christmas ever. Then, just before New Year she turned up again. She acted like nothing had happened. The same thing happened in the middle of January and then again at the start of this month."

"I have to ask you this," Smith said. "Do you believe your wife killed those three men?"

"I don't know. It sounds terrible. She's my wife but you haven't seen her at her worst. Anything's possible. I don't know what to think - it's like she turns into somebody else when she doesn't take her medication."

"We'll find her. I don't think she's gone too far."

"What will you do to her?"

"We'll bring her in for questioning, and if she's innocent we'll know. Don't worry. She's going to be alright. How long have you been married?"

"Seven years," Ian said. "We met at University in Leeds."

"What about her family? What do you know about her family?"

"She didn't talk much about her childhood, and I didn't pry. She obviously had her reasons. From what I gathered, her parents are both dead and she has no brothers or sisters."

"So, you know nothing about where she grew up?"

"Nothing. I don't know how to handle this. After seven years of marriage it's hard to accept that my wife is some kind of monster."

"We don't know that yet," Smith said. "We'll do everything we can to try and find her."

"What do you want me to do now?"

"Nothing," Smith said. "Go home and try to stay calm. If she gets in touch with you call us straight away."

Smith opened the door to his office and sat down behind the desk. He was still finding it hard to believe that the woman who had helped them on the murder investigation was now their number one suspect. He picked up the phone and dialled Grant Webber's number."

"Webber," Webber sounded very irritated.

"Have you had a chance to look at the watch yet?" Smith said.

"I don't know what you think I am. I'm not some kind of miracle worker. What did you expect me to find on an old watch?"

"What about the black hair? There was a long black hair stuck to the clasp. Did you compare it with the other hair samples?"

"There was no hair," Webber said.

"Are you sure?"

"I'm not stupid. There was no hair. All I received was a watch in a plastic bag. No hair."

"Crap," Smith said.

He hung up.

The hair must have fallen out somewhere, he thought.

Smith switched on his computer and brought up the photograph of Selene Lupei when she was a young girl. He zoomed in and studied her face. Her eyes were striking. They seemed to stare straight through him. Smith had to admit that the girl in the photograph did bear a slight resemblance to Jessica Blakemore. He turned off the computer and left the office. He needed some advice. He walked down the corridor and knocked on Chalmers' door.

"What?" Chalmers shouted in a gruff voice.

He was obviously in a foul mood.

Smith opened the door and went inside. The office smelled vaguely of cigarette smoke.

"Can I have a word, boss?"

"Make it quick, I've got a report to finish for old simple Smyth. The man's driving me mad. I've been thinking up ways to get myself demoted."

"I could give you a few tips," Smith said. "I need some advice."

"Sit down."

Smith sat down opposite him.

"Out with it then," Chalmers said.

"It's this Jessica Blakemore thing."

"The shrink?" Chalmers said. "Have you found her yet?"

"No."

"You don't think she did it do you? I've seen that look on your face before. You're having doubts."

"All the evidence points to her - the days she disappeared, the scratch on her face."

"But."

"But no, I don't think she's our killer. I think all the other stuff is just coincidence."

"There's no such thing as coincidence. You should know that by now. You said you wanted some advice? Go out there and find her. Only then will you get some answers and you can stop this namby pamby pontification."

"Thanks, boss," Smith said.

"If that's all, can I get back to this bloody report?"

"What's the report about?"

"Immigration matters. What else?"

## CHAPTER SIXTY NINE

### Monday 14 February 2011

After two days of frantic searching for Jessica Blakemore, Baldwin was more surprised than anyone to find herself face to face with the suspected serial killer early in the morning of Valentine's Day. Blakemore was very pale, and she seemed extremely agitated.
"I need to talk with DS Smith," she said.
Baldwin didn't know what to do. Half of the York Police Department had spent the whole weekend looking for the woman in front of her. She picked up the phone and dialled Smith's number.
"Smith," Smith answered.
"Sir," Baldwin said. "I need you at the front desk right now."
"Give me ten minutes. I've just got a few emails to finish off."
"I need you here now, sir."
She realised her voice sounded very shaky.
"This had better be important," Smith said and rang off.
　　When Smith saw Jessica Blakemore standing by the front desk he thought he was seeing things at first. Baldwin looked absolutely terrified.
"Jessica," Smith said. "Where have you been? We've been worried about you."
"I needed time to think things over, but I'm ready to tell you everything."
"What do you want to tell me?"
"Everything," Blakemore smiled.
The smile sent a shiver down Smith's spine.
"I want to confess," she added.

"Baldwin, I want you to inform everybody of the situation. We'll be in interview room four."

"Follow me," he said to Blakemore.

Smith led Jessica Blakemore through to the interview room. He opened the door.

"Take a seat," he said. "Would you like something to drink?"

Blakemore didn't reply. She sat down and stared at the wall. She had a vacant expression on her face.

"Jessica," Smith said. "We're just going to have an informal chat."

He sat down opposite her. The expression in her eyes was starting to unnerve him.

"Have you been taking your medication?"

"I stopped taking it. I don't need it. It makes me forgetful."

"What do you want to tell me?"

The door opened, and Brownhill entered the room.

"Jessica," she said. "Are you alright?"

Blakemore looked at her and her facial expression changed completely. Smith could see hatred in her eyes.

"Get out," she screamed.

"Jessica," Brownhill said.

"Get out," Blakemore screamed again. "Get out, get out, get out."

She started to pull at her own hair. She threw large clumps of it onto the floor."

"Get out," she cried.

Smith nodded at Brownhill and Brownhill turned around and left the room.

"OK, Jessica," Smith said. "It's just you and me. What do you want to tell me?"

"I can't take it anymore," Blakemore said in a much calmer voice. "I want it to all go away."

"What do you want to go away?"

"The numbness. I can't stand it anymore. My whole body feels numb. I killed them all. Did you know that if you stare at the moon for long enough, you see faces eventually?"

"Why did you kill those men?"

"You know why, I had no choice. The faces in the moon are different each time you know."

Smith didn't know what to say. He remembered something he had practiced over the weekend.

"Selene," he said. "Selene Lupei. Unde te-ai nascut?"

Blakemore looked at him with interest. There was a sparkle in her eyes and she smiled.

"Am fost nascut in Borsa desigor," she said.

Smith's heart sank. He had asked her where she was born, and she had replied in fluent Romanian that she was born in Borsa. There could be no doubt - Jessica Blakemore was Selene Lupei. Smith had found his serial killer.

## CHAPTER SEVENTY

Jessica Blakemore confessed to the murders of Christopher Riley, Arnold Mather and Luka Gravov. She described the killings in such detail that there was no reason to doubt her word. She claimed that she couldn't carry on any more and she was ready to face the consequences of her actions before the next full moon. When questioned about the unusual knife, Blakemore said she had thrown it in the river - she had discarded it once and for all. After the confession, Blakemore seemed to have cocooned herself in her own little world and she hadn't uttered a word since. She'd been taken away to a secure mental facility where she was under twenty four hour suicide watch.

Smith sat opposite Whitton in the canteen. Bridge and Yang Chu walked in and sat down. Nobody seemed to know what to say. Bridge sighed.
"I can't believe it's all over," he said. "I thought it would never be over."
"I still don't get it," Smith said. "We worked with the woman day in and day out."
"I can't believe we didn't notice something," Yang Chu said.
"She's a psychopath," Whitton joined in. "Her brain is not right."
"What do you think will happen to her?" Yang Chu said.
"She'll probably end up in a nut house," Bridge said. "She's a first class whacko."
"We should be celebrating," Yang Chu said. "We've just put an end to the most frustrating case in history."
"Does anybody really feel like celebrating?" Smith said, "I certainly don't."

"It's Valentine's Day," Bridge said. "I'm certainly not going to let all this put a downer on my plans. I've got a hot date lined up."

"It's my birthday today," Smith said. "One more year and I'll be thirty."

"That's old," Yang Chu said.

"Happy birthday," Whitton said. "I didn't know it was your birthday. Do you want to do something later?"

"Like a date?" Smith smiled at her.

"Maybe."

"Sounds good, I feel like a steak and ale pie and a few gallons of Theakstons."

"I'll pick you up at seven then. When's your car going to be fixed?'

"Wednesday. It'll be good to have the old banger back again."

DI Brownhill walked into the canteen with Chalmers. Brownhill looked very tired.

"Before you all head off for the day," she said. "We need to talk about damage control. What happened during this investigation stays between these four walls. Is that clear?"

"I agree," Smith said. "If the press gets wind of what happened, they'll eat us alive."

"I've got a birthday present for you," Chalmers handed Smith a small box.

"You shouldn't have," Smith said.

He opened the box. Inside was a small plaque. The words, 'DS Jason Smith. For outstanding commitment to the job 2010' were written in italics on the wood.

"I thought I'd save you the embarrassment of a ceremony. Smyth took a bit of convincing though. You owe me one."

"Top cop of 2010," Bridge said. "I think we should sing for he's a jolly good fellow."

"You'll do no such thing," Smith said.

He stood up.

"I'll see you at seven," he said to Whitton. "I'll see the rest of you on Friday. I've got three days off. If I don't take it, I'll lose it."

He walked out of the canteen.

"He seems a bit down," Yang Chu said. "It's his birthday as well."

"This investigation has left a bitter taste in all our mouths," Brownhill said. "Jessica was a friend. I for one certainly won't be celebrating this one."

"Can I give you a bit of advice?" Chalmers said. "Put it behind you. I'm afraid you're going to come across worse ones than this in the future - that's just the way it is."

## CHAPTER SEVENTY ONE

*Friday 18 February 2011*

Smith woke up to the telephone ringing on his bedside table. He rubbed his eyes. It wasn't quite light yet, but the sun was starting to rise. He realised that the ring tone on his phone was not his usual one.
"I'm still dreaming," he said.
He thought about what Jessica Blakemore had told him about controlling his dreams.
Here goes, he thought.
He got out of bed and opened the curtains. The sun and the moon were both out together. Smith closed his eyes and ran at the window. He crashed through the glass and felt a sharp pain in his arm. A shard of glass had sliced open his shoulder. He felt himself falling and landed on the pavement with a dull thud.
"Jesus Christ," Smith woke up in bed.
I need to practice that a bit more, he thought.
His phone was ringing on the table next to the bed. It was his usual ringtone. He picked it up and looked at the screen. It was Webber.
"Webber," Smith said. "Don't you ever sleep? It's still the middle of the night."
"I've got some bad news."
"Great," Smith said. "I was planning on being in a good mood today."
"I found the hair - the hair that was on the watch strap. One of my technicians decided to bag it separately and didn't have the common sense to tell me."
"Why's that bad news?"
"If it's Jessica Blakemore's hair it's bad news."

"What are you talking about?"

"I compared it to the other hair samples," Webber said. "The ones from the murder scenes and the owner of this hair is not the same woman who killed those three men."

"Are you sure?" Smith could hear his heart beating in his ears.

"Positive. And it gets worse. I wanted to make absolutely sure, so I compared the fingerprints from the last crime scene with the ones we took from Jessica Blakemore."

"They don't match, do they?"

"Nope," Webber said. "Looks like we've locked up the wrong woman."

"But she confessed," Smith said.

"I'm just giving you the facts. Enjoy the rest of your day."

He rang off.

Smith couldn't believe what Webber had told him. Jessica Blakemore had confessed to three murders she didn't commit.

Why would she do that? He thought.

He got dressed and went downstairs to make some coffee. While he was waiting for the kettle to boil he went outside and smoked a cigarette. He phoned Whitton.

"Morning," Whitton sounded wide awake.

Smith told her what Webber had said.

"You've got to be kidding?" Whitton said. "Why did she confess then?"

"I have no idea. I should have known. There was something gnawing away at me in the back of my mind - there was something just not quite right about the whole thing."

"What do we do now?"

"We go back to square one. The full moon will be out tonight. If Jessica Blakemore isn't Selene Lupei someone is going to be killed tonight."

"I'll see you at the station in half an hour," Whitton said.

"This isn't good at all," Brownhill said.

Smith, Whitton and Yang Chu sat in her office. Bridge had a day off and he had turned his mobile phone off.

"Jessica Blakemore is lying in a hospital bed drugged up to the eyeballs," Brownhill said. "She's been charged with three murders she had no hand in."

"Why did she confess?" Yang Chu said.

"I don't know. Her state of mind is not exactly stable. I think she's suffered some kind of serious breakdown. What I do know is there's a killer still out there and it's highly likely she's going to kill again tonight."

"Where's Bridge?" Whitton said.

"His phone is off," Brownhill said. "I can't get hold of him."

"How the hell are we going to find this woman?" Smith said. "We have until tonight. We've been working on this for months and we still have no idea where to look."

"Go through the immigration files again," Brownhill said. "There must be something we've overlooked."

"We found nothing in there," Smith said.

"It's all we've got to go on," Brownhill said much louder than she intended. "A man is going to die tonight unless we find this woman."

Smith opened up the familiar list of names again. They were running out of time. He went through all the names of the women who had arrived from Romania in ninety one and ninety two and reaped the same results.

She's not here, he thought, this is a complete waste of time.

He left his office and went to the canteen to get some coffee. He took the coffee outside and lit a cigarette.

This is pointless, he thought.

He took a long drag of the cigarette and exhaled a cloud of smoke.

Think, he thought, what haven't I thought of?

He'd gone through every single Romanian woman who had arrived in the UK in the two years in question and he had not managed to find anything.

Romanian, he thought, Romanian immigrants.

A thought suddenly occurred to him. He remembered something he had watched on the television recently - a droning voice lecturing him about the status of immigrants. He threw the cigarette butt into the distance and went back to his office. He picked up the phone.

"Whitton," he said. "Find anything yet?"

"Nothing," Whitton sounded dejected. "What about you?"

"I've come up with an idea. Forget about looking for Romanians."

"What are you thinking about?"

"Stateless citizens. I don't know why I didn't think of it before. I don't think Selene Lupei entered the country as a Romanian citizen. I don't believe she possessed a passport. She came in as a stateless citizen. We need to check every person of unknown origin who entered the country in ninety one and ninety two. Tell Yang Chu to get onto it too."

He rang off.

    Smith's heart was beating fast and his fingers were fumbling on the keyboard.

We're getting closer, he thought, I can feel it.

His optimism soon faded when he realised how many people of unknown origin had entered the UK in ninety one and ninety two. There were six hundred and eighty five of them. Of those, three hundred and ten were women and eighteen were of the age Selene

Lupei would have been in those years. He emailed the list to Whitton and Yang Chu, instructing them to take six names each.

Four hours later, having eliminated all but six of the names on the list, they met in the canteen for a break.

"It would have been easier if Bridge was here," Whitton said. "I can't believe he's switched his phone off."

"He's with that old woman of his," Yang Chu said.

"We'll keep going," Smith said. "Bridge doesn't even know what's going on. He'd be here if he knew."

He returned to his office and continued with the list. Half an hour later he was left with one more name. Emilia Lopez.

"Here goes," he said.

Emilia Lopez came into the country in October nineteen ninety one. She arrived in Dover with no passport or any other documents to indicate where she'd come from. She'd been taken in as an asylum seeker and spent the first six months in an immigration centre. After that, there was no further information about her.

"Damn it," Smith said.

He didn't know where else to look. He noticed that there was a telephone number on the screen - a number for general information. He picked up the telephone and dialled the number. He listened as an automated voice gave him a number of options. He pressed seven to speak with an operative.

"Immigration," a woman with a deep voice answered.

"Goof afternoon, Smith said. "My name is Detective Sergeant Jason Smith. I'm trying to find out some information about a woman who came into the country almost twenty years ago."

"We're not at liberty to give out that kind of information to just anybody," the woman said.

"I'm not just anybody, my name is DS Smith, and this is extremely important."

"I'm sorry, sir, but how do I even know you are who you claim to be?"

"Phone this number."

Smith gave her the number for the central switchboard.

"Ask to be put through to DS Smith," he said. "This is a matter of life and death."

Smith looked at the clock on the wall. It was half past two. In a couple of hours' time, the sun would go down and the moon would appear. The telephone on his desk started to ring.

"Smith," he said.

"DS Smith," the monotone of the immigration operative said. "What do you need to know?"

"A woman entered the UK in October nineteen ninety one. Her name is Emilia Lopez. I need all the information you have on her. Where she ended up. Everything. Do you think you can manage that?"

"Give me your email address, and I'll look into it for you. It should only take a couple of days."

"I don't have a couple of days. I have a couple of hours. A man is going to die unless I get this information now."

The line went quiet. Smith realised he had gone a bit far with his little outburst.

"I'm sorry," he said. "Please can you send me the information straight away?"

"I'll see what I can do," the woman said and hung up.

Smith spent the next half an hour staring at the screen of his computer. He'd opened up his emails and was waiting for the information on Emilia Lopez. No new emails had arrived. He picked up the phone and was about to phone the immigration department again when a familiar beep told him he had received an email. He clicked on it. It was from the woman he had spoken to on the phone. There was a file attachment with the email. Smith opened it up and a detailed file filled the screen. There was a photograph of a young girl. It was black and white and slightly out of focus but when Smith looked closely, there was no doubt about it - he had found Selene Lupei.

## CHAPTER SEVENTY TWO

Whitton, Yang Chu and Smith were sat round Smith's desk. They were looking at the computer screen.

"That's her," Yang Chu said. "That's the same girl as the one in the photograph Luka Gravov sent you."

"Emilia Lopez," Smith said. "She came here in October ninety one. She arrived at Dover and spent the next six months in a centre for asylum seekers."

He scrolled down the page.

"It says she was placed in foster care, and then lived with a family in Southampton for a while. Mr and Mrs Higgins. Martin and Lisa."

After that there was no further information. Smith looked at the clock. It was almost three. He picked up the phone and dialled the number for the front desk.

"Baldwin," he said. "I need you to find the numbers for every Martin Higgins in Southampton."

"You don't ask for much, do you?"

"I need the numbers two hours ago."

Ten minutes later, Smith was talking to the third Martin Higgins in Southampton.

"Mr Higgins," he said. "My name is DS Smith. Do you know a woman by the name of Emilia Lopez?"

"Emily?" Higgins said. "Of course. Lisa and I took her in about twenty years ago. What's this all about?"

"I'm trying to find her. It's important that I speak to her. Do you know where she is now?"

"We lost touch. We looked after her for just over a year, but she went her own way when she turned eighteen. What's this all about?"

"Do you have any idea where she went after she left you?"

"Emily was a wild one," Higgins said with a hint of pride in his voice. "But I believe she settled down eventually. Last I heard was she met this IT geek and got married. Hold on a minute."

Smith could hear he had put down the phone and voices were heard in the background.

"Riley," Higgins said eventually. "That was his name. We only met him once. The wife has a much better memory than me. Emily married a man called Christopher Riley."

Smith held the phone to his ear long after he had finished talking to Martin Higgins.

"Emily Riley is Selene Lupei," he said. "The first man she killed was her ex-husband."

"Bridge is with her now," Yang Chu said.

"And the sun is already starting to set," Whitton added.

Smith was out of his office and down the corridor in seconds. He barged into Brownhill's office.

"We've got her," he said. "Selene Lupei is Emily Riley."

"The ex-wife of the first victim?" Brownhill said. "Are you sure?"

"Positive, I've just spoken with the man who looked after her shortly after she arrived in the country. Bridge is with her now."

"What the hell is Bridge doing with her?"

"He's been seeing her for a while. I'm going over there right now."

"You'll do no such thing," Brownhill said. "Have you tried phoning Bridge?"

"His phone is still switched off. He's in danger. We have to get there now. I think Bridge is going to be the next one."

"You'll wait for back up. This woman is extremely dangerous. I want armed officers on the scene first."

"There's no time," Smith ran out of the office and headed for the door.

Smith drove as fast as he could through the rush hour traffic. The sun had already set, and the evening half-light was descending. The moon hadn't yet come out. He parked outside Emily Riley's house and turned off the engine. There was a light on inside the house. Smith knew he should wait for back up to arrive, but he also knew that Bridge was in grave danger. He got out of the car and slowly approached the house. The curtains were drawn so he couldn't see what was going on inside. He thought hard about what he was going to do. He didn't know if Emily Riley was inside or not. He tried the door handle. The door was open. He carefully opened it and looked inside. He could hear a strange noise coming from within. It sounded like somebody was counting slowly. It was a child's voice. Smith went inside and walked up the stairs. He stopped outside what appeared to be the main bedroom. He pushed the door open and looked inside. There was nobody inside the room. He was about to look somewhere else when he spotted something by the side of the bed. He moved closer to get a better look. Bridge was lying face down on the carpet.

## CHAPTER SEVENTY THREE

"Bridge," Smith said.

Bridge sat up and looked at Smith in utter disbelief. A young girl appeared in the doorway.

"What are you doing here, Sarge?" Bridge said.

"What are you doing?" Smith said. "Why were you lying on the carpet?"

"We're playing hide and seek," the girl said. "Do you want to play?"

"Not at the moment," Smith said.

Bridge stood up.

"What's going on, Sarge?" He said.

"Where's Emily?"

"She had to work. She's at the hospital. She'll be home later."

"Can I have a word in private?"

"Maggie," Bridge said. "It's your turn to hide. Don't make it too hard though - I'm not very good at this."

Maggie turned around and ran down the stairs.

"Emily Riley is Selene Lupei," Smith said.

"No, she isn't," Bridge said. "I thought Jessica Blakemore was."

Smith told Bridge everything.

When he had finished, Bridge sat on the bed with his head in his hands.

"Are you absolutely sure?" He said.

"I'm afraid so. I thought you were going to be the next one."

"This is too much to take in," Bridge said. "Emily is so kind. I was really getting to like her. What about Maggie? What's going to happen to Maggie? I can't believe all of this."

"We need to find her."

"She's at the hospital. She should be just about finished her shift by now."

A commotion was heard downstairs. The sound of Maggie's screams could be heard. Smith and Bridge ran down to see what was going on. Three armed officers had stormed the house and were busy searching the place. One of them pointed his gun at Smith.

"It's alright," Smith put his hands in the air. "She's not here. Bridge is alright."

Bridge put his arms around Maggie. She was staring at one of the armed officers.

"Is that a real gun?" She asked him.

"It is," the man said.

"Are you going to shoot us?"

"He's not going to shoot anybody," Bridge said. "Shall we see if we can finish your new jigsaw tonight? You go through and get it started."

"Can I start in the middle?"

"I wouldn't expect anything else," Bridge said.

"Go and get her," Bridge said. "Go and find Emily. I'll stay here with Maggie."

Whitton, Yang Chu and Brownhill walked in the house.

"Where is she?" Brownhill said.

"She's at work," Smith said. "She's at the hospital. I'm going to go and find her."

"Me and Whitton will come with you," Brownhill said. "Yang Chu, you stay here with Bridge in case she comes back home. One of the armed guys can stay with you."

Smith drove with Whitton in the direction of the hospital. Brownhill drove closely behind him.

"Do you think she's even at work?" Whitton said.

"Let's hope so," Smith said. "She'll be off guard there. We should be able to take her easily there."

He stopped in the car park of the hospital and turned off the engine. Brownhill parked next to him. They walked through the entrance of the hospital and headed for the reception desk.

"Hi," Smith said to the man behind the desk. "I'm looking for Emily Riley. She's a nurse here. Do you know if she's still on duty?"

"She's just knocked off," the man said.

"Do you know where she is?"

"How should I know? Probably on her way home."

"Who's the doctor in charge?"

"Doctor Simmons," the man said and started to leaf through a pile of papers.

"Where can I find him?"

He was starting to become impatient.

"He's probably in the staff room," the man said.

Smith followed the signs and found the hospital staff room. He went inside and spotted Doctor Simmons straight away. Pete Simmons had treated a young girl who was in a coma a few years earlier. The girl had made a miraculous recovery and proved instrumental in helping solve one of Smith's first murder investigations. Simmons was sitting on a chair with his eyes closed.

"Dr Simmons," Smith said.

Simmons didn't stir.

"Dr Simmons," Smith raised his voice.

Simmons' eyes opened, and he stared at Smith.

"I know you," he said.

"DS Smith, can I have a word?"

"You're the Australian," Simmons said.

"I thought you'd be lapping up the Pacific air by now."

Simmons had always expressed a desire to retire to Australia.

"Two more years," Simmons said. "Two more years of blood and guts and I'm off to the sunshine. What can I do for you?"

"We're looking for Emily Riley."

"She knocked off about an hour ago."

"Do you know where she went?"

"Home probably," Simmons said. "It was a rough shift. That pile up on the A19 was a right mess."

A nurse with thin hair in a ponytail and a silver ring in his nose walked in. Pete Simmons nodded to him in acknowledgment. The nurse sat down and opened up a book.

Smith took out his phone and dialled Bridge's number.

"Sarge," Bridge answered straight away. "Have you found her?"

"Not yet," Smith said. "I take it she hasn't come home then?"

"No, she should have been here by now."

"I'll let you know if we find her," Smith said and rang off.

"Do you have any idea where she might be?" Smith said to Doctor Simmons.

"Emily is an enigma," Simmons said. "She doesn't need the money. I don't know why she puts up with the crap that gets thrown at her in here."

"Are you looking for Nurse Riley?" The nurse with the long hair looked up from his book.

"Yes," Smith said, "do you know where she is?"

"She left with Derek."

"Derek?"

"Derek Grimes, I couldn't believe it. She asked him out for a drink. Derek's a real loser."

"What do you mean?"

"Derek is an orderly here," the nurse said. "He's a real sad case. He's over forty and I bet he's still a virgin."

"That's enough," Pete Simmons said.

"I need his address," Smith said. "I need it right now."

"He's got a crappy flat off Monk Gate. I don't know the number."

Ten minutes later Smith drove through the city headed for Monk Gate. He'd found Derek Grimes' address from one of the women in the hospital administration department.

Derek Grimes, he thought, sad, lonely and middle aged. It fits perfectly. Bridge was never meant to be her next victim.

The full moon had still not shown its face and Smith could feel a glimmer of hope rushing through him.

We might just be in time, he thought.

He parked outside the flat on Monk Gate and turned off the engine. Brownhill parked behind him and she and Whitton got out. They approached Smith's car. Smith got out.

"This is Derek Grimes' flat here," he pointed to a small place above what looked like a DIY shop. The lights were not on in the flat, but the curtains were open.

"Looks like nobody's home," Whitton said.

"I wouldn't be so sure," Smith said. "She likes to kill by the light of the moon remember."

It was as if the moon had heard him. An ethereal glow slowly filled the sky and the moonlight lit up the skyline of the city in the distance. Smith watched as it climbed higher in the sky. It had an orange tint to it.

"We need to go in now," Smith said.

"We wait for back up," Brownhill said. "This woman is a savage killer."

"There's no time. She's going to kill him if we don't go inside."

He crossed the road and walked up to the DIY shop. Brownhill shook her head and followed him. Whitton walked closely behind.

"Whitton," Smith whispered. "You come in with me. I hope your self-defence skills are up to date."

"Of course. What about yours?"

"Nope," Smith said.

He turned to Brownhill.

"Boss," he said. "You wait out here. In case she tried to make a run for it."

"So, I'm still the boss then?" Brownhill said.

"Of course," Smith looked around for the door to the flat.

A grubby blue door at the side of the DIY shop seemed to be the obvious choice. Smith tried the door handle. The door was locked.

"We need to get hold of the landlord," Brownhill said. "We need to get a key."

"There's no time," Smith said.

He walked back to his car and returned with two large screwdrivers.

"Try to be quiet," Brownhill said.

"I have done this before."

He inserted one of the screwdrivers next to the lock.

"Although it was a long time ago," he added.

He jammed the screwdriver in the door. He did the same with the second screwdriver and twisted it in the opposite direction. The door opened with a crunch. Smith looked inside. The whole stairwell was in darkness. He went inside and waited for his eyes to adjust to the blackness. Whitton stayed close behind him. They slowly walked up the stairs. Smith had to hold on to the rail, it was so dark.

They reached the top of the stairs and stopped. Smith put his ear to the door and listened. He could hear low murmuring sounds coming from inside.

"She's in there," he whispered to Whitton. "I'm going to kick the door in and we'll take her by surprise."

"What are we going to do when we get inside?"

"I haven't thought about that. We'll go on three. One..."

He took a deep breath.

"Two..."

He looked at Whitton and smiled.

"Do you fancy a drink after we're finished up here?" He said.

Whitton nodded. She looked absolutely terrified.

"Three."

Smith kicked the door as hard as he could and winced. The pain shot right up his leg. The door didn't open.

"Shit," he said.

He kicked the door again and it crashed open.

## CHAPTER SEVENTY FOUR

The light from the full moon outside the window lit up the whole room. An overweight, balding man was sitting on a chair next to the bed. His head was slumped down, and his eyes were closed. Emily Riley was standing with her back to Smith and Whitton. She was making strange mumbling sounds. Smith noticed that she was holding a knife in her left hand. It was the most unusual knife he had ever seen. The handle was made from a light wood and the blade was curved like the arc of a new moon. The moonlight was reflected in the steel. Emily turned around. The expression on her face was something Smith would never forget. She gazed at Smith and Whitton and then at Derek Grimes.
She said something in a language Smith didn't understand and raised the knife in the air. She crept closer to the unconscious man on the chair.
"Emily," Whitton said. "Put down the knife. Everything's going to be alright."
Emily moved a step closer to Derek Grimes.
"Emily," Whitton said again. "Drop the knife."
Emily grabbed Derek Grimes by his thinning hair and tilted his head back. She took a long look at the moon and placed the knife against his throat. A trickle of blood started to ooze down his neck. The knife was obviously very sharp. Smith didn't know what to do. Emily said something in the strange dialect again and looked at the knife.
"Selene," Smith shouted. "Selene Lupei."
Emily stopped moving. She looked at Smith in disbelief.
"Selene," Smith said in a calm voice. "We know why you're here - we understand but you have to stop."

Emily appeared to stop and think about something for a moment. She looked at the knife again.

"Selene," Smith said. "Natasha misses you. I've spoken to your sister. Natasha would like to see you."

Emily froze. Her whole body turned rigid. Her arms dropped to her side and she dropped the knife on the carpet. It landed next to the bed with a dull thud. She collapsed in a heap on the floor and started to sob. Smith bent down and picked up the knife. He was surprised by how heavy it was. He handed it to Whitton.

"Get this thing out of here," he said. "We need an ambulance here now."

Whitton turned and left the room. Smith leaned over the lifeless body of Derek Grimes and checked to see if he was still alive. His pulse was weak, but his heart was still beating. Emily Riley was sobbing uncontrollably on the carpet. The full moon had reached its peak of brightness and it lit up the whole room.

"Emily," Smith said. "I need you to come with me."

Emily stared up at him. There was no life left in her black eyes.

"Natasha," she pleaded. "Natasha."

Two of the armed unit stormed in and immediately pointed their guns at the figure huddled on the floor.

"It's alright," Smith said. "It's all over."

"Emily, I'm going to put handcuffs on you now. Please do not move."

He held out his hand to one of the armed officers and was given a pair of handcuffs. He held Emily Riley's hands behind her back and snapped the handcuffs on.

"Please stand up," he said to her.

She did as she was told. She was shaking.

"Take her downstairs," Smith said to the armed men. "Be gentle with her."

Two paramedics entered the room.

"I think he's been drugged," Smith said. "Probably Chloroform."

"We're going to need some help," one of the paramedics looked at Derek Grimes lying on the chair. "He's not exactly a beanpole."

Ten minutes later, Derek Grimes was wheeled on a stretcher into the back of an ambulance. Emily Riley had been taken away in a separate ambulance to be checked over. DI Brownhill had gone with her.

Smith went to his car and took out a packet of cigarettes from the glove compartment. He lit one and inhaled deeply. Whitton walked over to him.

"It's all over," she said. "The nightmare that lasted almost three months is over. I'm never going to forget this one."

"Does Bridge know what happened?" Smith said.

"Brownhill phoned him. Apparently, he's in a right state."

"Crap taste in women. He'll get over it."

"You're all heart."

"Speaking of crap taste in women," Smith said. "Are we still alright? I mean you and me?"

"Buy me a drink and I'll let you know," Whitton said.

Smith smiled. He opened the box of cigarettes and took one out. He took out his lighter from his pocket. A piece of paper fell out and landed on the pavement. Whitton picked it up and read what was written on it.

"Be very careful of wolf dressed as sheep," she said.

**THE END**

Printed in Great Britain
by Amazon